PATRICK
&
VICTORIA

ALSO BY J J FLANAGAN

Tambu

The Camel Cocktail

Rio Cobre

If She Were to Die

Z'Abaya

Patrick & Victoria

A NOVEL

J J FLANAGAN

LIVESEY BOOKS

NEW YORK

Published by Livesey Books

990 Avenue of the Americas, Suite 10E, New York, NY 10018

First published by Livesey Books 2008

Patrick & Victoria / J J Flanagan

ISBN 978-0-6152-1326-2

PUBLISHER'S NOTE

To dearest Jilly,
for following me all around the world.

. . . but at the tip-top,
There hangs by unseen thread, an orb'ed drop
Of light, and that is love.

JOHN KEATS
Endymion

ONE

Earlier that morning, there had been bright sun along the west coast of Ireland but by noon black storm clouds were building up across the sky, casting dark shadows over the land, turning the sea the color of gunmetal. The wind, becoming a gale, was violent and unpredictable, whipping ragged streaks of spray from the mountainous waves rolling endlessly in from the Atlantic.

A yacht, running before the wind a few hundred yards off the island of Ennismore, was racing towards the rocky headland at its southern tip.

"Slow down, Connor, please slow down," Victoria shouted, staring at her brother gripping the tiller with both hands. "We're going too fast. Something will break!"

"No it won't . . . we'll be fine . . . this time we'll beat the record . . ."

She turned again towards the island and the waves exploding along the base of the cliffs. Behind them stretched their wake, a swirl of white foam cutting through the gray sea, and although they were still in sunlight, immense rain clouds were closing in from the north.

The excitement that Victoria had felt when they set off from the mainland had now changed to fear, but she smiled bravely at her brother before opening the seat locker and reaching for the yellow life jacket.

The wind grew stronger, the ropes and sails strained to their limit and the yacht went even faster.

Connor threw back his head, laughing.

"The Equinox! The gales of September!"

Suddenly he braced himself and shouted: "Victoria! Hold the tiller! Must reef the mainsail . . ."

Over her brother's shoulder she could see a mottled pattern flickering across the water, coming straight at the yacht, but before she could grab the tiller a vortex of wind and sea burst over them, snapping the boom across so violently that the mast broke with a sickening crack and they heeled over in a tangle of sails and broken rigging.

For an instant she saw Connor's face, his eyes wide in disbelief as he tugged at the ropes around his body, then he was gone.

The next wave engulfed the yacht, turning it upside down, dragging Victoria under. Coughing and choking, she was trapped in a pocket of air, screaming alone in the darkness.

TWO

The older fishermen had warned against leaving the island that day but Patrick and his father would not listen and had taken their boat out, intending to stay close to the shore.

When they reached the northern tip of Ennismore, Patrick's father wanted to turn back but Patrick persuaded him to go a little further on, passed the lee of the island and out into the Atlantic where they might catch at least one good fish before heading home.

They rowed due west and their boat, a curragh made of wooden ribs covered with tarred canvas, rose and fell as the waves passed beneath. They slid down into deep troughs where the land was completely hidden from them, then moments later rose high on a crest and could see their village and the mainland beyond, clear and sharp in the sunlight.

When the wind began to veer north they decided it was too dangerous to continue and turned for home, but although they pulled on the oars until their muscles burned they were unable to reach the shelter of the island. Powerless to resist, they were driven relentlessly down the coast, pitching and rolling in the waves coming in from the Atlantic.

As they approached the southern point of the island the gale began to gust from different directions, driving them nearer and nearer the cliffs until the roar and crash of the waves became so loud Patrick could no longer hear the prayers his father was saying. He rowed almost in a trance, conscious only of the approaching rocks.

At last they rounded the headland, and sea gulls began circling their boat as they entered the quiet refuge of a small cove.

Patrick's father stopped praying. Neither of them spoke but lay across their oars until gradually they recovered their strength. When Patrick finally sat up he saw, about fifty yards away, a bright yellow life jacket holding a person's head just above the water.

"Look!" he shouted, pointing. "Look there!"

His father turned and shaded his eyes.

"God have mercy on us. It must be a survivor from a torpedoed ship," he said, starting to row again. "But I only see one, and usually there's many more."

He held the curragh steady into the wind while Patrick leaned over the side and pulled the body towards him. Gently he pushed back the hair and gazed into the face of a young girl.

"Is she alive or dead?" his father asked, crossing himself.

Patrick stared at her intently.

"I don't know father, I don't know."

THREE

Patrick was awakened the next morning by the shrill blast of a ship's siren echoing against the cliffs and through the hills behind the village. Sitting up, he pulled back the curtain and looked out.

A few hundred yards from the shore he could see a gray warship moving slowly just beyond the harbor, the red ensign flag at the stern hanging limp, smoke from the funnels rising almost vertically to the sky.

Hurriedly he pulled on his clothes then ran outside the cottage to where his father and mother were standing, gazing down at the ship several hundred feet below.

"What is it, father?" he asked.

"It's a British Navy destroyer. Must be from Bantry Bay."

The morning was still, the gale having died out during the night, and Patrick could hear the petty officer's whistle as a steam launch was swung over the side then lowered into the water. It pulled away, quickly gathering speed, cutting a vee-shaped ripple through the flat calm.

"Come on," his father said, starting down the steep path towards the harbor. "They'll want to talk to us."

The launch came alongside the jetty and a British officer stepped ashore.

"Who is in charge here?" he demanded, looking at the

people clustered around him.

Patrick's father pushed forward and said: "You'll have come about the girl. She's with the priest. I'll send for him directly."

The officer seemed to grow in stature.

"Tell me, my good man," he said, tilting his head back, "haven't they taught you to take your cap off when speaking to a British officer?"

Patrick's father had started to answer when an old woman cried out, pointing up the hill to the priest followed by a girl dressed in a sailor's suit and ankle-length skirt, the clothes Patrick remembered she'd been wearing yesterday now dried and pressed. The priest picked his way carefully down the narrow, winding path but the girl behind him walked with the agility and confidence of youth. As they came closer, she appeared to be about fifteen or sixteen years old. Her hair, a light chestnut brown unlike the women of the island, was pinned clear of her face exposing skin that was fair and smooth, not wind-burned like the islanders.

When they reached the jetty, the officer stepped forward and saluted.

"Lieutenant Beamish, at your service. Are you Lady Victoria, the daughter of Lord Stafford?"

"Yes, I am."

"We were told you were out sailing with your brother yesterday. Is he with you?"

"No. There's no news of Connor yet. I don't remember anything after the mast broke and we capsized. But we're sure he's been swept onto another part of the island," she said, her eyes beginning to glisten with tears, "and he'll be found safe and sound very soon."

Turning away she faced the priest and asked: "May I please meet the fishermen who rescued me?"

"Of course, my child," he replied, smiling at her. "It was Patrick Castelan and his father. They were the only men brave enough to go out fishing yesterday," he added, beckoning towards them.

Patrick took her hand, warm and vital now, so different from her touch when he pulled her cold and lifeless from the sea. Abruptly he remembered how her soaking clothes had clung to the outlines of her body, and a sudden stab of sensuality made him unable to speak for a moment or even hear properly when she said: "The name Castelan sounds Spanish or Portuguese rather than Irish."

"Riccardo de Castelano was a sailor with the Spanish Armada," the priest explained. "They were wrecked on Ennismore in the winter of fifteen eighty-eight trying to reach home by sailing around Scotland and the west coast of Ireland."

Victoria nodded politely then turned back to Patrick and his father.

"I'm so grateful to you both. How ever can I thank you?"

"It was the will of God," the priest interjected.

"The will of God? Well, yes," she answered, "I suppose it was."

FOUR

As they came alongside the destroyer Victoria glanced up at the British flag, the symbol of invincibility and power, and was glad to be back among her own people.

At the top of the gangway the First Officer was waiting and saluted as she stepped onto the deck beside him.

"Nigel Trubshaw," he said. "Glad to have you aboard. Captain's on the bridge. Let me lead the way."

Gripping the rail, she followed him up the stairway and into the wheel house. The Captain, a man in his late forties with graying hair, came forward to meet her.

"This is really a great honor to have you on my ship and to be of service to General the Lord Stafford. Would you care for some refreshment? Tea? Or lemonade?"

Victoria smiled and shook her head, then turned to look back at Ennismore.

"We were here earlier this year," the Captain went on, following her gaze, "picking up survivors from the liner 'Rangoon'. She was torpedoed last February."

"This terrible war, when will it end?"

"Next year," the Captain assured her. "Nineteen sixteen will see the end of the Kaiser. Did the islanders treat you in a proper manner?" he asked, changing the subject.

"Yes, they were very kind."

"Primitive lot but their religion keeps them in order."

Victoria nodded. "I suppose you're right," she said over her shoulder as she stepped out onto the open bridge.

She heard the Captain call out an order, the ship began to tremble then rapidly increased speed. Victoria could feel the breeze cool on her face as they came around in a wide circle and turned towards the mainland. The sea was flat calm, undisturbed by wind or wave except for their wake churning away behind them.

"Very beautiful," the Captain said, coming up beside her. "Beautiful and a little melancholy, like everything else in Ireland."

"Melancholy? I've never found Ireland melancholy."

"The native Irish tend to be rather a sad lot. It's the Catholic religion and their history. All that sort of thing."

"I'm afraid we live such splendid lives, we're not too conscious of the ordinary people," Victoria said, gazing at the island receding behind them. "I suppose that's very wrong of us."

She thought of the islanders she had met, particularly the fisherman's son. Most of them were thick-bodied and squat but he was tall and graceful, and reminded her of the dark and handsome Mediterranean sailors in the book about Lord Byron in the library of the Castle.

Feeling herself beginning to blush she took a deep breath.

"My family have lived here for hundreds of years," she said turning to the Captain again, "but we never really get to know the people."

"It's not necessary," he replied as they went back into the wheel house. "We can't possibly mix together. The only relationship can be that of master and servant. We're a very different breed."

Victoria slowly nodded.

"I suppose you're right," she said. "Perhaps we are."

FIVE

When the fishermen returned that evening they reported seeing a sail and pieces of rigging scattered among the rocks on the other side of the island.

As the sun began to set, Patrick and his father, accompanied by a group of men from the village, climbed down the cliffs and found the remains of Connor Stafford still entangled in the wreckage of the yacht.

For the next two days a westerly gale prevented any fishing boats leaving the harbor and the body had to remain lying in the church. But on the following morning the wind dropped, and in the calmness of the early dawn Patrick and his father set out for the mainland with the body wrapped in canvas, lying lengthwise in the bottom of the boat. After more than three hours of steady rowing they entered the harbor of Ballinahinch and tied up at the Customs House.

The Customs Officer, an Englishman, kept them standing in his office while they told him what had happened.

". . . the body of Lord Stafford's son? This requires very careful handling indeed," he said, cranking the telephone. "Exchange? Connect me with the Royal Irish Constabulary barracks immediately . . . yes I'll hold on . . . Is that you,

Mulcahy? We have a very serious matter on our hands. The son of . . . what's that? You already know!" he exclaimed, his forehead tightening. "Yes! Yes! All right then, be quick now with the hearse and tell the undertaker to bring his finest coffin."

Irritated, he sighed and replaced the telephone in its cradle.

"The RIC will be here directly," he said without looking up. "Wait outside."

A little later, a pony and trap with two policemen clattered over the cobbles. It was followed more slowly by the hearse pulled by a team of horses driven by a man in black clothes and a tall black hat.

Together they lifted the body and placed it carefully in the coffin in the back of the hearse.

"I'll take the lead," the Customs Officer said, his voice sharp and commanding. "You follow on behind, Sergeant, with the two fishermen."

The procession wound slowly through the streets of the town, donkeys and carts stopping before them and people crossing themselves as they passed. Clear of the houses they broke into a trot, moving swiftly along the Limerick road until they came to the turreted gateway of Ballinahinch Castle.

The gates were swung open and they continued along the driveway for about a mile, crossing bare, windswept bog land, then descended into a shallow valley, partly sheltered from the cold winds that swept in from the Atlantic.

In front of them was the Castle, dark and menacing, battlements and turrets outlined against the gray overcast sky, its granite walls as hard and enduring as the Cromwellian solider who built them. From the highest tower they could see the Stafford family flag was flying at half mast.

At the top of the stone stairs, under the portico of the main door, stood Lord Stafford dressed in riding clothes with a tweed cap pulled firmly down on his head. Even at that distance Patrick could feel the strength of his personality.

The Customs Officer was the first one up the steps.

"Your Lordship," he said, panting. "May I offer you my sincerest sympathy for your tragic loss."

Lord Stafford nodded, curt and short, then looked passed him at the hearse and coffin. Seeing Patrick and his father he called out: "Come up here you two!" as if giving a command to his soldiers.

Patrick was momentarily startled, but his father remained calm and self-possessed as he walked unhurriedly up the steps. "Lady Stafford and myself are beholden to you," Lord Stafford said, briefly shaking hands. "Both of you come with me."

He strode ahead of them into the Castle, the butler bowing low as he passed, Patrick and his father following closely as he marched across the hall, the thud of his riding boots on the bare flagstones echoing in the domed ceiling above. They continued on through double doors into the Morning Room, small and intimate with chintz-covered furniture, family photographs, and flowers.

In front of a crackling fire lay a cocker spaniel, stretched out beside Victoria's chair. She was leaning forward, stroking his head, and looked up the moment they entered.

Sitting opposite her was her mother, dressed in black, thin-lipped with grief.

"Clarissa," Lord Stafford said, "this is the fisherman, Castelan, and his son."

Lady Stafford made no move to get up or shake their hands so they remained standing awkwardly in the middle of the room.

After what seemed like a long time she said: "Thank you for saving the life of my daughter, and for bringing home the body of my son."

"You have my sympathy," Patrick's father said, "for I know the pain of losing a child to the sea."

He waited for her to say something but she remained silent.

"We must be resigned to the will of God," he continued, bowing his head.

"The will of God?" Lady Stafford murmured without conviction.

Again silence until Victoria spoke.

"Father, you haven't introduced Jeremy and Blaise."

Lord Stafford frowned at her.

"Mr. Castelan," he said, irritated. "My heir, Lord Blaise, and my youngest son, the Honorable Jeremy."

The boy standing behind Victoria's chair blinked at them through thick-lensed glasses, nodded, then looked down at the floor again. Beside him, sitting on the arm of a chair, was a tall, slim young man, smart and trim in his cavalry officer's uniform. He moved his head slightly when he heard his name but his expression remained distant and faintly hostile.

"There is nothing more to add," Lord Stafford said

abruptly, "except to thank you on behalf of my family, and to give you a reward."

"A reward?" repeated Patrick's father.

"Yes, please take it," Lady Stafford said, pointing to a small velvet money bag on the table. "There are a hundred gold sovereigns in there for you and your family."

"We don't need any reward," Patrick's father said, emphasizing each word. "It was God's mercy that we were there to rescue your daughter. I'm only sorry we're not bringing your son home to you, alive and well."

Lord Stafford picked up the money bag and held it out to them.

"Here! Take it!" he ordered

"No thank you."

"But you must. Surely people like yourselves have many uses for a hundred sovereigns".

"God provides all we need."

"We're indebted to you!" Lord Stafford said, his mouth tightening, his face becoming red. "And I won't be beholden to the likes of you!"

Instinctively Patrick put out his hand, but his father stopped him.

"Now, Lord Stafford," he said in a firm, clear voice, "if you'll excuse us we must take our leave. It's a long row back to Ennismore and we must hurry if we're to arrive before nightfall. Goodbye," he added, smiling at Victoria, "God be with you."

He nodded to Lady Stafford then turned away and walked towards the door. Patrick hesitated for a moment then followed. As they crossed the hall the butler took a step towards them as if to strike Patrick's father then stopped and glared at them as they passed.

"You should be horse-whipped," he whispered, his voice quiet but vicious, "for talking to his Lordship like that!"

They pretended not to hear, and walked unhurriedly on down the steps to the driveway where the Customs Officer and the Sergeant stood waiting.

Patrick put his hand on his father's shoulder.

"Why in the world didn't you take the hundred sovereigns?"

"Because they were treating us like beggars".

"But what about Maeve? What about me? With money like that I could have gone back to the Jesuits, finished school, and maybe won a scholarship to Trinity College like Uncle James and become a doctor."

"I wouldn't take their damned money even if we were starving."

"Father! I'm not going to spend my life as a fisherman on Ennismore."

"Quiet, son, be quiet, or you'll say something neither of us will be able to forgive or forget."

The sound of the butler closing the door made them all look up towards the Castle.

"You'd best be on your way, Sergeant," the Customs Officer said, "and take the fishermen with you. I shall stay. I'm sure his Lordship will wish to talk further with me."

They climbed in beside the Sergeant. The young policeman snapped the reins and the horse broke into a brisk trot down the drive to the main road. They rode in silence all the way back to Ballinahinch, the only sound the clip-clop of the horse's hooves and the rattle of the wheels passing over rutted portions of the road.

At the RIC barracks they made a statement which was laboriously written down by a young policeman. When it was finished and signed, the Sergeant asked them into the kitchen and insisted on giving them some tea.

"Why, in the name of God, didn't you take the hundred sovereigns?" he demanded. "Sure that's a fortune! With a hundred sovereigns you need never work again."

"It is a fortune, God knows, and we could surely use the money," Patrick's father replied. "But I couldn't take it from them, not with that attitude they have, expecting us to grovel like beggars. We rescued the man's daughter, brought back the body of his son all the way from Ennismore, and he doesn't even ask us to sit down in his house. To Hell with him!"

The sergeant became silent and thoughtful.

"I agree with you," he said. "But it's different for the likes of me. I have an oath of allegiance, and a pension to think of."

"I know. My brother, the clever one of the family, won a scholarship and became a doctor. He was in the Colonial Service in British West Africa. He too had mixed feelings at times."

The Sergeant sat forward, interested.

"Your brother is in His Majesty's Colonial Service?"

"He was, God rest his soul. He died of Yellow Fever in nineteen eleven. Buried in Lokoja. Hundreds of miles up the River Niger, far away from his own."

"I'm sorry to hear that."

"Ah! He was the hope of the family. Believed in the English, in what he called the fundamental fairness of the British System."

"He was right. The only way our people will advance is through the British system and Home Rule."

"But something has got to happen soon," Patrick's father said, anger hardening his face. "We can't take another seven hundred years of the Staffords and their like."

SIX

As soon as the butler closed the door, Lord Stafford said: "Damn it, Clarissa. I won't be beholden to fishermen!"

"A strange manifestation of pride," Lady Stafford said touching her chin. "Admirable, perhaps. A hundred sovereigns must be a great deal of money to people like that."

"There was a time when they'd be flogged for such impudence!" Blaise said. "Pity those days are over."

"That's in the past, dear. We don't treat them like that any more."

"Perhaps that's our mistake," he replied. "You know, we've had intelligence reports recently that some extremists are planning a rebellion. They think that we're so preoccupied by the war and with all our soldiers away in France we'll . . ."

"I'll offer him a job," Lord Stafford interrupted. "That's what I'll do. Give that son of his a start, a chance of getting out of the peasantry and bettering himself," he added, walking over to the fireplace and pulling on the bell rope.

"A handsome young man," Lady Stafford said, almost to herself. "Jet black hair, brown eyes, olive skin. One of the Black Irish."

"The Black Irish?" Blaise repeated, frowning then grimacing at his mother. "Who, or what, are they?"

"The Black Irish of the Atlantic coast, people descended from shipwrecked Iberian sailors of the Spanish Armada. You find them in different places from Donegal down to Kerry."

"Oh," Blaise said, disinterested.

A few moments later the butler knocked and came into the room.

"You rang, your Lordship?"

"Yes, Paisley. Tell the Agent I want to see him immediately."

"Father, there's something I don't understand," Victoria said going over to him. "Everyone on the island was so very kind and considerate to me yet you didn't even offer Mr. Castelan and his son anything to drink, or ask them to sit down."

"You can't ask them to sit down and have tea with us!" Blaise snapped.

"Why ever not?"

"Because they're bloody native Irish, that's why. It would be ludicrous. In any case their clothes were probably dirty."

"Blaise, what a foul thing to say about the two people who rescued Victoria," Jeremy said becoming flushed, determined to go on. "This is nineteen fifteen. Nowadays, we need the consent of the governed."

"Rubbish! Where did you hear that nonsense? The iron hand is what's needed."

He stopped abruptly as the Agent came into the room and stood waiting at the door.

"Ah, Robinson," Lord Stafford said. "Come in. It's about the fisherman's son. I want you to give him a job, looking after the yacht. Also train him as a groom. Give him the means of earning a living. Pay him well, double the going rate."

"Very good, m'lord. When would you like him to start?"

"Immediately."

As she listened to her father, Victoria thought again about Patrick and how she felt both times she saw him. A new feeling -- puzzling yet exciting.

She remembered the girl who had been expelled last term from her school in England. One of the teachers caught her climbing over the wall at three o'clock in the morning, having been down to the village to meet a boy. It was whispered that she was 'over-sexed': it sounded, she thought, as if it were some terrible disease. For one awful moment, Victoria wondered if she was suffering from the same thing. She blushed, and immediately leaned down to stroke the dog at her feet.

As soon as the Agent had left the room, Blaise continued haranguing Jeremy.

". . . the rulers must be harsh, otherwise they lose their authority and subsequently their power. The British Empire prevails because we stand no nonsense from the lesser peoples God has called upon us to rule. In the long run they benefit from our laws and . . ."

"Oh Blaise!" Victoria exclaimed, sitting up. "Stop being so dreadfully pompous. It's a terrible thing to say the Irish people are inferior."

"But my dear little sister, they are. They're a mongrel people. Providence has ordained that there shall be the rulers and the ruled."

Lady Stafford clapped her hands.

"Children! children! Stop it! What Blaise says is true, we all know that, but it's bad form to put it into words."

Victoria looked at her mother, then at Blaise, and then at the stern face of her father.

She had never really thought about the Irish people before: they had always been there, smiling and willing, just part of the background of her life. Confused, she turned away and gazed into the fire.

"We govern them well, very well in fact," Lord Stafford said. "We give them law and order and a measure of freedom within the Empire. To go beyond that, and give them Home Rule, would ultimately end up in the country breaking away, and reverting to a primitive, priest-ridden society. The Staffords have been here for more than two hundred and fifty years, and we've brought great benefits to the people in this part of County Clare."

Victoria looked up at him.

"But father," she said, "this was originally their country. Do we really have the right to be here?"

"Yes!" Blaise replied coming over to her. "We are here by right of conquest. We use these people for the benefit of the Empire and as part of this process they benefit themselves."

"We use them?" Victoria repeated, staring at him.

"Children! Children!" Lady Stafford said again. "This conversation has gone quite far enough. We're in mourning for Connor, dear Connor, and I won't have his brothers and sister arguing like this. Although people of our class don't show their feelings in public, it is a time of great sadness for our family. Please remember that."

Lady Stafford looked at each of them in turn, then she stood up.

"I won't be with you all for luncheon. I'm retiring to my room. And Victoria," she added, going over to her. "Please don't look so worried. We'll treat the fisherman very generously, that is if he'll let us."

At the jetty, Patrick and his father were about to cast off when the sound of horse's hooves made them look up.

"You there!" the rider called. "Wait! I have a letter from the Agent."

He reined in his horse, and leaning down handed an envelope to Patrick's father.

"Here son, open it. You read the English better than I do."

Patrick broke the wax seal and took out a piece of writing paper with the Stafford family crest on it.

> *Ballinahinch Castle*
> *County Clare*
>
> *10th September 1915*
>
> *Dear Mr. Castelan,*
>
> *As your son is an accomplished sailor I would like to offer him a job as an apprentice to Mr. Sharpe who is in charge of his Lordship's yacht. In addition, he could work as a stable boy and learn to be a groom.*
>
> *A salary of fifteen pounds a year would be payable and he would be provided food and*

*lodging of the same standard as the indoor
servants of the Castle.*

*Yours sincerely,
Malcolm Robinson
Agent to Lord Stafford*

"That's extraordinarily good pay, especially for a Catholic," the horseman said, "and you'll learn a trade. You should take it."

"I will," Patrick almost shouted.

"Son," said his father. "This is a family decision. We must talk it over with your mother, and the priest."

"But I want the job, father."

"Come on now," the horseman said, slapping his riding crop against his leggings. "Make up your minds!"

"We'll think about it and let you know," Patrick's father told him, stepping into the boat.

"Come back, damn you! I've got to have an answer."

"Tell the Agent," Patrick's father called over his shoulder as he grasped the oars, "that my son will arrive within a week, if he's going to arrive at all."

SEVEN

B laise stood in front of the mirror, preening himself. He held a cane in his right hand, and turning from side to side cut the air with it several times. Suddenly with a flick of the wrist he brought it down sharply on the bed pillow, leaving a deep crease. His throat went dry as he struck again, even harder.

A light knock on the door startled him. Turning quickly he swayed, and immediately conscious he'd drunk more brandy after dinner than he realized he straightened up, breathing deeply.

He lay the cane down, reached for his dressing gown and crossed the room to open the door.

Outside, a girl smiled cheekily at him.

"Good evening, your lordship," she whispered as she held out her skirts, making a deep curtsy.

"Rosaleen, you gorgeous thing. Do come in."

She slipped passed him and walked across to the bed, then abruptly stopped and looked down at the cane.

"Oh Jaysus not that your lordship!"

"Yes, it must be that tonight."

"It'll cost you a sovereign."

"A sovereign? But that's an awful lot of money."

"I know it is but that's what you gave me the last time

when you just had to do it."

"I did, did I? All right then, you little minx. I'll give you one again."

"It's in a good cause, your lordship. I'm saving my money so that I can emigrate to America."

"Well, I hope you're not planning to go too soon," Blaise said, his lips trembling, "because I'd miss you very much."

Frowning but resigned, she looked up at him.

"I'd better go and get the butter. I'll be back directly. Please put the money on the bedside table. I like to see it there close to me."

As soon as she'd gone, Blaise poured two large brandies from the decanter and started to drink one of them as he walked into his dressing room. Tension made him cough momentarily as he took the four old ties that he kept to one side of the rack. He hurried back into the room and threw them onto the bed.

A little later the door opened quietly and Rosaleen tiptoed in.

"There, your Lordship," she said putting down the butter dish. "Now I'd like my brandy, please. Oh, I see you've been kind enough to pour me some."

"Wait!" Blaise said. "Take your clothes off first."

"Why?"

"You've no idea, Rosaleen, how really beautiful you look with no clothes on. Your blonde hair and your blue eyes, you must be descended from Viking marauders who came to plunder and rape."

"Rape," she repeated. "That word has a cruel but exciting ring to it."

She paused, smiling at him.

"Eighth century Viking or twentieth century Ascendancy buck, sure the whole damn lot of you are all the same."

"Is that how you see me? An Ascendancy buck!"

"Whatever you are, I need some brandy if we're to go on. I'll compromise," she said, smiling. "One large one now and another even larger one when I'm undressed."

She gulped down two mouthfuls, gasped, then took another and emptied the glass.

"God! That's wonderful stuff. Beats potcheen any day."

"Potcheen? What in the world is that?"

"Irish moonshine," she replied with a provocative flick of her hip.

She went into the dressing room, took off her clothes and put Blaise's bathrobe on.

"Oh no," he said when she returned. "You look so much more beautiful naked. Please don't wear that."

"All in good time, your lordship. A little more brandy, please."

He hurriedly poured her some from the decanter, spilling drops onto the table. Then, taking hold of the robe slipped it over her shoulders and pulled it down around her waist.

"My God, but you're lovely!" he said as he bent to kiss her slowly on each breast.

"I thought I was meant to be a boy tonight."

"Yes, yes, you are. The beast must be satisfied, then everything will be fine."

Rosaleen sighed.

"Let me have my drink first," she said, tossing it back as she walked towards the bed. "All right then, your lordship, if you really must, I'm ready."

She lay down and allowed him to knot the ties to each of her wrists and ankles, securing them to the bed so that she was spread-eagled face downwards. She heard him swish the cane through the air several times, and clenching her fists tightly she waited.

At the first cut of the cane she sank her teeth into the pillow, squeezed her eyes shut and thought only of the golden coin that he had put on the table beside her, soon to be added to her savings account in the Post Office.

After eight or ten strokes her bottom was stinging and burning and beginning to turn numb. Then the blows stopped and she could feel him kissing and licking her, and murmuring as if speaking to someone else.

She managed to mask everything out and dream only of her plan of escaping from Ireland and emigrating to America but the noise of the dish being moved made her open her eyes and she saw Blaise's hand scoop up some butter.

"Bertie," she heard him say, "your bum is a really gorgeous shade of pink."

She concentrated hard on totally relaxing, trying to think of America and the New York skyline, repeating to herself that it would soon be over. She tensed momentarily as he entered her but with a determined effort she relaxed again. For the next few minutes it was as if she had left her body, and was only a witness to what was happening.

Suddenly Blaise shouted: "Damn you! Bertie, Damn you! Why do I like shafting you so! Damn you!" he shouted again, then finally lay limp and heavy on top of her. Moments later he withdrew, and standing up went into the dressing room without saying a word.

Rosaleen could hear the sounds of water running in the basin and Blaise washing. After a couple of minutes he came back, a bath towel around his waist, a cigarette in his mouth, smiling and relaxed.

"My dear girl," he said. "The beast is happy at last. Let me untie you."

He undid the ties, then very carefully Rosaleen slid off the bed and picked up the sovereign.

"So the beast is satisfied for a while," she said, smiling. "Expensive little devil, isn't he?"

She pushed passed him then went into the bathroom.

When she came back he was lying on the bed, naked, a glass of brandy in one hand and a cigarette in the other. Rosaleen noticed that he'd poured a very large brandy for her, and picking it up she sat down beside him.

"I think I'm drunk already, and I've only had a couple of these. You've been drinking all night."

"You get a lot of practice in the army. When we pull back from the line to the rest area it's the way we relax."

"It must be terrible in the trenches. Worse for the men than the officers."

"Probably, but damn it I'm going back in a few days. Don't let's talk about it now."

"I hope you don't get killed," Rosaleen whispered.

Blaise laughed. "So do I, my dear girl, so do I."

Suddenly he looked around at her, and frowned.

"Why ever did you say that?" he asked.

"Oh, I don't know, I'm so sorry. Make love to me, please. The proper way, right now."

"You usually charge me a minimum of half a crown."

"This one is for free."

"But what about your America fund?" he teased. "Are you sure you can afford it?"

Rosaleen's whole body suddenly craved him.

"We all have a beast to satisfy, Blaise me darlin'," she said, taking hold of his shoulders and pulling him towards her.

EIGHT

The following week Patrick, with his father and another fisherman, left Ennismore to row to the mainland. A light rain was falling but the sea was calm.

Patrick's Sunday clothes, together with a prayer book, Rosary and holy medals were wrapped in a piece of oilskin in the bottom of the boat.

With three of them rowing, they crossed to the mainland in less than three hours. As they pulled into Ballinahinch harbor the rain stopped and a watery sun brightened the town beyond.

"God be with you," his father said, watching him climb out of the curragh. "We'll pray for you. The seas will be too rough in the winter but you'll come back and see us, God willing, next Spring."

Patrick waited a few moments as they drifted away, then picked up his bundle and started to climb the steps up to the dock. He turned to wave but they had reached the mouth of the harbor and were soon hidden from view behind the breakwater.

He walked along the main street, looking briefly in the shop windows, then quickened his pace as he started along the road to Ballinahinch Castle and his future.

"There is a tide in the affairs of men," he said aloud,

"which, taken at the flood, leads on to fortune."

He repeated this over and over again, remembering the scholarly Jesuit and his English classes, and how he had given so much beauty and meaning to Shakespeare, and everything else he taught. Recalling also the bitterness of being forced to leave school and return to Ennismore, he quickened his pace along the road until he came to the turreted gateway of the estate.

He turned in, identified himself to the gatekeeper, and continued down the driveway. After about a mile it began to descend into a shallow valley and at last the Castle came into view. As he got closer he saw a large motor car parked under the portico at the foot of the staircase up to the main entrance. The chauffeur was holding the car door and Lord Stafford and Victoria were about to get in when they saw Patrick.

Victoria said something to her father, then walked quickly towards Patrick, smiling broadly.

"I'm so glad you've decided to take the job," she said. "I hope you'll be very happy here."

Patrick nodded. "I'm sure I will."

She was dressed in a shapeless schoolgirl's smock and had a white straw hat on her head with the badge of her school pinned in the center. She looked younger, almost childlike, as she stood there bright-eyed still smiling.

"Victoria!" Lord Stafford called, glancing at his watch. "We must hurry or you'll miss the Dublin train."

For a few seconds it was as if neither of them had heard him. Abruptly she said: "Goodbye" and ran back to the car.

Patrick stayed where he was until they'd started down the drive and the car had vanished over the brow of the hill.

"What the Hell do you think you're doing!"

Startled, Patrick spun around and saw the butler scowling at him from the top of the stairs.

"What's wrong?" he asked, taking off his cap. "I've come here to work. Lord Stafford himself . . ."

"I know very well who you are! But you're a servant and you've no right to be at the front of the Castle. If I find you around here again I'll give you a toe up the arse."

"But where should I go?" Patrick asked, trying to stay calm.

"Go back until you see a road to the right. Take it!"

Patrick hurried away and kept going until he came to the turning that lead to the stables and servants quarters behind the Castle. After several hundred yards it became a sunken road, about ten feet deep, where it crossed the view from the west side of the Castle towards the Atlantic then it sloped gently upward, the walls on either side tapering off until Patrick was on level ground again.

He stopped for a moment and looked at Ennismore partly hidden by rain. He thought of his family, of the warmth of their cottage, and the love and security of his home. Consciously he straightened himself and began walking again until he came to the arched gateway with its clock tower and weather vane, leading into a cobble-stoned courtyard.

All around were stables and garages, the rooms above for the stable boys and other outdoor servants. On the far side, away from the Castle, was the forge with its acrid smell of singed hooves, and the ring of anvil and hammer echoing through the yard.

Patrick reported to the Administration Office, and was

interviewed by Robinson, the Agent, a red-faced man who spoke with an English accent, but not quite the same as the Stafford family.

". . . Lord Stafford says you'll be employed and so you shall, but it seems at an excessively large salary."

He rang the bell on his desk, looking Patrick up and down as they waited.

There was a knock on the door, a subservient knock, and it was pushed open by an aging little man dressed in black clothes. His face was pale and bloodless, as if he never went outside.

"Mr. Evans," the Agent said, "this young man is coming to work at the Castle to help with looking after the yacht and to be trained as a groom. He will be paid fifteen pounds a year. Please start a file on him and arrange to have his photograph taken."

"A photograph?" Patrick said in surprise.

"Lord Stafford's instructions. We want to keep track of all young Papist men of doubtful loyalty."

"I don't understand."

"You don't have to. Now, be a good lad and go with Mr. Evans."

Patrick followed him to his office, along a passage between rows of desks with clerks sitting on tall stools. The moment they were inside, Evans sat down and immediately started to write.

"Name?" he asked.

"Castelan."

"Christian names"

"Patrick Riccardo."

"Riccardo?" Evans repeated, taking the pince-nez off his

nose and rubbing his eyes. "What do you mean, 'Riccardo'? This is a British household. From now on you'll be 'Richard'".

He began writing again, looking up from time to time at Patrick.

". . . about six feet, maybe a fraction more, black hair, thin features, brown eyes. How much do you weigh?"

"I don't know. Please sir, why are you asking all these questions?"

Evans ignored him. "Can you read and write the English language?"

"Yes. I can read and write English, Gaelic, French, and Latin."

"You're very well educated. Where did you go to school?"

"For a while to the Jesuits in County Dublin."

But Evans wasn't really interested and began reading what he'd written on the form. Satisfied, he turned it around to Patrick.

"Sign here."

Patrick wrote his name in Gaelic script.

Evans sighed and shook his head sadly.

"No hieroglyphics, please. Sign in the King's English."

Patrick hesitated, then signed again.

"A word of advice to you, young man. You seem to be a fine upstanding lad and you should be all right if you watch your step. But you don't look like the usual Irish boy. In fact, you look somewhat foreign. The young ladies may like it, but around here, and in wartime too, I'd be very careful if I were you."

NINE

"He's a charmer, isn't he?" O'Shaughnessy said when he escorted Patrick away from Evans's office. "He's known as 'Dry Balls' to his friends. We love him, and all the other Northern Ireland Orangemen here too."

"Sounds as if you're a Catholic."

"Of course I am. One of Mr. Evans's serfs. As the most junior, I have the honor of looking after the new arrivals. Like you."

"There seem to be an awful lot of clerks here."

"You need them to handle an estate of one hundred and thirty eight thousand acres."

They went through a small doorway and upstairs to a room over the forge.

"This is where the beginners start. If you behave yourself you'll get moved to a better room away from the stink of burnt horse hoofs, but it won't be much better because you're a Catholic."

"And if you're a Protestant?"

"If you're a Prod then life is very different. They have all the good jobs and all the power around here. But nobody gives you power," he added, his voice dropping to a whisper, "you've got to take it."

"How?" Patrick asked.

"The way it's always been got. By force, by force of arms. The Germans will send us guns. Then the people will rise."

"Redmond is the best hope for the Irish people," Patrick said, shaking his head. "He'll win Home Rule for Ireland once the war is over."

"You're a bloody West Briton."

"I'm sorry, I don't understand."

"West Briton. An Irishman who's sold out to the British."

"Redmond will win Home Rule."

"Like Hell he will! There must be a rebellion," O'Shaughnessy replied, getting excited. "Successful revolutions are made by a few determined people. Just a few, that's all we need. Many people are prepared to talk, but damn few are prepared to fight, and to die if it is necessary. At least on our side. Are you prepared to join us?"

Patrick shrugged his shoulders. "I don't know. This is the first I'd heard about a possible rebellion. I thought all that belonged to the history books. In any case I believe in John Redmond."

The next morning Patrick was awakened by the stable boys he shared the room with falling all over each other in their hurry to get dressed.

"What's wrong?" he asked, leaning on his elbow.

"Time to get up. Better be quick! You'll get a fine if you're late."

After breakfast there was a roll call. At the end, Patrick heard his name, followed by instructions to report to Mr. Sharpe, the Head Groom.

"I suppose as a fisherman you haven't had much experience riding a horse," he said when Patrick found him. "Do you think you can handle this animal?"

He nodded towards the stable boy tugging at the reins of a large and formidable horse, trying to hold him still.

"Yes, I think so," Patrick said, grabbing the pummel of the saddle.

The horse bucked and swayed as he mounted, trying to unseat him but remembering the lessons he'd had at school he hung on, determined not be thrown. He followed Sharpe across the yard, the horse raising on his hind legs then pitching forward trying to throw him. Sharpe pretended not to notice and continued on through the archway. Patrick's horse seemed to sense that he'd met his master and passing under the arch became calmer.

Drawing level Patrick asked Sharpe: "Where are we going?

"To the yacht. It's where you'll stay in future. Usually the person who has that job is a Protestant. I hope you realize how lucky you are to have it so soft."

They went along the main driveway for about a quarter of a mile, then branched off down a road leading to the sea. Fifteen minutes later they crossed a ridge and dropped steeply to the harbor.

"There's the boat house," Sharpe said, pointing with his riding crop. "Actually, it's a proper house really. Built by Captain Stafford, hero of the Battle of the Nile against Napoleon, when he was invalided out of the Navy."

It was constructed of the same granite blocks as the Castle, with miniature castellated walls and turrets.

"The real boat house is on the other side, in front of the

slipway. That's where the smaller sailing boats are kept. You will have access to it for your work but the rest of the building's out of bounds."

Ahead of them the east arm of the harbor extended out into the sea for a couple of hundred yards to a lighthouse at the end. Moored about half way along was a large and graceful two-masted schooner.

"That," Sharpe said, "will be your main concern. Keeping her spotless at all times will be your only reason for living."

On the other side of the harbor a dock stretched several hundred yards straight out from the land. About half way along was a large warehouse, it's windows boarded up.

"This seems to be a very big harbor for a yacht."

"It was originally built when they were going to develop the lead mines up in the hills," Sharpe replied. "They would have shipped the ore from here to the smelter in Limerick but the rebellion of seventeen ninety-eight broke out and they abandoned the scheme. Bloody rebellious Irish again."

They walked the horses along the jetty and dismounted in front of the yacht. A young man stood on the deck, looking up at them.

"Good afternoon, Mr. Sharpe, sir," he said, bounding up the gangway. "And to what do I owe this honor?"

"This is Patrick Castelan. He will be taking over from you."

"First I've heard of it."

"Don't worry. We have a good job for you at the Castle."

"Thank you, Mr. Sharpe. I know you always take care of your own," he said, shaking Patrick's hand in a peculiar manner which ended with a slight twist.

"What's that?" Patrick asked.

"Our Masonic sign, the Orange Lodge of . . ."

"Castelan here is a Papist."

"Damn!" he retorted, standing back, rubbing his hand as if it were contaminated. "I might have known it with a name like that. But Mr. Sharpe, sir, this job is not open to Papists."

"Lord Stafford's instructions. Pack your things. We'll make a quick inspection then be on our way."

They started in the Owner's Cabin at the stern, a large room with windows across the back and a connecting bathroom and dressing room. There were four other double cabins, and forward of the main saloon the galley and crew's quarters.

"This will be where you'll sleep," Sharpe said to Patrick as they looked into the small triangular-shaped space in the bow.

From another of the crew's cabins they heard the young man snigger as he packed his clothes. Patrick was about to ask why he wasn't being given the same cabin, but decided not to.

At the stern of the yacht was the cockpit with a seat all around, and a steering helm that duplicated the controls in the wheel house. After describing the various tasks that Patrick would have to do and showing him where everything was kept, Sharpe turned to the young man and said: "You take your horse. Castelan here will be making the journey every day on foot."

That evening, after he had finished work, Patrick locked the yacht and started up the road. When he had almost reached the Castle, Blaise and Jeremy came cantering along the driveway and passed him.

Immediately Jeremy reined in his horse.

"Blaise!" he called, "Wait a minute, here's Patrick Castelan."

Blaise shouted something about being late and cantered on, but Jeremy turned and trotted back.

"So you've started work," he said. "Good."

"It's my second day," Patrick replied.

"Why are you walking?"

"I don't have a horse."

"Why not? The young man who looked after the yacht before you had one."

"He was a Protestant," Patrick explained, smiling noncommittally.

Jeremy looked embarrassed, then laughed.

"What! No horses for Catholics! Sharpe seems to have forgotten the Penal Laws were repealed in eighteen twenty nine. I'm so sorry, I'll make sure he finds you something good."

TEN

The train lurched, and began moving slowly forward. Blaise leaned out of the window to wave to his mother standing on the platform. When he kissed her goodbye, he had been surprised to see tears glistening in her eyes. Normally, Lady Stafford was a person completely in control of herself -- emotion in public was something she would never permit.

He leaned out further and waved again, but she had turned away and was walking back into the station. Taking hold of the leather strap he pulled the window closed and sat down, staring at the opposite side of the compartment, rocking with the motion of the train.

The tears in his mother's eyes were so unlike her. He felt his heartbeat quicken and perspiration tingle on his forehead as he began to wonder if she had some premonition about him.

The warning sound of the engine's whistle as the train approached the level crossing on the Limerick road made Blaise glance outside. Behind the closed gates of the crossing a group of people were waiting for the train to pass. Among them he saw Rosaleen, her head turning from side to side as she tried to see into the carriages.

Blaise jumped up, flung open the window and put his

head out. He started to wave but she was looking the other way. He shouted her name but a moment later they had rounded the next curve and he could no longer see her.

Slowly he shut the window and sat down. Taking a cigarette from his case he tapped it on the lid, hardly noticing the bare countryside slipping passed. He remembered soldiers he'd known who began to think they were going to get killed, and invariably they were. It was as if the idea took hold and became self-fulfilling.

He lit the cigarette and inhaled deeply.

It was necessary, he knew, to be absolutely and unshakably convinced that you were not going to die. You must believe without any doubt whatsoever that you would be one of the survivors. He repeated this several times to reassure himself but, as he sat back in the corner of the seat, a feeling of helplessness and terror began to take hold of him.

The fact that Rosaleen had come to the level crossing, hoping to catch a glimpse of him, made him think that she too, like his mother, had some inkling she might not be seeing him again. The native Irish believed in leprechauns and magic, and some of them were said to be clairvoyant.

"I'm not going to get killed!" he shouted to the empty carriage. "I am going to survive this war, inherit my father's title, and live to a ripe old age."

He laughed aloud, but somehow the sound of his laughter rang hollow. Looking out at the windswept landscape he drew deeply on his cigarette, wondering if he would ever see County Clare again.

The troop train was due to leave Charing Cross Station

at half past four in the afternoon, and they would cross the channel in darkness when there was less risk from the U-Boats. Blaise and a group of officers had a long lunch at his club. Everyone drank heavily but no one got drunk, and they all arrived at the station bright and talkative, as if they hadn't a worry in the world.

Blaise recognized several officers from his regiment who were being seen off by wives and girl friends. They were laughing and talking loudly to each other, consciously exuding the confidence and leadership of their class, setting an example to the Tommies crowded together further down the platform, families crying and hugging each other, saying what they really felt.

Blaise's batman found him, confirmed all his gear was on the train and said he would come to him again when they reached Dover.

Lighting another cigarette he stared fixedly across the station to the gateway at the back. He could just see the first of the ambulances parked outside, waiting for the trainload of wounded that would arrive as soon as they had left.

As the guard blew a warning on his whistle a Bentley sports car came weaving through the line of taxis onto the platform, the young woman at the wheel frantically sounding the horn. Beside her sat a young officer, his cap tilted at a rakish angle.

"Bertie!" Blaise shouted. "Over here! For God's sake hurry up or you'll be shot as a deserter!"

The train whistle echoed through the arched roof of the station, the carriages lurched then started to move forward as Bertie came running alongside the open door and Blaise swung him aboard.

Laughing and waving to the girl in the Bentley, he blew her kisses until the curve in the track hid her from sight.

There was a strong wind blowing up the channel and the troop ship rolled and pitched violently. Although most of those around him were getting sick Blaise felt fine, but by the time they'd docked in Boulougne the soothing effect of the brandy was wearing off and he began to worry again.

The troop train waiting for them had a few very old passenger coaches for the officers and cattle trucks for the Tommies. It pulled out of the station in the total darkness of the black-out and was soon clear of the town.

Bertie turned to Blaise in the crowded carriage and said: "You seem very preoccupied, old chap, since we left London. Is everything all right?"

"Of course it is. But going back to the front after leave isn't much fun, is it?"

"No it's not. A bit like going back to school. Extraordinary to think it was only two years ago since we were there together. It seems more like a hundred, doesn't it?"

ELEVEN

Two hours later the train arrived at the base camp near Arras and as soon as they stepped out on the platform they could hear the artillery up at the front line and see the flashes of guns in the night sky.

Half asleep, stumbling in the darkness, they made their way to the transit camp, wooden huts and tents set out in lines beside the railway track.

Blaise lay on the wooden bunk in his clothes, trying to sleep but found it impossible. Just before reveille at six o'clock the noise of the guns grew louder and more intense. Several of the men sat up, listening.

"That's a rolling barrage," one of them said. "They're getting ready to attack. Either us or Jerry."

There would be no more sleep for any of them that night and they began to get up and go outside into the chill morning. The distant gun flashes were growing fainter in the brightening sky but the noise of the barrage continued relentlessly until about seven o'clock when abruptly the rumble of gunfire ceased and everything went quiet. In the eerie silence somebody said: "The attacking infantry are going over the top." Another muttered: "Poor buggers,"

At eight o'clock they assembled in the mess tent for breakfast. The continuing silence made everyone uneasy and tense, and nobody had much interest in eating. Blaise and Bertie went outside and stood with a group of the others, smoking cigarettes and looking northwards in the direction of the front line. They were beginning to disperse when they heard the sound of a motorcycle. A dispatch rider was approaching and they watched him ride across the parade ground and stop in front of the command center. Pushing his goggles up onto his cap, he got off and went inside carrying a leather dispatch case.

Fifteen minutes later all the officers were assembled in the briefing room, waiting for the Colonel. When he came in, everyone rose to their feet. Walking to the center of the dais he picked up a pointer and said: "Gentlemen, please be seated and I'll brief you on the situation that's developing."

Bertie and Blaise looked at each other as they sat down.

"This is the present front line in our sector," the Colonel continued, tracing the pattern of the British and German trenches plotted on the wall map. "We are here, approximately seven miles back from the front. The terrain in this area favors defense. So far, we have not attacked the Germans, nor they us. Until today that is."

He turned to face them.

"We've been taken by surprise. There were no intelligence reports of an impending German attack and our reconnaissance aeroplanes had not detected any particular build-up on their side. This morning, however, after a very heavy barrage German infantry attacked in strength at three minutes to seven. They overran our first line of trenches and are now massing along our second line. We have no reserves in this area and it will be several days before we can deploy enough troops to meet them in equal numbers. In the meantime, if they break through again they'll be into open country and could wheel around in a westerly direction, threatening our whole defensive system in the area."

The Colonel traced the line of a possible German advance, making a hooked motion on the map with his pointer.

"I have here a dispatch from Headquarters, ordering me to get every man in the transit camp moving up to the front. I realize many of you are cavalry officers, pilots in the Royal Flying Corps, and I even see some Navy people with us."

Everyone laughed, and Bertie leaned over and whispered, "Blazer, old chap, I never thought we'd end up as bloody infantry, did you?"

". . . about three miles from here towards the front," continued the Colonel, "there's the village of Sainte Marie, located in a shallow valley with a small river, and behind it a ridge of high ground, a good defensive position. I need an officer to hold the north part of the village until the bridge is mined and fortifications are constructed. Could I have a volunteer, please?" he asked, looking around.

Nobody moved as his eyes swept across their faces. Then he looked at Blaise.

Immediately, he stood up.

"Stafford, sir. Cavalry. Seventh Dragoons."

"Stafford? Lord Stafford's son?"

"Yes."

"I was with your father in the Second Afghan Campaign. Please come up here so you can see the map better."

By eleven o'clock they were ready to go and Blaise

started along the road, walking ahead of about forty men from various services, marching in some sort of order. Behind them came an artillery limber loaded with explosives, drawn by a team of horses.

After about an hour, as they were approaching the village of Sainte Marie, the sound of aircraft made them all look up. With terrifying speed, two Fokker tri-planes, one behind the other, dropped down out of the sky and flew straight at them a few feet above the road. Puffs of dust raced ahead as machine-gun bullets hit the ground until the lead plane passed directly over Blaise's head with a stunning roar of engine and guns.

The screams of men behind him, and the awful sounds of dying horses tangled in their harness, made him turn. Numb with shock, he stood in the middle of the road and stared at the scene before him. The noise of the second plane diving at them finally hit home and he sprang to the side of the road, rolling over and over until he fell into the ditch.

He lay there, listening to the planes growing fainter. Almost immediately he heard the roar of another approaching, and sitting up saw that the first one had already wheeled around in a wide circle and was starting to make a second strafing run down the road, empty now except for dead and dying soldiers, and horses struggling to stand on their shattered legs.

Blaise leaped to his feet, pulled his revolver out of its holster and fired at the plane as it passed over his head before making a climbing turn to the east, towards the German lines.

Suddenly calm, he began to take charge. He called for

stretcher bearers and first aid for the wounded, shot the dying horses, organized the men into squads to unload the explosives from the artillery limber, and started them moving up the road again. A few miles further on, they descended into a valley and entered a deserted village.

It was completely quiet and still, everything in order, nothing damaged, as if a silent plague had carried off the inhabitants and they had died without a murmur.

Blaise led the men along the main street of the village to the bridge at the other side of the town. Under his direction, they barricaded the street with overturned carts, and filled sandbags to make firing positions. The engineers mined the bridge and laid the detonating wire about a hundred yards down the street into a wine shop. The owner had left in such a hurry that he had forgotten to lock the door, and his cigarettes and matches were still on top of the cash register.

The engineer officer put the detonating plunger on the counter in front of Blaise, connected the wire from the bridge to it then said: "There'll be quite a bang when it blows. Make sure you get all your men back over this side before pushing down that plunger. I'd like to leave one of my men to help you but there's too few of us."

"Don't worry," Blaise said. "I can handle it."

"Right then. She's all wired up and ready to go."

Glancing over Blaise's shoulder at the rows of bottles and the wine barrel behind the counter he said: "Let's have a drink."

"Looting?" Blaise asked, raising his eyebrows in mock surprise.

"Hell, no! I wouldn't do that."

Blaise took two glasses from the shelf and filled them

with strong dark wine from the barrel.

The officer dug into his pocket and pulled out some money then put a few coins on the counter as he threw back his head and drained his glass.

"You're cavalry," he said, looking at the flashings on Blaise's uniform.

"Yes, I am."

"You and your men are in a difficult position here. When the Huns attack you're going to have to retreat back up that hill. You'll be exposed all the way up to the top, until you get to the ridge."

"What do you mean?"

"It's not good to be in a position where your only line of retreat is up a hill behind you. If I were you," he continued, "after you get your men back to this point and blow the bridge, run like hell immediately after the explosion and don't wait to set up defensive positions."

"Why not?"

"Because for a minute or two, the enemy won't be able to see you through the smoke and falling debris. The moment it clears, though, they'll be able to pick you off like sitting ducks if you're strung out up the hill."

After he'd gone Blaise drank another glass of wine, then went out into the deserted street and looked towards the high ground rising behind the town. The officer was half way to the top of the ridge and clearly visible. Frowning, Blaise turned and started walking towards the bridge.

He crossed the river and made an inspection. The men had worked hard, reinforcing the barricade with furniture taken from houses on either side of the street, and now had a formidable obstacle to slow down the German advance.

Feeling happier, he stopped in the center of the bridge and leaned over the wall. A trout darted through the water and for a moment he saw its speckled back as it swam upstream and passed beneath him. The river, though twenty feet wide, was shallow.

It would be easy for the Germans to cross on either side and surround those defending the bridge, probably annihilating most of them. The more he thought about it the more uneasy he became. He remembered his mother's tears when he left Ballinahinch station, and Rosaleen at the level crossing.

A premonition of his death?

Straightening himself, he looked at his watch. It was five o'clock. The shadows were beginning to lengthen, and a slight chill was in the autumn air.

He went back to the wine shop. He knew he shouldn't drink on duty but decided to have one more drop to steady his nerves. As he started to pour he saw a bottle of brandy on a lower shelf.

After his second glass he began to feel calm and quite philosophical. If he was to be killed defending the bridge of Sainte Marie then so be it. He would be remembered as someone who had kept up the Stafford tradition and died an honorable death for King and Country. It all began to seem attractive to him, and he repeated aloud the words of Keats: 'Half in love with easeful death,' then wondered if he knew really what was meant.

He drained the glass then looked at his watch. The luminous dial showed half past nine. The desire to sleep was becoming overwhelming. Reminding himself that he must inspect the barricade again at midnight he allowed his

PATRICK & VICTORIA   53

head to rest for a moment on the counter.

Blaise awoke abruptly and sprang to his feet.

Outside, bullets ricocheted from side to side of the narrow street and he could hear shouting and firing from the direction of the bridge. Flailing around in the darkness he found the plunger and pushed the handle down to its limit.

Silence.

Thinking something had gone wrong, he straightened up at the instant the explosion shattered the windows of the wine shop and the concussion hurled him backwards. Recovering his balance he groped his way outside and staggered towards the bridge, pieces of brick and debris falling all around him.

When the smoke cleared he could see, in the light of early dawn, the barricade with the British soldiers trapped on the other side of the river. They were desperately firing at the mass of German infantry advancing steadily down the street towards them.

TWELVE

Every Sunday morning the Protestant staff of the Castle attended the church on the estate but the Catholics went to Ballinahinch in large, horse drawn open carriages provided by the Staffords ever since Catholic Emancipation in 1829.

On his first Sunday, Patrick dressed carefully and assembled with the others in the yard promptly at nine o'clock. The day was overcast and the air chilled with the first hint of the coming winter.

The driver of the first carriage cracked his whip and they moved off, passing under the arch and breaking into a trot down the driveway.

The more senior Catholic staff sat quietly in the first two rows while the younger stable boys and maids chattered and laughed in the rear. Patrick kept to himself, watching the scenery roll by, lulled by the rhythmic clip-clop of the horses' hooves.

As they approached the town he heard the bells ringing for Mass. People were converging from all directions towards the church, towering above the surrounding white-washed houses and cottages. They stopped in front of the gate and as they started to get down the driver warned them he would be leaving for Ballinahinch Castle at exactly half past eleven. Anyone who was late, he said, would have to walk.

Just before ten o'clock a large carriage glowing with fresh paint and varnish pulled up, and a heavyset man in a fur-collared overcoat and bowler hat got out. His fleshy face was turkey-red from whiskey, and his double chin almost covered his tie and the winged collar of his shirt. He glanced at the crowd then turned to help a fat woman, dressed in Sunday finery, step down from the carriage. She was followed by a girl about Patrick's age, then a young man of about twenty and two boys who looked much younger.

As they walked up the pathway to the main door of the church, Patrick noticed people moving respectfully out of the way for them. Men were tipping their caps, and women making quick curtsies as they passed.

"Who are they?" Patrick asked O'Shaughnessy.

"That's O'Malley, the Gombeen Man, and his brood. He owns most of Ballinahinch. Bog aristocracy of the very highest order."

At the end of Mass, Patrick waited until the O'Malley family filed out. The daughter, though not pretty, was graceful and feminine, with large bright eyes dominating her face.

He tried to edge through the crowd and keep them in sight but when he finally reached the door of the church their coach was already moving off.

"We have half an hour," O'Shaughnessy said. "Like a walk through the metropolis?"

Although most of the shops were closed, the people

were milling up and down the main street in groups, talking among themselves, the younger men and women eying each other with lively interest.

"O'Malley looks to be a very rich man, almost as rich as one of the Ascendancy," Patrick said.

O'Shaughnessy snorted with laughter.

"Richer than most of them. Since he's made his money he tries to ape them. You've already seen his big coach. He's just finished building himself an enormous house, and now has a huge staff of servants. Huge everything."

They were nearing the center of the town.

"Look, I'm off to Hanrahan's Bar for a quick drink before we have to go. Coming?"

"No thank you," Patrick replied. "I don't drink. I've taken the Pledge."

"Why in the name of God did you do that? It's one of the only pleasures us Irish have left."

"The priest on the island made me take it before I went away to school."

"Went away to school?" O'Shaughnessy repeated. "What do you mean?"

"Boarding school."

"Where?"

"Clongowes Wood."

"But that's the best Jesuit school in Ireland. With an education like that, why on earth are you working as a stable boy with the likes of me?"

"I didn't finish."

"Finish what?"

"School. I had to leave when I was fifteen."

"Why was that?"

"Oh, it's a long story," Patrick replied, suddenly angry and resentful. "You enjoy your drink. I'm going to take a look at the rest of the town."

After he had been walking for some time he saw a group of the young maids from the Castle coming down the other side of the street towards him. The prettiest, a blonde girl with light blue eyes, stopped when she saw him and came over.

"Hello, handsome," she said, allowing her body to sag into a saucy and provocative shape. "My name's Rosaleen. I've been dying to talk to you. Tell me, is it true that you rescued Lady Victoria the day her brother was drowned?"

"Yes, it is."

"And they offered you a big reward and you didn't take it?"

Patrick nodded.

"Don't you think that was rather silly?" she said, a hint of mockery in her voice.

"My father is a man of principle. He doesn't like to take money unless he's earned it."

"Principle? Lunacy I'd call it. People like us sometimes get one chance. It must be grabbed because it never happens again."

THIRTEEN

During the following weeks the Castle became very quiet. All the family had gone away to their house in Dublin, and Patrick's life developed into a routine of work broken only by the Sunday visits to Ballinahinch for Mass.

In early December it was announced that all the family were coming home for Christmas. Patrick was told that he'd be expected to help in the dining room and carry drinks and refreshments at parties because the staff had been reduced by the departure of many of the servants for war service. Such work, Patrick felt, was beneath him and he decided to leave. But after thinking about it for a couple of days he realized he should stay because of the money. Also, he admitted to himself, he wanted to see Victoria again.

During the week before Christmas the weather became very cold, the nights freezing and the days clear in bright winter sunshine. By mid-morning the sun had melted the frost except for the shadows of the trees and buildings etched in white on the hard ground, and by four o'clock it was beginning to get dark again.

On the afternoon the family were due to arrive, the house servants -- now reduced to thirty -- were assembled in the hall in two lines graded in declining importance. Patrick rated a position about half way down one line: on the other side, at the extreme end, was Rosaleen. She caught his eye and winked slowly, pressing her tongue into the side of her cheek. Embarrassed, he looked away as the butler began to speak.

"His Lordship will be arriving in about ten minutes," he said looking at his watch. "When they telephone from the gate you will all walk through the door and form two lines either side of the stairway. Most of you have done this before and know the drill. The female staff will curtsy as his Lordship and the members of the family pass, and the male staff will nod the head in a slow and respectful manner. In the unlikely event any of you are spoken to, you will keep your answers short, and speak in a quiet and respectful voice."

At that moment the telephone rang and the butler hurried to answer it.

"Lord Stafford is here," he announced. "Everyone get a move on."

They all filed out and took their positions down the sides of the stairway. The setting sun, low on the horizon, brightened their faces and cast long shadows in saw-toothed patterns diagonally across the stone steps.

A few minutes later the Rolls Royce came into view, its wheels crunching on the gravel as it glided slowly around the circle of driveway. It pulled up at the foot of the stairs and the chauffeur got out. He opened the door, then stood back as Lord Stafford emerged, imposing in his General's uniform.

Holding the veil on her hat, Lady Stafford took her husband's hand and stepped out with studied grace. Blaise followed, his face set in a rigid expression. Jeremy came next, smiling agreeably, and then Victoria.

They came forward together in a group, sedate and unhurried, acknowledging the more senior servants with a barely perceptible nod of the head. Victoria saw Patrick immediately and paused for a moment as they passed.

"Hello," she said. "How nice to see you again."

Surprised, not sure what to say, he murmured, "Welcome home."

"Thank you. I'm so glad you decided to stay with us."

She smiled at him, her eyes wide and friendly, then turned and ran up the stairs after the others.

FOURTEEN

On Christmas Eve the Staffords always gave a lunch party, and guests began arriving soon after eleven o'clock in the morning. Those who lived nearby came in carriages and on horseback, while those from further afield came in motor cars. The last to arrive was a rakish and elegant Hispano-Suizza sports car, its canvas hood open despite the cold. It was driven by a young woman wrapped in furs, a Cossack hat pulled down on her head like a Russian princess. As she skidded to a stop at the foot of the stairs Blaise ran passed Patrick and bounded down to meet her.

"My darling Pippa," he called, "how are you, my pet?"

A footman stood waiting at the bottom step. He moved forward but she'd already pushed open the car door and got out, leaving the engine running for the footman to deal with. She and Blaise came up the steps arm-in-arm, laughing and talking, happy and stimulated by each other, and strode past Patrick as if he wasn't there.

He stared after them, then whispered to a servant standing beside him: "Who is Pippa?"

"Lady Philippa Tremayne," he replied, speaking without moving his lips. "She's the eldest daughter, and Lord Tremayne's heir because there's no son. They think she'll marry Blaise. Gorgeous, isn't she? What I wouldn't give to have a night with her."

He stopped short as he saw the butler hurrying towards them.

"That will be the last of the guests," he said, sharp and authorative. "Remember what I've told you. Everything must be perfect."

Patrick went into the banqueting hall and joined the other servants making last minute preparations.

On either side were cavernous fireplaces with huge logs burning and crackling and radiating heat out into the room. Down the center was the banqueting table, extended to take twenty four people on either side. Clusters of glasses and silver were grouped in front of each chair with napkins folded like a bishop's miter forming long symmetrical lines from one end to the other.

Precisely at half past one the gong in the hall was struck three times, its muffled echo sounding throughout the Castle.

Patrick had been instructed to look after the three places near Lady Stafford's end of the table. Apprehensively he watched Blaise and Pippa approach. Blaise held her chair until with an elegant movement of her hand she swept her skirt to one side as he slid the chair forward. He then sat down on her right. On her left was a gray-haired old man with a fiery red face and beside him, Lady Stafford.

Patrick picked up two steaming bowls of soup and carried them carefully to the table.

"Excuse me," he said.

Without looking up, Pippa leaned away from Blaise as Patrick placed the soup in front of her. For an instant before he stepped back he was conscious of the faint scent of expensive perfume, of clean hair and fresh clothes, the aroma of wealth and privilege hovering all around her.

One course followed another, different wines were served and the conversation, loud and animated, continued at a steady pitch. Finally, about an hour later, they brought in the Christmas cake and wine waiters moved nimbly around the room, filling everyone's glass with champagne.

Patrick glanced up the table at Victoria and saw she was happily talking to a dashing young man about her own age. Looking away he stared directly in front of him, his eyes on the guests at the lower end of the table.

Pippa was leaning towards the old man, listening intently to what he was saying. Blaise, holding a champagne glass in his right hand, was talking to the woman opposite him. Patrick was about to look away when a slight movement drew his attention to the officer's flashing on Blaise's left cuff.

Mesmerized, he watched Blaise's hand slide over Pippa's knee to the inside of her thigh. She stiffened then widened her legs and continued talking as if nothing had happened.

The ringing sound of a piece of cutlery striking a glass made Patrick look up. People stopped talking and as the hall became quiet Lord Stafford rose to speak.

"My friends, Lady Stafford and I would like to wish you all a very happy Christmas. This year, because of the war, many of our friends are not with us, and many have given their lives for King and Country. Although they will never come back, their memories will be in our hearts forever . . ."

Patrick glanced down at Blaise, sitting stiff and upright. He had removed his hand from Pippa's thigh and was now clenching it tightly on the table beside him.

". . . and, with the help of God, the Allied armies will drive the Germans back across their own frontiers and victory will be ours in nineteen sixteen. God save the King!"

After a prolonged round of applause, everyone stood up then moved in groups out into the hall and across to the drawing room on the west side of the Castle.

All the thirty bedrooms were full over Christmas but on New Year's Day most of the guests started to leave. The following week Lord Stafford and Blaise returned to the war and only Lady Stafford, Victoria and Jeremy remained at home.

When Patrick was told that Victoria would soon be returning to Dublin he felt depressed. He knew it was irrational, and determined not to indulge in sexual fantasies about girls of the Ascendancy like some of the other servants, he resolutely cast her out of his mind. But, despite himself, on the day of her departure he arranged to be exercising one of the horses at the time she would be leaving to catch the train.

Hidden in a grove of trees some distance from the Castle he watched the car being loaded with luggage until finally he saw her appear with her mother at the top of the stairway.

As the car moved off he spurred his horse into a gallop and emerged a few minutes later on the driveway near the main gate. When the chauffeur saw him he immediately slowed down not to frighten the horse.

Patrick raised his hand tentatively at the car as it passed. Victoria immediately turned in her seat and looked out of the window directly into his eyes. She smiled and waved, mouthing the word "Goodbye" as they rounded the bend in the drive and were hidden by the trees.

FIFTEEN

After weeks of cold wind and driving rain, St. Patrick's Day dawned bright and clear. Soon after nine o'clock, the Catholic servants left for Mass, happy and laughing as today was their holiday.

"Did you mean it when you said I could come with you to the O'Malley's St. Patrick's Day party?" Patrick asked, turning to O'Shaughnessy beside him.

"Of course I did. I've already got the invite from Kevin."

At Mass, Patrick sat three rows behind the O'Malley family and could see obliquely through the rows of people in front of him the profile of Kathleen, intent on her prayer book.

She was not beautiful like Victoria, nor pretty in the provocative way that Rosaleen was, but she had a quality of wholesome femininity about her that made Patrick feel he was looking at someone quite special.

When the service was over, as on previous Sundays the congregation waited respectfully while O'Malley led his family slowly down the aisle of the church. Immediately they'd passed, O'Shaughnessy nudged Patrick with his elbow, encouraging him to push his way out of the pew.

Along both sides of the main street flags were draped on upstairs window sills or hanging over the pavement on poles. There were green flags of St. Patrick with Celtic crosses, pennants of the Knights of Columbanus, and Papal banners with the keys of St. Peter embroidered on them.

Everyone was in a festive mood, and many of the girls were dressed in traditional Irish green and red petticoats with black shawls around their shoulders. There were pipers playing, children dancing, and by the time they had walked through the town to the Limerick road they were as light-hearted as everyone else.

"Well, well, well," O'Shaughnessy said as they arrived in front of the recently completed gateway to the O'Malley's house. "Would you look at that!"

He pointed at the name 'Tara' chiseled on the gate pillars either side, the letters picked out in gold paint.

"Tara," he said, laughing. "The seat of the High Kings of Ireland. The vulgarity of the man, it's unbelievable," he added as they started up the driveway.

Outside the house there were ponies and traps, and horses tethered to the railings by the front door. Several of them had feeding bags around their heads or piles of hay at their feet. As Patrick went up the steps he could hear sounds of lively fiddle music and hand-clapping punctuated with loud laughter.

O'Shaughnessy beat out a tattoo on the door knocker, ending up with two resounding blows. Moments later a maid in a starched cap and apron let them in.

They followed her to the living room and stood in the doorway watching Kathleen and her two younger brothers dancing an Irish reel. They were dressed in green kilts with cloaks around their shoulders secured by large silver pins of traditional Gaelic design. Although they all danced well,

Kathleen gave it a rare elegance and style. Auburn hair slightly tousled, faces flushed, they came to the end and bowed in response to the applause. Kathleen, still breathing deeply, went over to her father and mother and kissed them both on their foreheads.

"Well, O'Shaughnessy, a hundred thousand welcomes," a voice behind them said in Gaelic.

Turning around they saw a young man in his early twenties who bore a marked resemblance to Kathleen, including the same auburn hair.

"I'm Kevin O'Malley," he said, shaking Patrick's hand. "I'm sure you two men could use a ball of malt."

"Ball of malt?"

"Yes," Kevin said. "A large glass of Irish whiskey.'

"This poor fellow has taken the Pledge," O'Shaughnessy said, grinning. "He only drinks lemonade."

They both laughed then went across to the bar. Uncertain what to do, Patrick decided to pay his respects to Mr. and Mrs. O'Malley who were sitting in two large chairs on either side of the fireplace. Some older people of their generation sat near them, while numerous men and woman stood nearby listening attentively to whatever they were saying and laughing at Mr. O'Malley's jokes.

Patrick went over to Mrs. O'Malley, a tightly corseted woman whose fat pale face was topped by a thin bun of graying hair.

"Patrick Castelan," he said, introducing himself. "I came with O'Shaughnessy, who was at school with your son, Kevin."

He held out his hand to her. She looked up into his face, suddenly interested.

"Are you the young man who rescued Lord Stafford's daughter the day his son was drowned?" she asked.

"Yes, my father and I had been out fishing."

"You're welcome to our house," Mr. O'Malley said, interrupting him. "You'll have a ball of malt?"

"No thank you, Mr. O'Malley. Your son has already offered me one but I took the Pledge a number of years ago."

"I wish you'd take the Pledge," Mrs. O'Malley said, nudging her husband, "and Kevin too."

O'Malley grunted something then took the cigarette from his mouth, spilling ash on his waistcoat. "What do you do at the Castle?" he asked.

Patrick told him.

"After saving their daughter's life you'd think they'd give you a better job than that. Now if you'd been a Protestant, the sky would have been the limit. But, in any case, if you've the drive and determination to better yourself come and see me about a job," he said, dismissing him.

Patrick wandered from room to room, through the crowd of prosperous Catholics. The men were all drinking heavily, their woman clustered together in little groups talking among themselves. The fiddler continued to play, his eyes darting through the crowd, frequently glancing over at O'Malley.

At three o'clock 'dinner' was announced and they all moved into the dining room to a lavish buffet of smoked salmon, pheasant, roast beef and lamb, and a large dish of pigs feet. Patrick picked up a plate and took some roast beef and vegetables.

"I think that's exactly what I want."

Startled for a moment, he turned and saw Kathleen standing beside him.

"Please have this," he said, offering his plate.

"Thank you. Would you like to sit down?" she asked, watching Patrick help himself. "There're so many people here today that we couldn't seat them all but come with me."

Patrick followed her into the conservatory, through a profusion of green plants and flowers, to a white wicker table and chairs with brightly colored cushions.

"This is very pleasant," he said looking around.

"It's my creation, within the house of O'Malley."

"Well, it's really very beautiful."

They ate in silence for a few moments, then both spoke at the same time, laughing with embarrassment.

"I was just going to say that this is our first St. Patrick's Day in this house. Last year we were still living over the shop. Now we're behaving like landed gentry."

"The new Ireland?"

"The emerging Bog Aristocracy. Hundreds of years of oppression have left their mark. Our people can accept the British being in charge of everything, but they're jealous when one of their own makes money and they want to pull him down."

"There's nobody rich on Ennismore so we don't have these problems."

"The loss of our Gaelic culture and language," she continued, serious and anxious to talk, "is what has really reduced us to serfs. If it wasn't for Lady Gregory, Yeats, and Thomas Moore there'd be nothing left. When I finish school next year I hope to go to Dublin to study at the Abbey Theater. I'd love to be in Gaelic plays."

"You want to be an actress?"

"Yes," she said with determination.

"There's not much call for play acting in Ballinahinch."

"I am not planning to spend the rest of my life in Ballinahinch," she said quietly. "I don't want my parents to know this but I intend to make something of myself and my life."

Suddenly she looked over Patrick's shoulder and saw her father striding into the conservatory.

"So, Kathleen, this is where you've been hiding yourself."

"I'm not hiding, father. We just wanted to sit down to eat our food."

"Well, now that you've finished," he said nodding at her empty plate, "you should go back to your other guests."

Kathleen blushed. She stood up abruptly and without a word walked quickly out of the room.

As soon as O'Malley was sure she had gone he turned to Patrick: "See here, young man, my daughter is a bright and intelligent girl. She'll make a great match for the right man one day for she'll have a very large dowry, so let me make this perfectly clear. My daughter will never be marrying a stable boy from Ballinahinch Castle."

SIXTEEN

Late in March, Victoria returned home with her younger brother Jeremy for the Easter holidays. Patrick did not see her arrive but heard the chauffeur say that she'd grown up a lot during the last few months and was no longer just a schoolgirl. She was becoming very beautiful he said, and looked like Lady Stafford thirty years ago.

It was several days before he saw her. She and Jeremy had been out riding and they came down to the harbor on their way back to the Castle. Patrick was cleaning the brass on deck, and hearing the sound of horse's hooves on the cobblestones he looked up and watched them approach.

"Hello, how are you?" Victoria called out as they stopped on the dock above him. "The yacht looks beautiful."

"So it should," he said smiling at her. "I'm wearing the metalwork away with all this polishing."

"Good morning, and God be with you," Jeremy said in Gaelic.

Patrick looked surprised. "I didn't know you spoke our language."

"More than that," Victoria said proudly, "Jeremy writes poetry in Gaelic as well."

"He does? That's most unusual. You must like languages," he said turning to face him.

"I do. People say I have a flair for them," he answered modestly. "Do they interest you?"

"Yes. I learned some French at school, as well as Greek and Latin.

"From the priest on the island?"

"No, I went to a Jesuit school for a while."

"Where?"

"Near Dublin."

"You're very well educated then."

"Not really. I left when I was fifteen."

"Why?"

"The fees were being paid for by my uncle in the Colonial Service. When he died his pension was only enough to support his widow."

"What a shame."

Patrick shrugged his shoulders, irritated at being reminded.

"Look, can I get you both something to drink? A cup of tea perhaps?"

"That would be lovely," Victoria said, slipping her riding boots out of the stirrups.

They tethered their horses and came down the gangway.

Taking off their hats they sat in the cockpit while Patrick went below to light the oil stove under the kettle.

"I'm afraid the Castle will be very full during the Easter holidays," Victoria called down to him. "We've got lots of Daddy and Mummy's friends coming as well as ours."

"Lots?"

"Yes. I hope it won't make too much extra work for you."

Patrick came up carrying a tray with empty mugs and a jug of milk. "We'll manage," he said smiling at her. "It's the nature of life. Some are born to serve."

"It's only an accident of birth," Jeremy said, awkward and defensive.

"My brother still believes that babies are made in heaven," Victoria explained, smiling at her brother, "and are waiting there in rows to come down to the world to be born."

"And some of us arrive on Ennismore, and others at Ballinahinch Castle," Patrick said, laughing.

"Have you been able to get home yet?"

"No. It'll be another month before the sea is calm enough."

"Does everyone on the island still speak Gaelic?" Jeremy asked.

"Yes, but the priest insists that all the young people learn English properly in case they emigrate to England or America."

Hearing the kettle whistle, Patrick went below to make the tea. When he emerged again carrying the teapot Jeremy stood up to help him.

"I should love to see Ennismore," he said, pushing the empty mugs across to Patrick. "May I come and visit your family next summer?"

"Of course. You'd be most welcome."

"Do you still have bards and story tellers on the island?"

"Yes. Most of the stories of great deeds aren't all written down, despite the efforts of the Gaelic League."

"Jeremy would like to record some of them and have them published."

The three of them chatted, easy in each others company, and didn't notice the dark clouds beginning to build up across the sky. The horses, smelling rain, were becoming restless, whinnying and pawing the ground.

"Victoria, we'd better be on our way," Jeremy said, glancing up at the sky, "otherwise we're going to get drenched."

Patrick watched them walk their horses to the end of the dock and mount. Victoria turned in her saddle and waved. Her tailored riding clothes, combined with the poise and assurance of the Staffords, made her look at least twenty years old.

By contrast, Jeremy didn't even look like a Stafford. His gold rimmed glasses, his sweetness of character, and his courtesy and diffidence in dealing with people like Patrick made some of the Protestant servants say he was a foundling and not one of the family at all.

SEVENTEEN

The next day, Good Friday, Victoria returned about the same time, alone. "Hello," she called out to him. "I've just been to church and the Vicar gave a very long and depressing sermon. May I come aboard?"

Since early morning the wind had blown strongly from the north and the waves from the bay outside came in the mouth of the harbor, making the yacht move uneasily in its moorings and the masts and rigging creak overhead.

Patrick again made tea and they sat in the wheel house, their elbows on the chart table, looking out to sea at the white-capped waves and banks of dark cloud partly hiding Ennismore.

"I've hardly been here any time at all but I suppose I'd better go," Victoria said picking up her hat and riding crop. "If I don't, Daisy and I will be soaked."

They went up the gangway to the dock.

She untethered the horse and led it along the jetty, Patrick walking beside her.

By now the storm was almost upon them and large drops of rain had already begun to fall, forming a pattern of black spots on the cobblestones and making the horse shiver and tug at the bridle.

"I'd better make a run for it," Victoria said, adjusting the reins and grabbing the pummel of the saddle. She slipped the toe of her boot into the stirrup and started to mount but the horse jerked away just as a sudden gust of wind caught them momentarily off balance, abruptly engulfing them in heavy rain.

"Let's shelter," Victoria shouted. "Where can we put Daisy?"

"At the back of the boat house, where I keep my horse."

The stable was warm and dry and smelled agreeably of hay and leather. Leaning on either side they looked out of the half-door and watched the storm until the wind, gusting and changing direction, blew sheets of rain in their faces.

"How long will it last?" Victoria asked, stepping backwards.

"Hard to say. It can't keep raining like this for more than fifteen or twenty minutes. I'm sorry there isn't anything for you to sit on."

"We'd be much more comfortable inside."

"I don't have a key."

"I know where there's one," Victoria replied. "We used to come here as children."

Walking over to the connecting door she stood on her toes and reached up, feeling with the tips of her fingers along the top of the door frame.

"Here it is!" she said triumphantly.

She unlocked the door, then put the key back in its hiding place. They walked through to the living room and sat down facing each other.

After a few moments of embarrassed silence Victoria said: "This boat house was constructed by the only Stafford who'd served in the Navy rather than the Army. He'd been with Nelson at the Battle of the Nile and was badly wounded. He came home to convalesce in seventeen ninety eight, just after the rebellion had been put down. They used prisoners to construct it . . ."

Abruptly she stopped talking as they both heard the sound of an approaching car.

"Who on earth can that be?" she exclaimed, walking over to the window facing the road from the Castle.

Patrick followed her and looked out.

Coming over the rise and down the hill was the Hispano Suizza sports car. Pippa Tremayne was driving, Blaise beside her in the passenger seat.

"My God!" Victoria cried out, her eyes staring in panic. "They're coming here!"

They both stood back from the window as the car passed. They heard it swing around the boat house and come to a stop outside. Mesmerized, they stared at the front door and heard the sound of the key being put into the lock.

Signaling with an upward movement of her eyes Victoria ran, quick and silent, across the room and up the stairs, Patrick right behind her. They had just reached the landing when Pippa and Blaise burst in with a rush of wind and rain, slamming the door behind them.

They stood for a moment, laughing and brushing the raindrops off their clothes. Then Blaise lifted Pippa off her feet, kissing her mouth, her neck, her cheeks as he slowly turned her around and around.

Pushing against him she broke free and whispered: "Blaise! You're absolutely enormous!"

"That's very crude and naughty of you to say so," he said, laughing as he peeled off her raincoat.

"I like being crude and naughty, particularly with you."

She stood still, holding her hands high above her head while Blaise pulled off her sweater. He threw it on a chair and started to unhook her brassiere.

At the top of the stairs, Patrick and Victoria were in a state of shock. Standing absolutely motionless, hardly daring to breath, they watched as Blaise began to kiss her breasts. Not knowing where to look, Patrick closed his eyes and started to pray.

A squeal of laughter from the room below and Pippa screaming, "Come on, you bastard!" made him grasp Victoria's arm and lead her backwards down the passage into one of the bedrooms, pulling the door almost shut behind him. Hearing the sound of them bounding up the stairs together, Patrick peered through the crack in the door and saw Pippa running, half-naked, down the passage, Blaise close behind.

"Not in there, you whore!" Blaise shouted, giving Pippa's bottom a resounding smack. "The double bed's in here!"

"Bastard!"

"Slut!"

"Rapist!"

"Fornicator!"

Panting and laughing, they fell into the room. Soon their shouts and grunts subsided and were replaced by a rhythmic pounding of flesh and creaking bedsprings. Victoria pressed the palms of her hands tightly against her ears and stared wide-eyed ahead of her. The sounds from the next room reached a crescendo and Patrick heard Pippa cry out: "Yes! Yes! Yes!"

Then complete silence -- except for the wind outside and

sheets of rain driven against the window panes.

Patrick cautiously looked out.

The passage was empty and he signaled Victoria to follow, but just as they started to move the sounds from the next room began again, although less frenzied this time. Victoria, her back to the wall, slowly slid down to a sitting position, her legs and arms limp as if she were exhausted. Closing her eyes, she let her head fall forward.

A sudden shriek followed by a low moan made her glance up and look at Patrick.

Unable to meet her gaze, he turned away. Fixing his eyes on the window he saw it had stopped raining and a watery sun was breaking through the gray, wispy clouds.

Sounds from the next room made Victoria stiffen but she went limp again as she heard Blaise say: "Come along, Pippa old girl. Put on your knickers. Mustn't be late for lunch. The Vicar will be there so we've got to be punctual."

Then Pippa's voice: "I'm absolutely ravenous," followed by the thump-thump of someone hoping up and down on one foot, "and I'm longing for some champers."

A minute later Patrick heard them running barefoot down the stairs and across the floor below. They stopped briefly to get the rest of their clothes on, then laughing and shouting things at each other they slammed the front door behind them.

From beneath the window came the sound of the car being started and the powerful roar of the Hispano Suizza's engine followed by the grinding of gears and skidding of wheels on the gravel as they accelerated away.

When the noise grew fainter, Patrick leaned down and put his hand on Victoria's shoulder.

"They've gone," he whispered, trying to help her up but she sprang to her feet and pushing passed him ran out of the room.

Patrick followed her down the stairs and out to the stable. He held the bridle of her horse while she mounted but she didn't say a word and jerking the horse's head around she cantered off up the road without even a backward glance.

That evening, Victoria walked across the hall into the small drawing room just as the clock struck seven. She was about to sit down in front of the fire when she saw Patrick standing behind the drinks trolley, dressed in his footman's uniform and white gloves, polishing glasses.

"Good evening," he said.

She was going to answer but suddenly she didn't know what in the world to say to him so she hurried out of the room, leaving the door open behind her.

She crossed the hall and went into the library. It was softly lit, the fire banked with slack so that it glowed and burned slowly. She sat down in an arm chair, stretched out her legs then closed her eyes.

Although she had tried to put the events of the morning from her mind they were still there, vivid and fascinating. Images of Blaise and Pippa running along the passage . . . the noises from the bedroom next door . . . other images that had formed in her imagination . . .

Abruptly she opened her eyes and stared up at the ceiling then murmured to herself the word, "fornication".

It sounded ugly -- but compelling.

She stood up, went over to the book shelves and

pulled out a dictionary. Turning the pages she came to "formidable", then "formula", and then with a little stab of excitement she placed her finger on the word "fornicate".

Whispering aloud, she read: "Commit fornication, voluntary sexual intercourse between unmarried persons. Fornicator, one who commits fornication. From the Latin, 'Fornix', a brothel."

Blushing, she closed the dictionary with a snap and quickly put it back on the shelf.

She gazed into the fire once more, visualizing again the shocking things that had gone on between her brother and Pippa earlier that day. Appalled yet intrigued, she thought of the words used to describe what they had been doing. Besides 'fornicate' there were others like 'copulate', 'coupling', and that awful four letter word which she and the girls at school occasionally used when they were feeling really wicked.

"Making love," she whispered aloud to the empty room.

That had a nice ring to it, too nice to describe what she had heard that morning. Making love? Blaise and Pippa had talked about being 'in love', and Victoria thought they would probably get married. But supposing Pippa had a baby before they did? Suppose Blaise decided at the last minute to marry someone else? Suppose he was killed in the war?

At school, the girl who was expelled had a collection of pornographic photographs which she would let Victoria and her friends see in secret. She had told them about being 'shafted' by a boy in the village and how absolutely excruciatingly delicious it had been. She had also described what a boy looked like when he had no clothes on and was about to shaft her.

The image of Patrick crossed her mind, and then Patrick with no clothes on.

Suddenly she heard her parents talking as they crossed the hall, and immediately feeling ashamed of what she had been thinking she shook herself and ran to the door to join them on the way to the dining room.

EIGHTEEN

On Easter Monday, Patrick and the servants who had worked the day before were given a holiday. Although it looked as if it would soon rain, everyone in the carriage going to Ballinahinch was in high spirits, making plans and talking excitedly about what they were going to do.

About a mile passed the gates of the Castle they heard the sound of an engine and a motor cycle came towards them from the direction of the town. The coachman, slowing the horses to a walk, pulled over to the side to let an army dispatch rider go by.

"I wonder what he's got in that." O'Shaughnessy said, pointing to the leather case strapped on his back.

Patrick shrugged his shoulders.

The carriage started to move forward again and a little later, as they approached the church, they could see a crowd clustered around the gate, agitated and excited and all talking at once.

". . . a rebellion . . . the IRA have captured Dublin . . . fighting all over the country . . ."

"Jesus Christ!" O'Shaughnessy cried out in a shrill whisper, "the rebellion was meant to start yesterday but it was called off. Something must have gone terribly wrong."

He grabbed hold of Patrick's arm and they joined the throng of people moving towards the Royal Irish Constabulary police station.

A large crowd was already blocking the street, everyone shouting and talking among themselves, rumors rippling back and forth:

". . . Dublin Castle burning, the Vice-Regal Lodge taken by the IRA and the Viceroy himself a prisoner. . . British warship sunk at anchor in the Liffey . . ."

A dangerous excitement was gripping the people, a savagery that you could almost smell.

A man climbed up on the window sill of a house and gripping the bars on the window shouted in Gaelic: "People of Ireland! Now is our chance! Seven hundred years of repression and injustice are about to end!"

There was a roar of approval and Patrick found himself shouting with the rest.

"Hang the RIC men!" someone yelled. "Scum of the earth."

From somewhere behind them, a rock came arching over their heads and thudded against the door of the barracks. A moment later another one shattered an upstairs window.

The crash of glass and the scream of the Sergeant's wife caused abrupt silence for a moment. Then everyone began shouting again and rocks went flying through the air. Within minutes all the windows on either side were shattered and the roadway sparkled with shards of broken glass.

At that moment a pony and trap came around the corner, driven by the young curate from the church. Sitting beside him was the parish priest, his arms folded, his face grim and angry.

They turned in a half-circle then stopped directly in front of the police station. The priest stood up and held his arms wide. He looked from side to side through the crowd, staring directly at the people he knew. Slowly they quieted down until they were completely still.

"Brethren!" his voice boomed out, authoritative and unchallengeable. "Whatever you feel about the British and your desire for the freedom of Ireland, which I most earnestly share with you, this is not the way for us to succeed. Violence begets violence, and if you persist there'll be terrible reprisals, prison, hangings, and suffering. Ireland's freedom must come some day, and we pray it's God's will that it be soon . . ."

"You and all the clergy are on the side of the British!" yelled the man who had been shouting earlier. "You want to hold us down, keep us in bondage and servitude . . ."

"We will now offer the Holy Rosary for the people of Dublin," the priest continued, ignoring him and motioning to the people to kneel down, "and for the brave men of the Irish Republican Army. Hail Mary, full of Grace, the Lord is with thee, blessed art thou among women . . ."

Slowly the people became calmer, and in ones and twos began to kneel. At the end of the prayers, the parish priest blessed the crowd then raised his hands, palms upwards, motioning them to stand.

"Go now in peace," he said, "go to your homes, to your families. Do not believe anything you are told unless it comes from me or one of my curates."

He waited until they all began to move, and when the

street cleared he followed them at a walking pace in the pony and trap up the street towards the church.

"I suppose there's nothing for us to do now but go back to the Castle," Patrick said to O'Shaughnessy as they neared the carriages parked outside the church.

"Like hell," he muttered, clenching his teeth. "History is in the making and I want to be part of it. Are you with us?" he asked, looking around at Patrick.

"With whom?"

"The I.R.A, of course. The Irish Republican Army," he said, forming each word carefully, almost reverently, as he stood up straighter.

Patrick hesitated, then said: "It's all too sudden. There seems to be no plan."

"Kevin will know what's happening. Will you join us?" he asked again.

Patrick paused then shook his head.

On the way back to the Castle most of the younger servants were in a high state of excitement, talking among themselves and speculating what might be happening. Opposite Patrick, Rosaleen turned to the two maids beside her.

"I'm going to join the I.R.A, the Women's Brigade," she said, "and fight like the rest of our soldiers. There's a place for us women in the rebellion. Maybe we should start by burning down the Castle. Oh God, the thought of it makes me feel so alive . . ."

"Shut up!" shouted one of the older servants sitting opposite her. Dropping his voice he whispered through clenched teeth: "Shut-up-you-little-slut!"

". . . like the French Revolution," Rosaleen went on, ignoring him. "The mob looting the homes of the aristocrats, taking their fine clothes, burning everything. We should loot the Castle thoroughly before we burn it."

Her face was flushed, her eyes bright as she looked directly at Patrick. "Your friend, O'Shaughnessy, has gone to join them, hasn't he?"

Patrick nodded.

"Then why the hell aren't you with him?"

"Will you shut up, you little slut!" the man opposite said again, shouting this time. "Isn't it bad enough that we've desecrated the Easter to make a rebellion against the British when they're fighting such a desperate battle in France? You don't need to add to it. We've stabbed them in the back. We deserve what we get!"

"What do you mean?" she cried, sitting forward in her seat. "You must hit the tyrant when he's off guard."

"God will punish you," the man said. "Your friends are scum and rabble, not heroes. Look at how well Lord Stafford treats us and now we're rebelling against him and his kind."

Rosaleen let out a howl of laughter. "Hundreds of years of oppression have produced the likes of you. You're a gutless eunuch."

Abruptly he lunged forward and slapped her hard on the face. Stunned for a moment she covered her cheek with her hand. Then she leapt to her feet and fought back, hitting and scratching with all her might.

Patrick grabbed her around the waist and pulled her away. Struggling, she fell against him, her flushed skin warm to the touch and tousled hair fragrant against his face. The man, shocked, sat absolutely still, staring straight ahead, patting the nail scratches on his cheek with the palm of his hand.

When Rosaleen became calmer, Patrick let her go and she flopped down on the seat beside him.

Just ahead they could see the entrance to the Castle and a crowd of the other servants, their suitcases and bundles on the ground beside them, standing outside the locked iron gates. As they drew closer they saw through the bars two of the Protestant servants holding shotguns, gazing out at them with contempt and loathing.

The carriage stopped and the assistant butler, the most senior of the Catholic servants, got down. He looked uneasily at the others, then hesitantly walked forward and called out: "What's happened?"

"No Papists allowed within the confines of the Castle until further notice," said one of the men inside. "There's been a rebellion in Dublin. For the moment, until we sort you bloody lot out, any Papists found on the Estate will be shot!"

"Without exception?"

"Without exception!"

"But I've had twenty-three years service with Lord Stafford and my father before me with his father."

"Without exception! Now clear the gateway, or as sure as God's my judge I'll fire into the lot of you."

The assistant butler raised his hands in a gesture of surrender and slowly backed away.

He climbed up on the carriage then called for silence.

"We must return to the town and await further orders from the Parish Priest. He'll tell us what to do."

NINETEEN

The carriage was overloaded on the journey back and those who could not find a place followed on foot. Through the rhythmic clip-clop of the horses' hooves, Patrick could hear somebody from the coach in front begin to sing a marching song from the 1798 rebellion.

> *"What's the news, what's the news,*
> *Oh my bold shelmaleer. . ."*

The singing grew louder and Rosaleen, flushed and excited, started to join in.

> *". . . Enniscorthy's in flames*
> *And old Wexford is ours, and*
> *Tomorrow the river we will cross."*

When they arrived in the empty street outside the church, everyone climbed down. From the middle of the town they could hear bagpipes, drums, people shouting and more singing.

"We should be there!" Rosaleen cried, her eyes glowing as she tugged Patrick's arm. "Are you coming?"

They pushed their way through the crowd into the

market square and saw a four-wheeled cart standing in the center with a flag pole attached to it flying the Irish tricolor. Four men dressed as officers were sitting on top in straight-backed chairs, and soldiers in badly fitting green uniforms were grouped all around it. The swirl of the bagpipes and the boom of a big base drum were infecting the people with a mood of war, violence, and success.

A little later a car came down the main street, horn blowing as it threaded its way slowly through the crowd and drew up beside the flag. A tall man in a senior officer's uniform got out. He had the stature and bearing of a leader as he stood rigidly to attention while the band played the national anthem of the newly proclaimed Republic.

The soldiers presented arms and the officers saluted as he mounted the steps to the top of the cart.

"Who's that?" Patrick called out to Rosaleen.

"I don't know, but I'd follow him to Hell and back."

The officer opened his arms wide and gradually the shouting and cheering died down.

"I bring you great news," he said, slowly, in a loud voice. "This morning a rebellion against British rule began all over Ireland, and I have here a copy of the Proclamation of Independence which was read to the soldiers of the Irish Republican Army and the people of Dublin this morning."

He unrolled the document in his hand and held it out before him.

> "Irishmen and Irish women: In the name of God and the dead generations Ireland, through us, summons her children to her flag and strikes for her freedom . . ."

Unconsciously, Patrick straightened himself to his full height as he listened.

> ". . . we declare the right of the people of Ireland to the ownership of Ireland . . ."

"You're damned right!" he heard Rosaleen say.

> ". . . the Irish Republic is entitled to, and hereby claims, the allegiance of every Irish man and Irish woman. The Republic guarantees religious and civil liberty, equal rights and equal opportunities to all its citizens to pursue happiness and prosperity."

Rosaleen nudged Patrick. "Those are wonderful words," she said. "But will they be able to live up to them?"

> ". . . we place the cause of the Irish Republic under the protection of the Most High God, whose blessing we invoke upon our arms, and we pray that no one who serves that cause will dishonor it by cowardice, inhumanity or rapine. In this supreme hour."

Patrick glanced at Rosaleen, at the joyous expression on her face as she looked up at the leader, her eyes shining hard and bright, proud for the first time in her life of being Irish.

> ". . . signed on behalf of the Provisional Government of the Irish Republic, Thomas J.

Clarke, Sean MacDiarmada, P. H. Pearse, James Connelly . . ."

The big base drum was struck three times and the pipers began playing again. Everyone started shouting and cheering, delirious at the thought of a new Ireland, free of English rule after seven hundred years.

Rosaleen turned to Patrick, kissed him full on his lips, then shouted at the top of her voice: "Up the rebels!"

Abruptly the pipes ceased, and the sound of the kettle drums rolled back and forth across the square until there was silence.

"People of Ballinahinch," announced one of the officers in ringing tones. "Our leader, Eamon Cahill, is Commandant for the Irish Republican Army for this part of Clare. He leaves us now to attend a council of war in Limerick. After he goes, we will be signing up volunteers to fight with us. We also ask the young women to join the Women's Brigade, and fight alongside the men as they are doing at this very moment under the command of Countess Markievicz in Dublin."

The leader held up his arms and the crowd began cheering wildly again as he picked his way carefully down the steps and got into the car.

A roll of the kettle drums brought everyone to order once more and another officer stood up.

"Sergeant Lynch is in charge of the roll book and will record the names and addresses of those of you who wish to join us. You will each be given a number which will later be used on your membership cards. After you have all signed, I will administer the oath of allegiance to the Irish

Republic. Once you have taken this oath, it is binding until the day you die."

Turning, he pointed to the woman in a green uniform who stood beside the cart.

"Moira Kelly here is in charge of the Women's Brigade for West Clare and she will take the names of those who wish to join. The women will take the oath of allegiance with the men and it will be equally binding."

"Come on," Rosaleen said, taking Patrick's arm. "Let's be the first to sign."

He hesitated, but still inspired by the words of the Proclamation he let her pull him through the crowd towards the cart.

Rosaleen was the first woman to enroll. Patrick joined the young men already in line. He watched her sign the book, her brows tightly knit as she concentrated then the woman in the green uniform kissed her on both cheeks.

Suddenly, Patrick thought he heard the sound of gunfire. The officers on top of the cart stood up, their faces pale and drawn as they listened.

"It's coming from the Limerick road!" somebody shouted.

"Silence!" the officer called in a loud but calm voice. "Silence! Until we have assessed the situation, you should all disperse to your homes at once and await further instructions. You should not assemble in large groups, particularly if there are British soldiers about."

Somewhere in the distance the shooting continued. Abruptly everyone began moving out of the square, pushing and jostling each other, trying to get away from the cart and its green-uniformed men, but the rumble of approaching vehicles made people stop and turn their heads.

"British Army lorries!" someone shouted.

Panicking, everyone started to run in different directions and the main street emptied rapidly. Patrick began to go with them but Rosaleen gripped his arm.

"Damn them to hell! I'll not skedaddle like a rabbit before the bloody British! This is my country and . . ."

Abruptly she stopped as a soldier on a motor cycle came around the corner, followed by a car painted khaki. One by one three open army lorries came into view with steel-helmeted soldiers sitting in rows in the back, sunlight flickering on their fixed bayonets.

The sound of the engines, deep-throated and menacing, grew louder and the pounding of solid tires on the street made the houses on either side tremble and shake.

When the motorcyclist passed he glanced through goggled eyes at Patrick and Rosaleen then continued on, but the staff car stopped when it drew level with them and a British officer looked out.

"You there!" he shouted, pointing at Patrick. "Which is the road to Ballinahinch Castle?"

"You're going the wrong way, sir," Rosaleen said in a loud voice, her eyes sparkling and a brazen smirk across her face. "You want to turn right around and go back the way you came."

Patrick squeezed her arm to shut her up.

"Straight ahead," he said. "About two miles."

They watched the soldiers pass, the acrid smell of exhaust smoke from the lorries making their eyes smart. As the rumble died away a few people began to reappear.

"Why the hell didn't you let me give them wrong directions?" Rosaleen demanded. "It could have been my first blow in the fight for Irish freedom."

"It wouldn't have done any good. Just caused trouble," Patrick replied, looking passed her down the road. "I wonder who they were shooting at? It sounded as if it were coming from somewhere near the O'Malley's house."

Rosaleen threw back her head: "I don't really see the Gombeen O'Malley shooting at British soldiers."

"But his son, Kevin, might," Patrick replied, starting off down the street.

Rosaleen, suddenly serious, fell into step beside him.

More people were coming back into the street, standing in groups, anxious, uncertain what to do.

They walked quickly through them and a few minutes later the bulk of the O'Malley house came into view.

"Oh my God," Rosaleen said in a shrill whisper as she pointed ahead. "Isn't that the Commandant's car?"

About a hundred yards ahead they could see that the car had smashed into O'Malley's massive iron gates. Several people stood near it, talking excitedly, staring in the windows. As they got nearer, Patrick recognized the rotund figure of O'Malley himself. Kevin was there also, peering through the back window, shaking his head.

Seeing them approach, O'Malley said looking at Rosaleen: "This is not something for a young girl to see."

He walked forward to stop her coming any closer but she darted passed him and went around the other side of the car, Patrick close behind her.

The door was open, and the body of the Commandant lay slumped in the back seat, his right hand still gripping a revolver, his green uniform stained red where the bullets had hit him. Blood was trickling down onto the running board, dripping to the ground, making a widening pool on the road.

In front of him was the driver, crouched over the steering wheel as if he'd fallen asleep.

"Jesus, Mary, and Joseph!" murmured Rosaleen, moving away.

O'Malley took her arm and led her away as Kevin nervously lit a cigarette, inhaling deeply.

"They came around the corner going fast. Saw the British soldiers. No time to stop. Driver tried to ram the gates but they were too bloody strong. The Commandant started shooting. You can see what happened."

There were scores of bullet holes in the car, neat round holes with the paint flaked around each, exposing bare metal beneath.

"It's all a complete shambles," Kevin continued. "The whole country was meant to rise as one man on Easter Sunday morning, then it was canceled, then it seems the orders were changed again to Easter Monday. Maybe the rest of the country did rise up but something went very badly wrong in West Clare. Even I didn't know the Commandant was coming here this morning."

TWENTY

"God! I'm starving," Rosaleen said as they walked slowly back to the town. "I know it's a terrible thing to say after what we've just seen but I wondered if a bit of food might cheer us up. Would you like to come home with me, Patrick? I know my parents will give us something to eat."

They went out of the square and down the side street that passed the police station. The bricks and broken glass had been swept up into little piles, and a carpenter was at work boarding up the broken windows on the ground floor. A young policeman stood on top of a ladder fixing the Royal Irish Constabulary shield back in its place, watched by the sergeant.

Rosaleen's parents lived in the dock area, in a small two-story house in a row of similar ones that looked more like a Welsh mining village than a town in the West of Ireland. In the kitchen at the back her family were having supper around the table.

Patrick was introduced to all of them in turn.

Rosaleen's mother, still pretty though her hair was graying, fussed around them, kissing and hugging her daughter. She insisted they go into the parlor where she would bring them something to eat.

They went into a tiny hall and into the front room, musty from infrequent use. Over the fireplace hung a picture of Christ displaying a bleeding heart. On the mantelpiece was a statue of the Blessed Virgin and a model of an ancient Irish round tower.

"I hope your mother can spare the food," Patrick said as they sat down at the small mahogany table in the window, covered with a lace cloth.

"Don't worry. At least we'll get some potatoes."

Lying on the floor beside the armchair was a newspaper. Patrick picked it up and laid it on the table.

"It's the 'Irish Independent' dated today," Rosaleen read aloud over his shoulder. "It says nothing about the rebellion. The papers would have been put on the train in Dublin very early this morning."

Patrick nodded. "The headlines are mostly about the war in France," he said. "French Verdun Gain, British Tigris Attack Fails, Four Allied Ships Sunk off South Coast of Ireland, Sofia bombed by Allies . . ."

"I'm sorry," Rosaleen butted in, "but somehow I can't get worried about the Bulgarians at the moment."

"What about the death of Field Marshal von der Goltz? It says here he died on April 19 in Turkey of spotted fever."

Rosaleen burst out laughing.

"The poor man," she said. "God forgive me, I know I shouldn't laugh but it seems such an inglorious end for a German Field Marshal."

Patrick opened the paper and continued reading aloud.

"If you were in Dublin this weekend you could see Kathleen ni Houlihan by W. B. Yeats at the Abbey Theater, or if you preferred something lighter, the Gondoliers at the

Gaiety, or we could go to the moving pictures and see Charlie Chaplin in The Tramp."

"Oh Patrick darlin', I'd love to live in Dublin, all the excitement of a big city. I'm sick and tired of being a maid at Ballinahinch Castle. Marry me, Patrick *alana*, make a lot of money and whisk me off to Dublin on a flying carpet. If you don't, I'm going to emigrate to America as soon as I've saved enough for the fare."

Patrick smiled at her then turned the page.

"The Roll of Honor," he read out. "Listen to this, Rosaleen, last week's dead and wounded on the Western Front listed by their regiments. The Royal Irish Rifles, Irish Fusiliers, Connaught Rangers, the Inniskillings, Dublin Fusiliers, Royal Irish Regiment, the Leinster Regiment, the Irish Guards, the Munster Fusiliers."

He paused and looked up at her.

"One gets the impression from this," he said, dropping the paper to the floor, "that it's the Irish who are fighting the war on behalf of the English."

"And we're having a rebellion here. It doesn't make a lot of sense, does it?"

At that moment Rosaleen's mother came into the room carrying two plates of steaming food, mostly potatoes and green vegetables.

"Have it while it's hot," she said. "Your father and I will be in directly to hear all the news from the Castle."

Patrick and Rosaleen crossed themselves and said Grace almost as a reflex action, then started to eat.

A light patter on the window made them turn and look out at the rain, driven in sheets down the darkening street by a sudden squall coming in from the Atlantic.

"That must have been ordered by the British Army," Rosaleen said. "You can't keep up revolutionary fervor in people who are soaked to the skin."

TWENTY-ONE

"We'll say the Rosary," Rosaleen's mother said after they had cleared up the supper dishes.

The children turned their chairs around from the table and knelt down, devoutly pressing the palms of their hands together.

"In the name of the Father, the Son, and the Holy Ghost," she began. "As it's Easter time we will say the five joyful mysteries of the Rosary, the first joyful mystery, Christ rises from the dead . . ."

Rosaleen glanced across at Patrick. He would make a handsome priest, she thought, smiling to herself.

". . . Holy Mary Mother of God, Pray for us sinners now and at the hour of our death, Amen. Hail Mary, full of Grace," her mother began again and Rosaleen realized she had not said the response to the first Hail Mary with the others.

The rhythm and familiarity of the prayers were such that she found she was saying them automatically. Her mind began to wander as she looked around at her family, at the innocence and purity of them all compared to her. At eighteen she felt old and used. Instead of being fresh, untouched and full of hope, ready to marry a young man, have a family and lead a decent life, she was a laundry maid at the Castle, taking money from Blaise to satisfy him in ways that girls of his own class would not be prepared to do. The word for a female who takes money for having sex with men was, she knew, 'whore' -- a strong and ugly word but she quickly told herself that she wasn't a whore, she was a 'courtesan'. It sounded much pleasanter, and rather romantic -- Madame Dubarry and the court of Louis XIV she was thinking when the words of the Rosary broke into her thoughts and brought her back to the tiny kitchen and her family at prayer all around her, making her feel guilty and unclean once more.

She began to console herself with the thought that the end justifies the means. The money from Blaise would buy her a ticket to America and a new life. Money earned there would be honestly earned, and could be sent back to help the family. As soon as she had fourteen pounds in her Post Office savings account she would tell Blaise to go to Hell. Then she would make a complete confession to the Parish Priest, cleanse her soul and, fresh and innocent be reborn again.

But would God's forgiveness be so easy? Thoughts of her first encounter with Blaise came back to her and she began to worry. She'd always tried to believe that he practically raped her but in moments of honesty she knew she had encouraged him. For the son and heir of Lord Stafford to notice her and be excited by her body -- the only thing she really owned -- gave her a delicious sense of power in a life that was otherwise humiliating and degrading.

The first time she and Blaise had met face to face was early the previous summer when he returned home after his final year at school for four weeks holiday before joining the army. Rosaleen was stripping the sheets off his bed when she became conscious of him standing in the doorway. Keeping her eyes downcast, she'd picked up her laundry basket and started towards the door.

"Excuse me," she said, trying to pass him.

Raising her head slowly she had looked him straight in the eye then said again, "Excuse me, your Lordship, but you're in my way."

"What's your name?" he'd asked, smiling, his white teeth clenched on a cigarette.

"Rosaleen, your lordship."

Closing the door behind him he came across the room. She stepped back, swinging the laundry basket protectively in front of her.

"Put that down. I want to kiss you."

"Why?" she asked, a smile slowly spreading across her face.

"Because you're so damned attractive."

She made a deep, mock curtsy to him, still holding the basket in front of her.

"Would you like to earn some money?"

"What would I have to do?"

"Something you might enjoy"

Rosaleen felt herself blushing, suddenly embarrassed.

"The chambermaids are probably waiting outside in the hall, your Lordship. I think you should open the door and let me go."

"Will you meet me tonight?"

She shook her head and remained silent.

"Yes, you will. Tonight, midnight, upstairs in the

nursery," Blaise had said, standing to one side and opening the door for her. "Please come," he whispered as she slipped passed him. "I assure you I'll make it worth your while."

She had gone to the nursery that night, frightened yet excited, thinking how clever women throughout the ages had used rich and powerful men to advance themselves. As she climbed the servants stairs to the top of the house she reminded herself that she'd always been prepared to do anything to escape life as a laundry maid. This perhaps was her opportunity.

She opened the nursery door, listened, then went inside.

The furniture was covered with dust sheets: the beds, cots and rocking horses all carefully preserved, awaiting the arrival of the next generation of Staffords. She went into each of the rooms but there was nobody there. Taking the cover off an armchair, she sat down to wait.

She had dressed with particular care that evening and brushed her blonde hair for a long time trying to give it an extra sheen. Finally, she had put on some expensive cologne that had remained in a bottle thrown out from Lady Stafford's room.

After almost an hour she decided to give up and was about to leave when she heard the creak of the nursery door.

"Rosalind? Are you there?"

"No, I'm not!" she snapped. "I got tired of waiting and left half an hour ago."

She heard Blaise laugh softly in the darkness and saw the glow of his cigar.

"Sorry I'm late. Father wanted to talk and I couldn't get away. Is there any light in here?"

He took the cigar out of his mouth and kissed her. He tasted of port, and his shirt smelled of a mixture of clean linen and cigar smoke. "We must find a light. I want to be able to see you."

Rosaleen led the way into the Nanny's bedroom and closed the curtains. Groping for matches on the mantelpiece, she lit the candle. In the glow she could see Blaise, slim and elegant in his dinner jacket, pushing the door closed then turning the key in the lock.

"Is that to keep me in or others out?"

"So that we can be alone, my wild Irish Rose," he said as he stubbed his cigar out in an empty flower bowl and went over to her.

"Do you mind if I call you 'Rosalind' rather than 'Rosaleen'? Somehow it seems to describe you better."

"It has a better ring to it, I grant you. Less native."

"That's not what I meant at all," he said putting his arms tightly around her. He staggered, and laughing they both fell on the bed.

"How much port have you had, your Lordship?"

"Not too much," he replied starting to undo the buttons down the front of her dress.

"What do you think you're doing?"

"I'm trying to take your clothes off."

Pushing him away she had stood up, then looking directly at him undid the buttons herself and stepped out of her dress. Determined to keep the initiative, she took off her underclothes and stood in front of him with nothing on but her shoes and the green ribbon in her hair.

"There," she said holding out her arms and turning around.

"Good God!" he murmured looking away. "I'm overwhelmed."

She pulled him to his feet and kissed him on the mouth. "Now, your Lordship, you take your clothes off."

"Rosalind," he said running his hands around her waist and down the curves of her hips, "you're absolutely flawless."

She remembered how frightened and confused she'd really been but she'd kept up her brazen, forceful posture, afraid that if she stopped he would take charge.

Flushed with excitement, Blaise too had taken off his clothes and stood in the middle of the room in only his socks.

"You're a fine example of an Ascendancy young man, your Lordship," she had said, standing back to look at him. Excited and confused they had clutched each other and struggled on the bed, neither really knowing what to do.

Suddenly Blaise sat up.

"Actually, Rosalind, I've never done this before with a girl. Also, damn it, this is Nanny's bed! I feel she's watching us."

They had got up and dressed in silence, Blaise flushed with embarrassment but Rosaleen seemingly at ease, an impudent smile on her face.

He unlocked the door and went out ahead of her, saying quietly over his shoulder: "I've left a little present for you on the dressing table."

TWENTY-TWO

Patrick spent the night on the floor of the living room and was awakened early in the morning by the sound of children playing in the street outside. Hearing Rosaleen and her mother talking quietly in the kitchen he dressed and went to join them.

"Good morning," Rosalind said. "I hope you managed to get some sleep on that mattress. Come and have breakfast while I go and pack a few things. Then perhaps we should go and see if they'll let us return to work."

Patrick ate in silence as Rosaleen's mother busied herself at the sink.

"We should be off, Ma," Rosaleen said coming back into the room then giving her a big hug. "Kiss Da goodbye for me. He's fast asleep and I'd hate to wake him."

They walked up the hill together. Outside the church a group of the servants were standing around the two carriages from the Castle.

"It looks like they're getting ready to leave," Patrick said as they stopped in front of O'Shaughnessy who was leaning against the wall, his eyes half closed.

"You look terrible," Rosaleen teased him.

"I feel terrible. I've never drunk so much in my life."

"What's happening?" Patrick asked. "Is there any news?"

"Rumors, only rumors. Some people say the whole country is up in arms, but others say there's only fighting in Dublin and that the rebellion has been botched."

"Are we allowed to go back to the Castle?"

"That's what I hear," he said closing his eyes and leaning his head against the wall again. "The Stafford family are leaving on the Dublin train. When they've gone, we murderous Catholic rabble will be able to return."

"What time is the train?" Patrick asked.

"Ten o'clock. We have another half an hour to wait."

Patrick nodded then abruptly said: "Look, I'll be back in a little while. If I miss the carriage, don't worry."

Rosaleen frowned at him but he gave no explanation and set off down the hill to the lower part of the town, walking quickly towards the railway station.

On either side of the entrance stood British soldiers with a sergeant questioning each passenger who tried to get inside, demanding their business and why they were traveling to Dublin that day. If satisfied with their answers he directed them to the group outside. If not, he told them to clear off.

Patrick asked one of the group: "What's happening?"

"Nobody's allowed into the station until all the bloody Stafford family are safely on board in their private coach," the man was saying when the rumble of a British Army lorry, a sound everyone in Ballinahinch now recognized immediately, made them all turn their heads and look up the street.

A motor cycle came first, followed by a truck-full of soldiers, then the Stafford's Rolls Royce, and finally a second truck with more soldiers.

Lady Stafford was the first to get out of the car, followed by her husband, then Blaise and Jeremy, and finally Victoria. The family stopped in a group at the entrance while the station master spoke to Lord Stafford. Victoria had her back to Patrick, standing to one side with those waiting to board the train.

She was wearing a dark blue straw hat straight on her head, her chestnut hair braided into a single plait tied with a piece of crimson ribbon. Her ankle length dress gave the impression she was already a young women. She was about to follow the others into the station when she glanced around and saw Patrick. Immediately she waved, and walked over to him.

"I'm sure we'll return soon," she said, smiling, "and then everything will be normal again."

"I hope so," he was saying when the sound of the approaching train made her look away as the engine came around the curve, black smoke billowing from its funnel. "All of us will..." he started to say but the engine whistle drowned his voice as jets of white steam shot vertically into the air.

Victoria glanced nervously about her, gave him a brief smile, then ran into the station.

As the train pulled clear of the platform, Victoria leaned her head against the window so she could see the road outside. She caught a glimpse of Patrick, his head and shoulders just above the crowd, but he quickly vanished from her sight as the train gathered speed.

The Stafford's private carriage was like a drawing room, luxurious and very comfortable. Lady Stafford lay on a couch to rest, Jeremy sat at a table writing a letter, and Lord Stafford and Blaise stood in front of the bar drinking whiskey.

Victoria curled up in an armchair. She closed her eyes and soon became mesmerized by the rhythmic click of the iron wheels on the track. Relaxed, she began thinking of Patrick, then of Blaise and Pippa in the boat house. She had tried to forget about everything that had happened that day but she couldn't, her memories of the noises coming from the other bedroom were too vivid and overpowering.

When she first realized what they were doing she was shocked, then terrified they would find her. How could she have explained to them, and to her mother, what she herself was doing there, alone with a young manservant? Nothing she could have said would have excused that.

She remembered becoming very conscious of the nearness of Patrick and the need to hide her feelings from him, particularly when Pippa and Blaise started making love the second time. Her intense curiosity and fascination with what was going on had shut out everything else and she'd soon stopped being afraid they would find her. She remembered her back sliding down the wall until she sat on the floor, her eyes tightly closed, almost sick with excitement.

If she had been with a boy of her own kind there was no telling, she realized, what might have happened. But with Patrick, incredibly handsome though he was, it was unthinkable: the native Irish were different from the British, as were the natives in all the British Empire.

Different, she repeated in her mind. Did that mean inferior? An awful word to use about Patrick. Less equal sounded better.

She opened her eyes and sat up.

A native. Different? Inferior? But would it matter just once? Perhaps it could be part of her education. Help her to grow up and become an adult. The girl at school had said that it was the most marvelous experience a girl could ever have, assuming of course you had the right kind of lover.

Was Patrick the right lover?

He was certainly tall and strong and handsome.

Did she have the courage?

TWENTY-THREE

"The following," the Agent said a few days later to the Catholic servants assembled in the hall before him, "is an army communique that I want you all to listen to very carefully. It was issued yesterday, Wednesday the third of May, nineteen sixteen, and reads as follows:

> Three of the signatories of the notice proclaiming the Irish Republic, P.H. Pearse, T. Macdonagh, and T.J. Clarke have been tried by the Field General Court Martial and sentenced to death. The sentence having been duly confirmed, the three above-mentioned men were shot this morning. The trial of further prisoners is proceeding. Yesterday, there were still some disturbances in the South and West of Ireland in which some casualties have occurred. The rest of Ireland is reported quiet."

Taking off his glasses, the Agent looked up.

"This statement," he said starring back and forth at those listening, "was signed by the General Commanding Troops, Ireland."

There were several seconds of complete silence as his eyes continued to sweep back and forth across the room.

"No matter what rumors you hear, the communique I've just read to you is the truth. It is the official bulletin put out by the British Government about the present situation in Ireland and anything else reported will be false. You may all go now. I just wanted to make sure that every one of you understood the situation. God Save the King!"

To Patrick and the others it all seemed unreal. The rebellion had hardly begun when it was over and the leaders executed. The only visible changes in Ballinahinch were the soldiers bivouacked around the Castle and the British Tommies patrolling the streets of the town.

The following Monday morning, O'Shaughnessy gave Patrick a copy of a newspaper.

"Here's the Sunday Independent. It's very depressing. It seems there was no proper organization. That's what comes from having poets and dreamers and school teachers leading us rather than soldiers. Next time we need professionals, real killers."

Patrick took the paper with him back to the yacht. He spread it out on the chart table and began to read.

> *Sentenced to death but commuted to penal servitude for life, Countess Constance Georgina Markievicz, James Plunkett, Liam Cosgrave, Michael Collins, Arthur Wilson, Patrick Beehan... Peppard... Norton... O'Kelly... Mulligan... O'Brian... McNulty...*

The list went on and on. Patrick turned to an inside page and saw John Redmond's strong condemnation of the rebellion and the harm it had done to Home Rule for Ireland. There was also a report by his brother William Redmond, serving in the British Army on the Western Front. It said the Germans had been putting up notices opposite the trenches held by Irish regiments which read:

Irishmen! In Ireland's revolution, English guns are firing on your wives and children. Throw away your weapons. We give you a hearty welcome . . .

He turned to the next page. There was an article about the surrender of Countess Markievicz and the garrison in the burned out shell of the Royal College of Surgeons, describing how she had kissed her revolver before handing it over to a British officer, a member of the Ascendancy like herself, someone she had known socially before taking up arms in the cause of Irish freedom.

Dropping the paper on the floor, Patrick lay back in the chair. None of it made much sense. In Dublin, Irishmen were shooting at British soldiers: in France they were fighting with them, killing Germans.

The following week, O'Shaughnessy was arrested and taken away to Limerick with thirty or forty other young men from Ballinahinch. He returned to the Castle about six weeks later, pale and gaunt, missing his top front teeth. The Agent immediately gave instructions he was to be sacked and cleared off the estate.

TWENTY-FOUR

During the night of the first of July the wind veered to the southeast, bringing hot dry air from Africa that spread across Europe as far as the west coast of Ireland. An eerie calm settled over the Atlantic and its surface became unruffled and glassy in the warm breeze blowing in from the sea.

Day after day the heat wave continued, and by the time Victoria returned in the second week of July the fields had become sear and were turning different shades of brown. It was several days before Patrick saw her, but one morning she and Jeremy came down to the boat house after an early morning ride and walked their horses along the jetty, stopping just above the yacht.

"How are you?" she called down to him. "May we come aboard?"

Patrick took off his sailor's cap with an exaggerated sweep of his arm, and bowed.

She laughed, then swung her right leg over the horse's neck and, facing him, slid to the ground.

"Good morning," Patrick called up to Jeremy, who replied as usual in Gaelic.

They tied the reins of the horses to the railing and came down the gangway.

"I'm so pleased to see you," Victoria said rather formally, but it was obvious she really meant it.

Patrick became conscious of her cologne, and the fragrance that seemed to surround her, the smell on her hands from the leather bridle of the horse, her clothes, her hair, even the riding boots she wore.

He felt a blush creeping up his face and quickly moved away.

The three of them sat in the cockpit, facing the sun. Victoria unbuttoned her jacket then flapped the lapels back and forth trying to cool herself, her breasts outlined in the white shirt she wore.

"Tea?" Patrick asked.

Jeremy nodded, smiling and looking around him. "The yacht looks splendid."

"The family should use it more," Patrick said, starting below to put the kettle on. "With the new sails I don't think she could ever have been in better trim."

"Yes, we should," Victoria called down to him. "We used to sail often when we were children. We'd go along the coast, then up the Shannon estuary to Castle Tremayne and stay the night there. Daddy and Uncle Henry would race their yachts against each other and Daddy would become furious if he lost. Oh, Jeremy, let's do that again this summer. We'll ask Pippa and the others at lunch today when we can arrange it."

Patrick came up into the cockpit carrying mugs of tea. He put them down on the chart table beside the riding hats, now rocking back and forth as the yacht moved in its moorings.

"Connor enjoyed sailing so much," Victoria said quietly,

looking out across the harbor to the open sea beyond. "It was so terrible that he drowned. He was going into the Navy, you know, the first Stafford in more than a hundred years."

Suddenly she stopped talking, and Patrick thought she was about to cry.

"But he's dead, and I know he wouldn't want us to be sad on his account. He'd like to think of us all out sailing and being happy. We must arrange it. It's a pity Blaise won't be with us."

"I don't think he'll get any leave this summer. The Imperial General Staff," Jeremy explained, "are planning a big offensive in Flanders soon. I'm sure he'll be in it."

Patrick nodded. "Perhaps the war will end this year. Both sides have lost so many men."

"I hate the war," Jeremy said, vehemence and disappointment in his voice. "But I'm also fascinated by it. They won't let me join up, you know, because of my bad eyes. Poor father, I'm such an embarrassment to him."

"Please stop it, Jeremy. Don't let's talk about the fighting, or Blaise, or your weak eyes," Victoria said, leaning across the table, patting his hand. "Let's plan this trip instead."

"All right. Look, why don't we go sailing this afternoon?"

"Today? All the way to Castle Tremayne?"

"No, silly! Just around Ennismore."

"What a wonderful idea. Patrick, we're having a lot of people to lunch and I'm sure some of them would love it. We could be here about three o'clock, if that's all right."

Sharpe arrived about an hour later in a very bad temper,

followed by three young men from the Castle.

"They'll be here in no time," he snapped at Patrick. "How will we ever get her ready before they come?"

Just before three o'clock a car appeared over the brow of the hill. It was the Stafford's Bentley shooting brake with twelve people squeezed into it.

"Good God!" Sharpe exclaimed, putting his hand to his head. "Where are we going to fit such a crowd? We don't even have enough life jackets!"

The young people got out, laughing and joking, leaving all the doors open behind them, and started along the dock. The chauffeur went to the back of the car and started to take out several large wicker hampers.

"Go and help Mr. Carthew," Sharpe ordered Patrick. "It looks like they want that stuff on board. Where are we going to put it?" he muttered, shaking his head in a hopeless gesture.

"Hello, Patrick," Victoria said, smiling as she came down the gangway. "Isn't this fun?"

"Yes, it is. You seem to have a lot of guests. You should have booked the 'Mauritania'."

"They all wanted to come."

At that moment the Hispano Suizza arrived, driven by Pippa Tremayne, with two young men squashed in the front seat beside her.

With fifteen guests on board it was difficult for the crew to move around. There were people in the wheel house, others clustered around Sharpe in the cockpit, and several had gone down below to the main cabin. Pippa and the two young men she'd arrived with insisted on being up front in the bow.

Patrick started the engine then cast off and they moved out of the harbor into the open sea. Pointing into the wind they hoisted the sails. The engine was turned off, the shuddering vibration ceased and in the silence Patrick could hear the wind in the rigging as the sails filled and snapped taut. The yacht heeled and they started to tack out towards Ennismore.

The conversation of Victoria and her friends was quick and staccato, and not particularly coherent. The wicker hamper was opened. Bottles of wine, beer, whiskey and gin were taken out and passed around.

The young men were all just below military age, about seventeen or eighteen, but to a man they drank steadily as they sailed along. After about an hour they cleared the island and headed out into the Atlantic.

The waves were becoming higher and the wind stronger. The yacht rose and fell, and bursts of spray passed down either side of the bow each time they pitched forward. The laughter and high spirits soon began to fade, and drinks were left unfinished or emptied overboard.

"I think we should go back," Victoria said to Sharpe. "It's getting a little too rough."

"Yes, m'lady," he replied and called out orders to Patrick and the crew.

The yacht came around into the wind and the sails began to go slack.

"Stand by to go about!" Sharpe shouted at the top of his voice spinning the wheel so the yacht changed to the other tack and the sails began to fill and become taut again.

Ten minutes later they sailed into the lee side of Ennismore where the water was calmer and they were sheltered from the full force of the wind.

"Patrick," Victoria called to him from the cockpit. "You haven't been home for a long time. Why don't we stop and go ashore for a while?"

There was a chorus of approval, all the young men and women on board anxious to get off the rolling and pitching of the yacht, and the risk of letting themselves down by being sick.

When some of the fishermen saw the yacht getting nearer they put the repair of their nets aside and crowded along the jetty. Soon their wives and children came streaming from the village and watched the yacht tie up, fascinated with Victoria and her friends and the strangeness of it all. When lines fore and aft were secured the gangway was lowered, and Victoria led her guests jostling and laughing as they stepped onto the quay, grateful to be on solid ground again.

"Patrick," Victoria said, "I'd like to see your father once more. Do you mind if I come with you?"

"Of course not."

"Can I come too?" Jeremy asked.

"My parents would be very pleased."

Pippa pushed forward. "I'd like to come as well," she said, her voice loud and self-assured as she joined them.

Victoria faced her: "There'd be far too many of us."

"But I've never been inside one of their little mud huts, and I'm very curious. Of course, Victoria, Ennismore Island belongs to the Staffords so if you don't want me . . ."

"My family would be delighted," Patrick broke in. "Please come with us."

"Are you sure, Patrick?" Victoria asked, touching his

arm.

"Yes I am. Come on."

Patrick led the way, Pippa immediately behind him and Victoria following with Jeremy and the others, up the steep winding path to the village. When they reached Patrick's cottage everyone was breathing deeply.

"Marvelous exercise living up here," Pippa said, holding her chest, "and what a view."

Despite the blue sky and brilliant sun the mainland was in the soft focus of the heat haze.

"Patrick," Victoria said, coming up behind them. "On a clear day you must be able to see Ballinahinch Castle?"

"It's too far, and anyway the Castle is hidden in the valley, protected from the wind."

Patrick's mother, his sister Maeve, and the three youngest children were standing at the door to welcome them. Without a word she stepped forward, put her arms around her son and held him close. Standing back she said: "You're looking well, thank God. What a pity your father's out fishing. He'll be so sad that he's missed your visit. And I'm very pleased to meet you again," she added, turning to Victoria. "You've grown up a lot since I last saw you."

"It's so nice to see you, Mrs. Castelan. You were so kind to me last time I was here."

The memory of that day troubled Victoria and she turned away to face the children. "Is this your family?"

Mrs. Castelan introduced Patrick's sister, Maeve, then each of the children in turn. The smallest child, a little girl, made a sort of curtsy, giggled and ran behind her mother, hiding her face in her long skirt.

"This is Lady Pippa Tremayne," Victoria said.

Pippa held out her hand, palm down, as if she expected Mrs. Castelan to kiss it.

"And my brother, Jeremy. And all these other people are my friends, too many to introduce."

Everyone smiled, and a few waved in acknowledgement.

When Jeremy greeted Patrick's mother in Gaelic she looked startled for a moment then said: "There's not many of the Sasanach who speak our language. You say the words with a different but lovely accent."

"Thank you," Jeremy said in English, his expression shy but pleased.

"Now please come in and I'll get you some tea. Mind your head, for the door is very low."

"No, no, Mrs. Castelan," Victoria said, "we're far too many."

Mrs. Castelan smiled at her.

"I think perhaps that's true."

Pippa stepped forward. "May I peep inside?" She asked. "I've never been in one of these."

Victoria frowned at her but she persisted. "May I, Miss, Miss . . . I'm so sorry, what's your name again?"

"Castelan," she replied, her voice flat as she turned away, bowing her head under the doorway to enter.

The cottage was, as always, spotlessly clean and the mud floor freshly brushed. Pippa glanced around her, at the spinning wheel and the few pieces of furniture, the small window at the back and the large bed in the corner. She recoiled slightly at the picture of the Sacred Heart over the mantlepiece, then stooped to see into the fireplace and the blackened kettle hanging from a hook in the chimney.

"What a quaint little house you live in, Mrs. Castelan,"
Pippa said, her smile becoming a supercilious smirk as she
glanced up at the low ceiling. "How in the world do you all
fit in here? It's only one room."

"With God's help we manage. May I offer you a cup of
tea?"

"Thank you, no." Pippa replied.

"The only other drink we have in the house is a drop of
potcheen."

"Potcheen? I've heard of that, but never had any. Let me
have a little."

"Pippa!" Victoria said sharply.

"It will be a new experience. I'm always interested in
new experiences," she said, watching Mrs. Castelan go over
to the cupboard and take out a bottle with no label on it.

"Well, I hope you like it," she said, pouring some white
spirit into a glass then handing it to Pippa. "But don't tell
the Royal Irish Constabulary or we'll be arrested."

"I promise not to," she said and took a sip. As soon as
she swallowed she grimaced in pain.

"Fire," she gasped, "liquid fire."

"Perhaps you'd rather have some tea."

"I've started this," Pippa said in a hoarse whisper, "and
I'm damned well going to finish it."

She did, then handed the empty glass back, laughing: "I
won't be asking for another, Mrs. Castelan. You know, your
name sounds foreign."

"My husband's of Spanish descent."

"Really? What is his connection with Spain?"

"Riccardo de Castelano was our ancestor," Patrick said.
"He was one of the few survivors off a galleon of the

Spanish Armada, wrecked in fifteen eighty-eight on the other side of the island. It was impossible for him to get home to Spain so he had to settle on Ennismore."

"My father has a collection of Spanish artifacts at Castle Tremayne from an Armada ship wrecked near Kilkee. What things do you have that your Riccardo brought with him?"

"Not much. A dagger and a couple of pistols. A few ornaments and souvenirs of America.   Also some gold coins, presumably his pay."

"Gold coins? Was he a captain?"

"No, a gunnery officer."

"Not an ordinary seaman," she said, looking at Patrick with some interest. "I'd like to see what you have."

"If you want to."

Patrick walked over to the bed then reached beneath it and pulled out a small wooden chest with corroded metal handles either end. He carried it across the room and placed it on the table. The hinges were rusty and he had some difficulty with the clasp.

"Can you manage?" Mrs. Castelan asked. "Goodness knows how long it is since it was last opened."

With a final tug, Patrick lifted the lid then took out a pistol.

Pippa leaned in front of him and pointed to something at the bottom of the chest.

"That looks like a face, about the size of a human face, with holes for the eyes. By God it's weird," she said lifting it out. Holding it up to her head she peered through the eye-holes. "A mask of some sort, cast in silver."

"If my husband were here he could tell you more about it," Mrs. Castelan commented.

Pippa turned it over in her hands. "Really extraordinary. It certainly doesn't look Christian. Definitely Pagan. And it's fascinating. I want it. It would make a marvelous present for Lord Tremayne's collection. How much?"

"We're not in mind to sell it," Mrs. Castelan replied.

"But I want it," Pippa said again. "Fifty sovereigns is a good price. I'll arrange payment in the morning."

Patrick stepped forward.

"Our ancestor, Riccardo de Castellano, left instructions in his papers that it should remain in the family. It's Aztec. Came from the palace of Montezuma. He said it had once saved his life."

"How?"

"He didn't explain."

"His talisman," she murmured. "Look here, I don't want to haggle. Mrs. Castelan, I'll give you a hundred sovereigns. Do you have something to put it in?"

"Money's not the issue," Patrick said, holding out his hand to take the mask back.

"What do you mean, money's not the issue? Money is everything. How much do you want? A hundred and fifty? I want to be generous to you and your family. Two hundred gold sovereigns."

Victoria, her face flushed with anger, went in front of Pippa and grabbed the mask from her.

"Cousin," she said. "Do shut up! You've had too much potcheen. We're now returning to the yacht."

She handed the mask to Patrick.

"This is ridiculous," Pippa said to no one in particular before stooping to go through the doorway. "Thank you for the fire water, Mrs. Castelan. I'll send someone over in the morning with the money."

Victoria apologized to Mrs. Castelan for the behavior of her cousin, making a joke of it by blaming the potcheen. "We'll go on," she then said to Patrick, "and let you say goodbye to your family on your own."

Patrick turned to his mother. There were tears in her eyes when he kissed her and said goodbye. Hugging his sister, Maeve, he told her to be sure and tell his father how sorry he was to have missed him. He cuddled each of the children and carried the smallest one outside. He lingered at the door of the cottage, reluctant to leave, then handed the child back to his mother and with a final wave hurried down the hill after Victoria and the others.

When everyone was on board, Sharpe ordered Patrick to start the engine and they motored out until they were clear of the lee of the island. Patrick turned off the engine. The wind became stronger and drove them swiftly across the channel towards the mainland. Except for Pippa and the two young men she came with sitting in the bow, everyone had gone below. Sharpe was at the stern, intent on steering the yacht while Victoria sat, alone, at the front of the cockpit. Seeing Patrick, she beckoned him to come over. Sharpe's face tightened and his mouth became a thin line when he saw what was happening. Powerless to do anything about it, he fixed his eyes on the mainland. Patrick sat down beside Victoria. The high-pitched hum of the wind in the rigging, combined with the rush of water down either side, made it impossible for Sharpe to hear what she was saying.

"Patrick, I must apologize for Pippa's behavior. Quite frankly, although on the outside she's a grown woman, inside she's a spoilt little brat."

"I don't think she's as bad as that."

"Let me have my say then we'll never refer to it again. Most of the Ascendancy behave properly with the Irish. Pippa's one of the exceptions. I've seen her become a heartless bully with people who can't defend themselves. Nauseating. She's an ugly member of the aristocracy. And I'm sorry."

"But is she likely to make a problem with my family and send someone over to the island?"

"No, the Staffords own Ennismore. I'll talk to our Agent and make sure that doesn't happen."

They were approaching the harbor of the Castle. Jeremy was the first to come up from below. When the yacht was tied up and the gangway lowered the others appeared and streamed off onto the dock, relieved to be on dry land again. Victoria walked behind them with her brother. When they approached the boat house she stopped.

"Oh bother!" she exclaimed. "Jeremy, I've forgotten my scarf."

"I'll get it," he said but Victoria was already walking quickly back towards the yacht.

Patrick and the crew, intent on cleaning up and folding the sails, didn't see her until she reached the gangway. Sharpe was sitting in the cockpit, gazing out to sea, smoking his pipe and a glass of whiskey in his hand.

"Hello," Victoria called. "Patrick? I'm sorry but I've forgotten my scarf. It's downstairs in the main cabin. Could you get it for me?"

Sharpe spun around and said: "Lady Victoria, I will bring it to you directly."

"No thank you, Mr. Sharpe. Patrick will fetch it."

Patrick found the scarf on the bunk of the Owner's Cabin. Carefully he picked it up and held it to his face. The feel of the silk and the faint smell of Victoria's cologne made him pause.

"Castelan!" he heard Sharpe call out. "What's taking you so long?"

Patrick came up the steps two at a time into the cockpit and continued onto the gangway without acknowledging Sharpe.

"Thank you," Victoria said taking the scarf, then added under her breath: "Walk a little way with me."

Not quite sure what she had said, Patrick hesitated before falling into step beside her.

"Do you stay on the yacht every night?" she asked when they were out of earshot.

"Yes."

"Then I'll come back later, about midnight."

TWENTY-FIVE

That evening Patrick stayed at the Castle after supper, playing cards with some of the servants but at eleven o'clock he left, and rode back to the harbor apprehensive yet excited.

The night was clear and the arc of moon in the western sky outlined Ennismore in silhouette. He put the horse in the stable, closed the half door, then walked along the dock. It was completely still and silent except for the lapping of the water and the noise of the halyards striking the masts as the yacht rocked gently in its moorings.

He looked out to sea, then up at the dome of sky pierced by the moon and stars, and began to think of Victoria, going over in his mind the various times they had met and what she had said. He became lost in his own thoughts until the sound of the yacht's chronometer ringing one o'clock startled him.

She's not coming, he decided. Either he had dreamed the whole thing, or she had changed her mind.

He looked once more along the dock towards the boat house, shrugged his shoulders, then went below to his cabin. He started to undress, then paused when he heard the distinct clicking of a bicycle freewheel and the sound of footsteps on the cobble stones.

Silently he pushed open the forward hatch and put his head out. Victoria stood on the dock, looking down at him.

"Hello," she whispered. "I'm so sorry I'm late. I couldn't get away."

"I didn't think you were coming," Patrick said, crossing the deck and starting up the gangway. Taking the bicycle from her he leaned it against a bollard. They stood side-by-side for a moment, too shy to speak.

"It's a beautiful night," Victoria said finally. "We don't have many nights like this in an Irish summer."

"It's the heat wave."

"It seems to go on and on."

There was another pause, then Patrick asked: "Would you like a cup of tea?"

They both burst out laughing.

"Of course I would! What a wonderful idea."

She followed him along the gangway. He laid out some cushions and while Victoria made herself comfortable in the cockpit he went down to the galley to put the kettle on.

"It was a lovely sail today."

"Yes it was," Patrick called from below.

"I was so pleased to see your mother."

"So was I. It's almost a year since I saw her," he said as he put the two steaming mugs on the table.

They sipped their tea in silence: Patrick began to feel uncomfortable.

"Have you been into the boat house?" she asked. "Recently, I mean?"

Patrick was about to lie, but decided not to.

"Now that I know where the key is," he said smiling at her, "I sleep there when the nights are cold."

"So you've been there since . . . since . . ."

Victoria looked down in embarrassment.

"Since that day," Patrick said, "when your brother . . ."

"Yes, Blaise and Pippa, we heard them making love."

"I believe that's what they call it," Patrick replied picking up his mug of tea, then putting it on the table again untouched.

"I'd like to go there," Victoria said. "Now."

Dry-throated, his heart pounding, Patrick followed her across the gangway. She stepped onto the jetty then turned around to face him.

"I'm sorry," she whispered in a hoarse voice unlike her own. "It's no good. I feel so shy and terribly inadequate. I think I'd better go home."

"Well, it's up to you".

They walked in silence along the dock, then abruptly Victoria went ahead of him into the stable. The horse, startled by their entry, whinnied and pawed the ground.

Patrick took the key from its hiding place and unlocked the door, holding it open for her. Victoria hesitated, then walked slowly inside.

"There's a lamp and matches in the bedroom," he said groping his way across to the staircase. "I'll get them."

"I'll come with you."

They felt their way up the darkened stairs to the landing above, then down the passage and into the bedroom at the end. The mirror over the dressing table reflected the window and the starlit sky outside, giving just enough light for Patrick to see the oil lamp.

Lifting the glass funnel, he struck a match and lit the wick. He looked around at Victoria. She was standing, stiff and tense, staring at him. Slowly she took off her raincoat, revealing a strapless black dress.

Suddenly she shook her head.

"Patrick, I've thought about this for a long time but now I'm losing my nerve. I hope you know what to do because, honestly, I don't," she added, her voice trailing off as she sat on the bed.

Patrick had never made love before and had only the haziest idea of what was involved but his pride was at stake. Trembling a little, he turned down the lamp until there was only the faintest glow.

"Extinguish it altogether," she whispered.

He cupped his hand over the top of the funnel and blew out the flame, leaving a whiff of burnt paraffin hovering in the air. Hesitant and unsure, he crossed the room and sat beside her.

Fumbling and awkward, they put their arms round each other and kissed, pressing their mouths together, tightly closed. They remained like that for some time, rigid, not knowing how to continue. Then abruptly Patrick stood up and, lifting Victoria with him, began to undo the buttons at the back of her dress. With difficulty he slipped it down to her waist. Leaning against him and balancing on one foot, she managed to step out of it.

"I don't think this is going to work, Patrick, I really don't."

"We've come too far to stop now," he replied, gently pushing her onto the bed. She lay against the pillows and covered herself with the sheet.

He took off his clothes, then catching sight of himself in the mirror he suddenly burst out laughing.

"What's wrong?" Victoria asked.

"It's these British Army undershorts they give us at the Castle. They're private soldiers issue, loose and baggy for tropical Africa," he added marching bow-legged, across the room.

Victoria started to giggle, then threw back her head, laughing with him. He fell on the bed, weak from laughter, and they clung together rocking backwards and forwards until tears ran down their cheeks.

Patrick could feel her corset beneath the silk of her slip and it began to excite him. She felt his reaction, and became very quiet and still. Taking off her remaining clothes, he ran his hands lightly over her body and around her slim waist.

"You're so beautiful," he whispered, "why on earth do you wear a corset?"

"Mother insists. It's bloody uncomfortable."

They kissed again, their lips still tightly closed. Slipping off his undershorts, Patrick rolled on top of her and they made love. It was over very quickly. Conscious that he had deeply disappointed her and feeling ashamed, he wondered how quickly they could both get dressed and go.

"Victoria?" he said, turning to her.

"Don't say anything," she said softly, putting her hand over his mouth.

He bit her index finger lightly, then kissed her palm and she felt the touch of his tongue. Tenderly she took his hand and placed it on her mouth. Mimicking him, she bit one finger, then another, then kissed each one in turn.

He knew his body was reacting but was powerless to control himself. Slowly he kissed her breasts, then her throat, her chin, and the tip of her nose. Finally he kissed her on her mouth and their lips parted and he could taste her saliva and smell the sweetness of her breath. She began opening up to him and he made love to her with such intensity that she shuddered, and cried out with joy. Entwined in each others arms they fell asleep.

Patrick woke with the light of the eastern sky in his eyes. His left arm was still around Victoria, and she lay across him with her head resting on his chest, breathing lightly and evenly.

Gently he shook her until she opened her eyes.

"What time is it?" she asked, sitting up.

"I don't have a watch, but it'll soon be dawn. The first light is in the sky."

"Oh no! I've got to get back to the Castle without being seen," she said, slipping out of bed and looking around for her clothes.

Patrick lay still, watching her as she bent down and picked up her black dress, her slim body and womanly curves exciting him all over again.

"Please don't go yet," he whispered.

They made love once more until utterly spent they lay in each others arms, longing to drift back to sleep.

"You must go now," Patrick said lifting her tenderly and kissing her closed eyes. "It's morning."

Dressing quickly, they went downstairs and hurried outside. Although the rising sun had not yet broken the horizon, the sky glowed warm and golden with the coming of the new day.

"Dawn, the fourteenth of July, the anniversary of the fall of the Bastille," Victoria said, smiling wickedly at Patrick.

"A date I'll always remember."

Her bicycle was wet with dew and Patrick rubbed the saddle dry with the sleeve of his coat.

"If someone sees me, how do I explain riding a bicycle in a dinner gown in the early morning?"

"I've no idea."

"Nor have I," she said, laughing. "But, Patrick darling, no matter what happens, it was so utterly wonderful, I can't find the right words."

"Nor can I. I'm not sure they even exist."

He watched her cycle off up the road. At the brow of the hill she turned and waved before pedaling on.

TWENTY-SIX

Patrick flung his arms in the air as he walked back along the dock. He felt so happy he wanted to dance and sing, so light-hearted he let his spirit soar. He was reborn. His mind and heart were filled with Victoria -- her touch, her fragrance, the sound of her voice.

He stopped just before he came to the yacht. The rising sun, warm on his face, cast long shadows of the masts and rigging all around him on the cobblestones. When he looked across the gangway, he felt he could see her sitting in the cockpit, dressed in riding clothes, her hat and crop lying on the chart table.

Slowly he raised his hand to his lips. The scent of her cologne was still on his palm, and he remembered how she looked after they had made love, the shadowy outline and curves of her body in the light of the oil lamp. Wondrous, impossible thoughts came tumbling through his mind, joyous intoxicating feelings. He wanted to give her the world.

Savoring an extraordinary sense of happiness and well-being, he paced back and forth along the dock, confused by what it all meant yet totally elated as well until the chime of the yacht's chronometer broke into his reverie and he knew he had to hurry to the stable and quickly saddle his horse if he were to make roll call.

After breakfast he returned to the yacht, bringing with him a Dublin newspaper, several days old. He sat down in the cockpit, and spread it out across his knees.

'General Rawlinson's Fourth Army Advancing' the headline read, 'Successful Attacks along the Somme', and lower down the page was a prediction that this would be the decisive battle of the war and the Central Powers would be defeated in 1916.

He tried to read on but he could not concentrate. He looked up and gazed out across the harbor but all he could see was Victoria.

The priest on the island had told them about Eve tempting Adam, of the Devil presenting young unmarried people with 'occasions of sin' leading them to forbidden pleasures and unforgivable transgressions of God's law. The Jesuits had been less precise, and spoke in an abstract way about Holy Purity.

'The Devil presenting occasions of sin', Patrick repeated to himself, visualizing the bedroom in the boat house and the evil face of Satan lurking in the corner, his forked tail curved behind him.

Patrick laughed aloud, and the sound of his laughter echoed back from the dock wall. Although he knew he was thinking like a superstitious peasant he began to feel guilty. Reaching out for the paper, he scanned the heading: 'Casement Sentenced to Death for Treason'.

He wasn't sure who Casement was but he read on: 'Sir Roger Casement stated to the court he believed that without a German expedition to Ireland the rebellion was doomed to failure . . .'

He looked up. It was no good, he just wasn't interested. He could think only of Victoria. When would he be with her again, feel her near, touch her, kiss her? Would there be another time? Or had it been one amazing, extraordinary night, never to be repeated?

Resolutely, he turned back to the paper once more: 'Casement was knighted in 1911 for services to the Empire, but the traitor is now being held in Pentonville Jail, waiting to be hanged.'

That certainly did not seem to make sense, Patrick thought as he tossed the newspaper to one side. Anyway it didn't really matter, nothing seemed to any more, except Victoria.

Forcing himself to think of the work he had to do that day, he climbed down the steps to the engine room. He looked at the level of fuel in the tanks, then turned over the engine two or three times, cranking it by hand. He checked the batteries, and seeing that they were down he started the engine, running it out of gear until he saw the needle on the battery charger move upwards.

Climbing up the steps, anxious to get away from the heat and noise, he pushed open the hatch and looked out. The first thing he saw was Victoria, looking down at him from her horse.

"Did it really happen?" she asked, shaking her head slowly from side to side, her eyes glowing with the magic of it all. "Did it really happen?" she said again.

"Yes, I think it did."

"Patrick, darling," she said, "what in the world are we going to do?"

"I don't know. Can you stay now?"

"No, I'm afraid not. Jeremy and the others are with me."

"Tonight?"

"Yes. All right. The summer house on the south lawn. About midnight?"

Patrick nodded.

Smiling, she blew him a kiss and as he watched her go he could see several horses and riders standing on the brow of the hill, waiting.

That night soon after the yacht's chronometer struck twelve, Patrick set off, charged with excitement. It was hot, almost breathless, the end of the second week of the heat wave.

He tethered the horse well out of sight and reached the summer house without being seen. Only a few lights glowed in the upstairs windows of the Castle, otherwise all was quiet. It was not long before he saw Victoria walking carefully across the lawn towards him, moving through moonlight one minute then hidden by the bushes and trees the next. A dog barked and she froze where she was. Abruptly it ceased and she began to walk again then run when she recognized Patrick's silhouette outlined against the sky. She threw her arms about him and they kissed each other as if they had been separated for a long time.

"Where shall we go?" she whispered.

"Away from here, away from that damned dog."

Hands clasped together, they ran across the lower lawn and skirted the lake, the moonlight etching their flickering shadows on the ground. They stopped and kissed again, then ran on through the field to the grove of trees where

Patrick had hidden the horse.

He mounted. Leaning down he cupped his hand to make a stirrup for Victoria's foot and swung her up behind him. She put her arms around his waist, and leaning her head on his shoulder she whispered: "Patrick, my darling, I think I'm terribly in love with you."

He turned then kissed the top of her head: she squeezed her arms tighter in response. Patrick snapped the reins and the horse trotted a few yards before breaking into a canter across the field, anxious to get back to his stable. Victoria held Patrick tightly and they moved together with the rhythm of the horse as if they were one entity rather than three.

As they approached the harbor, Victoria raised her head from Patrick's shoulder and said: "It's so hot, wouldn't it be marvelous to have a swim? Let's go to South Cove. I haven't been there for years."

They continued on passed the boat house, the horse picking his way carefully along the narrow cliff path that led to the inlet where a small stream entered the bay. Before starting to descend, Patrick reined in and they stopped.

Below them, in the moonlight, they could see a ruined cottage and behind it a valley terraced either side with stone walls where potatoes once had grown.

"When I was young I asked why people didn't live there anymore," Victoria said in hushed voice, "and was told that grandfather had decided to clear a lot of the estate during the eighteen forties, preferring to farm on a big scale rather than having thousands of tenants. Lord Cardigan and Lord Lucan apparently were doing the same in County Mayo and other parts of Ireland. It seemed terrible that the people should be driven out like that, men and women and children and old people, everyone. It made me very sad. The English haven't always behaved well in Ireland."

"So I've heard," Patrick murmured.

"But all that stuff doesn't apply to us, does it? We mustn't let it come between us."

Patrick nodded in the darkness as they gazed at the white sandy beach and the waves lapping in from the calm sea. Then he flicked the reins and the horse began picking his way tentatively down the steep, rocky path to the cove. They tethered him to a tree, then walked hand in hand towards the water's edge.

"Last person in is a donkey!" Victoria suddenly shouted, starting to undress.

Patrick hesitated but seeing her unbutton her frock he began to undo his shirt. She ripped off the rest of her clothes, and with a shriek of delight rushed by him and dived in.

"Donkey! Donkey!" she shouted as she turned over and began kicking up sprays of sparkling foam.

He splashed through the surf then swam a few strokes below the water and emerged beside her.

"Who do you think you're calling a donkey?" he teased, placing his hands on her shoulders and pushing her under.

When her head appeared above the surface again she blew a mouthful of salt water that arched high into the air over him.

"I haven't done that for so long," she said laughing, putting her arms around his neck, kissing him.

They swam out, side by side, into the calm water beyond the waves and floated on their backs, their faces aglow with moonlight.

"This isn't real, is it darling?" Victoria whispered. "Are we actually here or is this just a lovely dream?"

"It must be a dream, and we're both in it."

They continued on but the water became colder as they neared the open sea so they headed in once more.

"Last person on the beach is a Double Donkey!"

Victoria swam swiftly and gracefully passed him, her arms glinting as they rose and fell, cleaving effortlessly through the water in front of her. Patrick soon realized he hadn't a chance to win and by the time he finally waded ashore she was waiting for him, standing with her legs apart and her hands on her hips, her body glistening with an almost ghostly sheen in the moonlight,

"Triple Donkey if you don't beat me to the point!"

Laughing, she took off up the beach, running swiftly along the water's edge, clods of wet sand arching into the air behind her flying feet, her hair bouncing as she ran.

Patrick, stung by his defeat in the swimming race, was determined not to let it happen again and charged after her, running faster than he'd ever run before. Heart pounding, leg muscles burning, he overtook her with still fifty yards to go.

He stopped abruptly and turned to face her. She slowed down for the last few steps then breathing too deeply to speak threw her arms around his neck and collapsed. Stumbling, he lost his balance and they both fell backwards onto the soft, loose sand.

He could feel her breasts and pounding heart on his chest, and her tummy and legs pressed against his. Slowly his hands caressed the warm skin on her back until they slid across her shapely bottom. They lay there motionless, still unable to speak until eventually they recovered their breath and became calmer.

Victoria started brushing her mouth over his, then began moving her body gently yet rhythmically on top of him.

"Let's make love," she murmured.

It was sweet and tender, and afterwards she stayed where she was. Drowsy and warm they remained entwined in a cocoon of tranquility and happiness, separated from the rest of the world, unaware of time passing. A little later, she became completely still. Patrick raised himself slightly and saw that she was asleep, breathing evenly through slightly parted lips, so he lay his head on the sand once more and looked up at the stars through half-closed eyes, enjoying her warmth and her nearness. Utterly content, he felt at last he understood the meaning of the word Nirvana.

Abruptly Victoria shuddered, her face almost against his, her eyes wide and startled.

"What's wrong?" he asked.

"I think I was dreaming."

"What about?"

"Something silly, something about all this being only temporary. But then everything in life is temporary, isn't it?"

"Carpe diem."

"What does that mean?"

"That's Latin for 'seize the day'."

"Oh my darling Patrick, to hell with the day. I intend to seize the moment," she cried, her eyes bright and intense as she joyfully began making love to him again.

Later, as they walked along the beach to the place where they'd left their clothes, Victoria said: "Darling, don't let's get dressed. If I live to be a hundred I'll never have another chance to ride, naked like Lady Godiva, on a horse in the moonlight with a beautiful young man."

"As my lady wishes," Patrick replied lightly slapping her bottom.

"What will we do with our clothes?"

"I'll make a bundle of them and tie them to the saddle," he replied as they started walking to the ruined cottage where the horse was tethered. They mounted, Victoria in front this time. Reluctant to leave, they plodded slowly up the path. At the top, Patrick wheeled the horse around for a final glance at the cove.

"Whatever happens," Victoria said, laughing, "this has been simply gorgeous, hasn't it? And I think I now under-stand why Lady Godiva smiled that lovely smile."

When she got back to the Castle, Victoria was too excited to sleep. Wide awake, she stood at her open bedroom window, her arms folded on the sill, watching the sky brightening in the east, thinking how incredibly happy she was.

It was July the fifteenth, the beginning of yet another hot day. By now the sun had risen over the rim of Western Europe and shafts of sunlight were creeping across the battlefields of northern France, into the trenches along the Somme.

She thought of Blaise, and started to worry about him. Then remembering the Staffords luck in wars, she stretched and yawned, and peacefully went off to bed.

TWENTY-SEVEN

Blaise was jolted awake by the rumble and crash of an intense artillery barrage. The flashes of the guns in the darkness lit up the canvas sides of the tent, flickering across the sleeping soldiers, giving their faces a ghostly pallor.

"They've decided to go ahead with the night attack," he whispered, shaking Bertie. "It's a risky gamble. There's never been one on a large scale before. How can you control a battle if you can't see where your men are?"

"It was Rawlinson's idea," Bertie replied, reaching for a cigarette. "Haig and the General Staff were against it. But perhaps it might work."

They sat in silence as the noise became more intense, the distant flashes brighter, the canvas walls swelling and snapping tight with the concussion.

Blaise had just started to light a cigarette when the guns abruptly stopped. In the eerie silence, the sound of him striking a match was startling and loud.

He looked at his watch.

"Exactly twenty past three. The Tommies must be about to go over the top. If they punch a hole in the German defenses and can hold it open long enough for the cavalry to charge through to open country, we could wheel north and fan out far behind enemy lines."

There was no more sleep that night for the Seventh Dragoon Guards or the Indian cavalry. They had been camped for weeks a few miles behind the lines, waiting for the infantry to make their move. Now, at last, they were to have their chance.

Keyed up after months of inactivity since the bridge at Sainte Marie, Blaise was anxious to rid himself of the terrible sense of shame and guilt he felt. Many times since then he had wished he would be killed before the survivors, captured by the Germans, could tell their story.

At seven o'clock they heard the bugler.

"Time to mount up," Bertie called out as they climbed on their horses. "A day of glory. Another Balaclava, another charge of the Light Brigade."

"They were counted in their hundreds, but we're in our tens of thousands. If the General Staff would only let us all go. Take the risk! The finest British and Indian cavalry are all here, just waiting, but for some reason only ourselves and the Indian cavalry are going up to the front. Why only us? The Hussars, Lancers, Life Guards, the Royal Horse Guards, the Second Indian and the Poona Horse, even the brigade of Canadians, they're all being held back in reserve. Wars are won by surprise and courage, not by caution. If Haig would commit us all in one bold strike, a charge by three full divisions of cavalry would be irresistible."

"I wonder? Horsemen against machine guns? It hasn't worked to date."

"Only because the cavalry has been used piecemeal, not in sufficient numbers," Blaise replied.

In response to bugle calls they formed up into

squadrons, Indians on the left flank and British on the right. Bertie and Blaise wheeled their horses round and took their place behind the standard bearer of the Guards.

Just after eight o'clock they moved forward into flat untended farmland, parallel to the Montauban road, which had been left clear for motorized traffic and infantry moving up to the front.

By eleven o'clock they were approaching Carnoy, and descended into the valley with the sun beating relentlessly down on them out of a cloudless blue sky.

The noise of battle grew louder as they plodded on through parched fields, sweating under the weight of their equipment, the legs of the horses hidden in a layer of dust stirred up by thousands of hooves.

They stopped at noon just south of Mametz Wood, less than two miles from the front line, to feed and water the horses but almost immediately were ordered to mount up again and prepare to attack. Their orders: storm High Wood and break out into open country beyond.

Ready and alert, they waited. An hour passed. Then the report came through that German machine gunners were still in Longueval and Bazentin, two villages about a mile apart immediately ahead of them.

They were ordered to dismount and wait again.

By five o'clock the heat of the day was waning, the men and horses tired from their long ride up to the front followed by hours of tension and inactivity but just before seven the bugles sounded. Excitement and relief rippled across the massed cavalry.

"Thank God," Blaise said. "At last, we're finally on our way!"

Staying close to the standard bearer, he and Bertie cantered through fields of corn that had never been harvested and had gone to seed. They passed close to the village of Montauban, then fanned out across open country, the thud of thousands of hooves on the hard ground blended with the ring of harness and equipment, forming a rhythmic beat against the continuous rumble of artillery and the staccato bursts of machine-gun fire. A euphoria seemed to take hold of them as they rode steadily on, expressions of great calmness on their faces, as if detached from their surroundings.

As they approached the Longueval to Bazentin road, a German field battery behind Delville Wood got their range and shells began bursting ahead of them. Suddenly, Blaise saw men and horses going down all around him as heavy machine guns started firing from the ruined villages on either side.

Ahead of them was a road, tree-lined, with ditches either side. A thousand yards beyond, the dark mass of High Wood dominated the skyline.

The standard bearer, followed by Blaise and about twenty horsemen, jumped the ditches ahead of the others and broke into a full gallop across rising ground, bugles blowing, pennants flying, lances and sabers glinting in the evening sun.

The shell-fire became intense. Men and horses were dropping around him but Blaise felt and heard nothing -- he could see the shells exploding but they were silent, as if in a dream.

About five hundred yards from the wood he came out behind the barrage, almost on top of the German trenches.

Just ahead of him a burst of machine-gun fire cut down the standard-bearer's horse, throwing its rider to the ground. Reining in, Blaise abruptly turned and trotted back. Unable to stand, the man thrust the flag upwards to him. Blaise grabbed the pole, sank his spurs into the horse's flanks and broke into a gallop, Bertie and a group of cavalrymen right behind.

Still in a trance, he saw the shell burst on his left and felt his horse go down, cut open by shrapnel. For a long moment he could see High Wood directly in front and the German machine-gunners firing straight at him, but slowly the wood began to revolve until it seemed to be upside down. Then, overwhelmed with pain, he began to lose consciousness as he felt himself falling into endless darkness.

TWENTY-EIGHT

A few days later, Patrick was riding to the Castle to have breakfast when he heard the sound of a motor cycle coming up the driveway. He pulled his horse over and a soldier in a khaki uniform and goggles rode by.

That evening, the news spread through the servants hall that the dispatch rider had brought a message from Army Headquarters in Limerick that Blaise had been badly wounded during the second big attack in the Battle of the Somme, and for the last six days had been in a forward field hospital barely holding onto life.

Services were held the following Sunday in the church on the estate, and the ten o'clock Mass in Ballinahinch was to be dedicated to all those men from Ireland, both natives and members of the Ascendancy, who were fighting and dying in France.

The priest's sermon that Sunday was circumspect and he chose his words carefully when asking everyone to pray for the Irish soldiers lying wounded in France, including "his Lordship's heir, Roger Edward Anthony Blaise Stafford."

Outside, after Mass, Patrick went over to Rosaleen as they waited for the carriage to take them back to the Castle. She was dressed in dark clothes, and looked pale and dispirited.

"Did you pray for Blaise and the others like the priest told us to do?" she asked, her eyes puffy as if she'd been crying.

"No," Patrick replied.

"Why not?"

"I've given up praying, and anyway I thought the Ascendancy were our enemies."

"Well, I prayed for him!" she said defiantly.

"You seem very upset. Is it because of Blaise?"

"I don't give a damn about an Ascendancy buck like him. It's the war, all this killing."

She pushed passed and hurried into the carriage. Patrick was going to follow when someone tugged at his sleeve.

It was O'Shaughnessy, grinning his toothless smile.

"How are you?" Patrick asked. "Did you get a job yet?"

"I'm kept busy enough," he answered, abruptly becoming serious. "Listen, there's a meeting tonight. They want you there."

"What meeting? Who wants me?"

"You know who. Just be there. That's all that matters."

"Have they asked for me by name?"

"Yes," O'Shaughnessy replied.

Patrick shrugged his shoulders, then slowly shook his head.

"Got something better to do?" O'Shaughnessy asked, a hard expression glinting in his eyes.

"Yes, as a matter of fact I have."

That night, clouds hid the moon. The weather had changed and the heat wave was finally ending. As Patrick went to meet Victoria, a moist wind was blowing in from the sea and he knew it would soon rain.

He made his way carefully to the summer house, then sensing someone was watching him, he stopped outside.

"Is that you, Victoria?" he whispered.

"Yes," she replied.

She came to the door and Patrick could see her outlined against the white trellis. She put her arms around him and held him close. "It seems ages since I last saw you, darling, but I couldn't help it. We're all so upset about Blaise."

"Is there any further news?"

"Yes, there is. They think he'll live but he's been terribly wounded. Mother hasn't slept for nights and Jeremy and I are going with her tomorrow to Castle Tremayne. It will be easier for her if she's with Uncle Henry."

"I'm so sorry."

"We'll be back in about two weeks. By then Blaise hopefully will be a little better and . . ." her voice trailed off and Patrick thought for a moment she was going to cry.

They sat down on the chaise and he kissed her tenderly.

"I always thought Blaise was a lucky person, that nothing terrible could happen to him," Victoria said. "I know it's very important to believe in luck, to believe in yourself. We're lucky, aren't we, Patrick? Everything will work out for us, won't it? We must never doubt each other. For, my darling, 'if the sun and moon should doubt, they would surely go out.'"

Patrick smiled then shook his head. "What is that you're saying?"

"Some silly poem we learned at school."

Victoria reached into her jacket pocket, took out a small silver flask and unscrewed the top.

"This is some of Daddy's best brandy," she said. "I think you'll like it."

"I'm sorry but I can't drink alcohol."

"Why ever not?" she asked in surprise.

"I've taken the Pledge."

"What on earth is that? Are you ill?"

"No. It's a promise to God never to take any alcoholic beverage."

Victoria threw back her head, laughing.

"Darling, you can't spend all your life without having a drink! Wine, brandy, and champagne are all part of the pleasures of living. Here," she said handing him the flask. "Just try a little. It's really such a good brandy I'm sure God won't mind."

Patrick took it and had a sip. The burning liquid trickled down his throat and felt agreeably warm in his stomach.

"You know, I thought if I ever did that, a thunderbolt from Heaven would kill me on the spot."

Victoria laughed.

"I don't see any thunderbolts," she replied.

Patrick took another sip then handed the flask back to her.

"I hope you don't mind but I've brought you a present," she said.

"A present for me? Why?"

"Because you're my love, and it's also very practical. It's a watch with a little alarm bell. I hope you like it."

She took a gold watch from her pocket and handed it to him.

"It's beautiful!" he said, holding it up, trying to see it more clearly. "Where did you get it?"

"In Limerick. I had them put an inscription for you inside the case."

"What does it say?"

"Our names, Patrick and Victoria, and a date, the fourteenth of July nineteen sixteen, the night we first made love."

"Victoria," he said taking her in his arms. "It's so kind of you to give me this but I can't accept it. If I were ever found with something so valuable I'd probably be arrested. People earning fifteen pounds a year don't have gold watches."

"I know that, darling, but please keep it. It will remind you of that night every time you look at it. Now I must go in case Mummy needs me," she said standing up.

She started to move away from him, then just before she was hidden in the darkness she paused.

"Always remember, my darling," he heard her say in a voice scarcely above a whisper, "How much I love you."

TWENTY-NINE

"Get out of my way!" Rosaleen snapped when she was stopped in the passage by a stable boy named Malone. She tried to push passed him with her heavy basket of wet laundry but he stood his ground and forced her to listen.

"I've got an important message for you," he said. "Sweeney wants to see you."

"Who the hell is he? I don't know anyone by that name."

"He's from the Central Committee in Dublin," he whispered, "and outranks our local Commandant."

"Commandant of what? Look, Malone, I don't know what you're talking about."

"Don't you now, my lovely. Remember the register of Women's Brigade which you signed on Easter Monday?"

"Oh, that," she replied quickly. "Well, what of it? It didn't mean anything. It was all in the heat of the moment."

"But you signed! As far as the IRA are concerned you're one of us now and under our control."

"Oh don't talk such damned nonsense!"

Malone shook his head slowly and deliberately. "Don't be a fool, girlie. It could be dangerous, and might even be fatal."

Rosaleen was silent for a moment.

"Well, what do they want me to do?" she asked, frowning.

"They haven't told me. My instructions were just to make sure you meet with Sweeney."

"Where?"

"The back room of Hanrahan's."

"When?"

"Tonight."

"Tonight! Oh don't be silly! How can I get out tonight?"

"You'll find a way. We'll meet on the Ballinahinch Road. You know the place where it's easy to climb the estate wall?"

"No I don't."

"You bloody well do. Look, Rosaleen," he said in a quieter, more persuasive voice, "take my advice. You must treat the IRA, and particularly Sweeney, very seriously indeed."

Rosaleen thought for a moment, then nodded.

"All right then," she said, "I'll come if I have to, but only this once."

"Good girl. I'll meet you at eleven o'clock, sharp. Don't be late. I'll have a bicycle waiting for you."

THIRTY

A light drizzle had been falling all evening and by the time Rosaleen had walked across the estate and climbed the wall onto the Ballinahinch road her clothes were damp and she could feel a trickle of water around the collar of her dress.

Malone had a man's bicycle for her but without comment she hitched up her long skirt and climbed on. Fifteen minutes later they were outside the bar and Malone was knocking on the door in a prearranged code.

"I'll leave you here," he said.

The door was opened and Hanrahan signaled her to come inside with a nod of his head. She followed him into the back room, small and stuffy, smelling of pipe smoke, Guinness and men's clothing. Two men were sitting at the opposite side of the table. Rosaleen recognized one of them -- Murtagh, the headmaster of Ballinahinch School. The man beside him reminded her of a ferret. His jaw was distorted, as if it had been broken and knitted badly, pulling his lips slightly to one side. In the corner of his mouth was a trickle of saliva that seemed difficult to control.

"I'm Sweeney, from the Dublin Central Committee," he said.

Leaning forward he held out his hand but did not stand

up. His eyes, small and quick, flickered back and forth from her face to her bosom.

"Rosaleen here was one of my brightest pupils," Murtagh said, glancing at Sweeney. "It's the great pity, girl, that you had to leave school so young. But there'll be opportunities for all of us in the Movement."

Rosaleen looked at him in surprise. "I didn't know you were one of them?"

"He is," Sweeney said, straightening up, "and now that you're actively engaged with us you should know that I'm Commandant for West Clare."

"Oh!" Rosaleen nodded, suddenly worried at the way they all assumed she was deeply involved with them.

"You look soaked through, me girl," Sweeney said. "Sit down there opposite me and I'll give you a drink. Whiskey?"

Rosaleen hesitated, then said: "Make it a large one."

Sweeney poured a measure of whiskey into a glass and pushed it across the table to her.

"It was a fine and good thing you did last Easter Monday, signing up for the Women's Brigade," he said, putting the cork back in the bottle then driving it home with a blow from his clenched fist. "The Movement needs more brave colleens like yourself."

"I didn't really mean . . ." Rosaleen began, but Murtagh leaned across and put his hand heavily on her shoulder. She stopped talking.

Sweeney's mouth tightened in a little smile, then he continued. "We suffered a grave defeat in the recent rebellion because of bad organization and confused orders. That won't be repeated."

"They're not going to try again, are they?" Rosaleen asked in surprise. "It was such a fiasco last time."

"There will be another uprising. There's no shortage of determined men. All we need are guns."

Rosaleen gulped down a mouthful of whiskey, paused then drank some more. "What do you want of me?" she asked very carefully. "I shouldn't be out all night."

Sweeney turned to Murtagh.

"If you'd be kind enough to leave us alone for a little while. I'll call you when we're finished."

As the door closed he leaned across the table and placed his hand on top of hers.

"We have an important assignment for you," he said. "An assignment that's vital to our success in this area. Are you prepared to do anything we ask?"

"It depends what it is."

"I was hoping that you'd say you would do anything we asked."

His expression changed and the look in his eyes hardened as Rosaleen pulled her hand out from under his.

"Let me put it this way, me girl. Once a man joins the IRA it's an irrevocable decision. The same applies to the Women's Brigade. Quite simply, and without any frills, if you don't follow orders you'll be knee-capped. If it's serious enough, you'll be executed."

He hit the table with his clenched fist and the noise made Rosaleen jump to her feet.

"Sit down, my dear, and drink your whiskey like a good girl."

He grabbed her glass and handed it to her.

"What is it you want me to do?" she asked as she sat

down again.

"It's about the young man you were with on Easter Monday. I'm told he was in the line of men anxious to join the IRA but the meeting broke up before he could enroll. We'd like him to be part of the Movement. We have a little job for him to do for us."

"Why don't you ask him yourself?"

"We think you'd be more persuasive. We're not too sure where he and his family stand in the fight for freedom. His uncle was a doctor in His Majesty's Colonial Service."

"Supposing he doesn't want to sign."

"There are no options. He must be made to, understand? This is too important for us."

"What is too important?"

Sweeney shook his head.

He leaned down and took a sheet of paper from his briefcase.

"Make sure young Patrick signs this," he said handing it to her, "then get it back to me".

"What is it?"

"It's an enrollment form for the IRA. You might say it's the one he didn't have time to put his name to on Easter Monday."

"I can't force him to sign this!"

Sweeney pushed back his coat, exposing a revolver stuck in the belt of his trousers. He lifted it out and laid it reverently on the table.

"A fine weapon, a Webley forty-five caliber revolver," he said. "Fires a heavy bullet. Does an awful amount of damage to a person."

"What happens if I fail?"

Sweeney looked at her in sudden anger, then the twisted smile returned to his face.

"Then you will be knee-capped for sure," he said then sighed, his face wrinkling in concern. "And that would be a terrible shame. A pretty young girl like yourself with those gorgeous, beautiful long legs. Knee-caps blown away by heavy caliber bullets never heal. I've seen it. Shocking. Crippled for life, constant pain."

"You wouldn't do that to me!"

"Necessity of war. You're not important, no individual is important. The only thing that matters is to serve the IRA. Now, my girl, you've got seven days. Do what you have to, but get him to sign this and be here before midnight next Tuesday. And remember, you can't ever get away from us. We'll always be able to find you no matter where you run."

"But . . ." Rosaleen began.

"I repeat, this application form must be signed. That is the only thing I can report to the Central Committee, that or to advise them we had to carry out a sentence on a female member of the Movement, one who failed to do her duty."

Over the next few days Rosaleen was sick with fear, her every waking moment filled with the worry of Sweeney's threats and the sense of guilt she felt whenever she thought about different ways to make Patrick sign the paper.

THIRTY-ONE

During the sermon at Mass the following Sunday, the parish priest made an impassioned plea for the missions in China.

"For only one penny a month," he said, stressing each word, "a person can adopt a Chinese orphan, provide food and clothing and turn them into good Christians."

Coming out of the church Rosaleen was given a number of printed forms for contributions, and asked to find twenty donors who would help the missions. Protesting it would be impossible for her to find that many people who would give her money she tried to hand them back, but the nun insisted it was God's work so reluctantly she stuffed them into her bag.

It wasn't until later, when she got back to the Castle, that she saw how similar in size they were to the form that Sweeney had given her.

That night, in the servants' hall after dinner, she worked her way up and down the tables asking everyone to make a contribution and thereby probably save their souls. Most of them laughed at her, but a few people actually did sign up. When she finally got to Patrick she sat down in front of him. For a moment she wavered but the image of Sweeney and his heavy caliber revolver drove her on.

"Me darlin' boy," she said, smiling determinedly despite the sick feeling in her stomach, "I want to give you the chance of saving your immortal soul by helping the mission to China."

She paused, then steeled herself to go on.

"Only one penny per month will feed and clothe a Chinese orphan . . ."

"I know, Rosaleen, I know. I heard all that at Mass today. But I'm saving every penny I can get hold of for charities nearer home. I've the greatest sympathy for the Chinese but I don't feel the least obligation to support their orphans on the other side of the world."

"Oh for God's sake, Patrick, please!" she begged, "just one penny a month! One shilling a year. Is that too much to give for God's work? And think, you'll earn all sorts of indulgences in Heaven. Where is your sense of human kindness?"

Patrick shook his head, laughing. "Pretty girls who use their charms to extract money from poor working men . . ."

"You don't understand, Patrick. This is so important to me. I promised I'd sell twenty of them, and I've only got rid of five so far. Most of the yahoos here wouldn't give a penny to save their lives, but I felt I could rely on you, me darlin'," she said, cocking her head to one side persuasively.

"One penny a month?"

"Yes, only a penny a month."

"All right. If it will keep you happy, Rosaleen, then it's well worth it. You can put my name on the dotted line."

"Oh thank you Patrick, thank you. You're an angel. You'll be told the name of the orphan and all sorts of details."

Suddenly she stopped, wondering if she could go on.

"Patrick, I don't want to force you into anything that you don't want to do."

He laughed and banged his fist on the table.

"You're really an expert saleswoman, Rosaleen. First you overcome my resistance, then when I'm ready to agree you draw back. Now I feel I want to force the money into your hand."

While Patrick had been talking Rosaleen had grown pale.

"What's wrong?" he asked. "You're not looking at all well. Are you feeling all right?"

Her left hand had slid down her leg and was now cupped around her kneecap. She stared at Patrick with unseeing eyes: for an instant she heard the revolver shot - felt the bone splintering . . . the agony and searing pain . . .

Shaking herself, she straightened.

"Yes, I'm fine, just worried about those poor little Chinese bastards who so badly need your money. Here, you skinflint," she said, turning the bundle of papers around to him, bending back the first few sheets. "This is where you sign."

THIRTY-TWO

"**C**ome with me to Hanrahan's and I'll buy you a pint," O'Shaughnessy said to Patrick as they came out of Mass the following Sunday. "There's someone there who wants to meet you."

"Who?"

"Someone important from Dublin," he replied in a quiet voice.

"I've told you before I'm not interested. You'll have to look for your recruits elsewhere."

"I can't go back to Hanrahan's without you, Patrick. I'm asking you as a friend."

Patrick frowned and looked at him. His face seemed unusually anxious and there was a troubled expression in his eyes.

"All right, I'll come with you if you want me to as long as you understand that I've no intention of joining them."

They walked quickly to Hanrahan's Bar and were ushered immediately into the back room. Sweeney was sitting at the table, alone.

"Patrick," O'Shaughnessy said. "I'd like to introduce you to Mr. Sweeney."

"Commandant Sweeney," he said correcting him in a pleasant voice then held out his hand to Patrick. "How nice of you to pay us a visit, Mr. Castelan. Do sit down and blow the froth off a pint of Guinness with me."

"I won't be staying long," Patrick replied, still standing, looking at the top of Sweeney's head, at the thinning red hair flaked with dandruff. "My friend O'Shaughnessy asked me to accompany him and that's the only reason I'm here. I have no interest in joining . . ."

"Mr. Castelan," Sweeney interrupted, wiping away the dribble from the corner of his mouth. "May I call you Patrick? Do sit down and take your ease. You'd be wise to blow the froth off a pint with me."

He was smiling and showing his teeth, but the glint in his eyes made Patrick uneasy.

"I'll call for the drinks," O'Shaughnessy said, hurrying to the door then shouting down the passage.

"O'Shaughnessy tells me you were great friends up at the Castle until he was taken away to Limerick barracks and the Orangemen kicked out his teeth."

"Yes. And we're still close friends."

"Of course you are!" Sweeney said affably. "And I know you want a free and united Ireland as much as any of us."

"I believe John Redmond will win Home Rule after the war is over."

"John Redmond, and that brother of his who's fighting in France, are traitors to the cause of Irish freedom."

"I won't stay here and listen to this," Patrick retorted, getting up.

"Mr. Castelan, Mr. Castelan," Sweeney said in a good-humored, patient voice. "Don't be in such a hurry. We have some business to discuss before you go. Sit down like a good lad and have your pint," he added, as the barman placed glasses of Guinness on the table.

Patrick saw the worried look in O'Shaughnessy's eyes, and slowly sat down again.

"Your health, Mr. Castelan," Sweeney said, smiling and raising his glass. "I'm sorry if I offended your sensibilities with my remarks about Mr. Redmond but I would remind you that Home Rule was almost won in nineteen twelve, then Lord Carson and the Ulster Volunteers sabotaged it, broke the law with impunity and in effect told the Parliament in Westminster to go to Hell. The British did nothing but cluck!"

"This time it will be different," Patrick replied. "So many Irishmen are fighting in France with the British Army."

"So they are, so they are, but we're not here for some long-winded political discussion. We're here to give you your orders as a soldier in the Irish Republican Army."

"What do you mean?" Patrick exclaimed, standing up again. "I don't belong to the IRA."

"Oh yes you do," Sweeney said taking a photograph out of a large envelope and handing it to him. "Take a look at this then shut up while I talk to you."

Patrick took the photograph and held it up to the light to read the Gaelic script then recognized his own signature. It was dated a few days before.

"I don't know what this is," he said firmly. "But it's obviously some sort of a forgery. I have never taken the oath of allegiance nor put my name to any such document."

Patrick's voice trailed off.

Rosaleen,

A penny a month,

The Chinese missions . . .

"You can keep that for your files," Sweeney said. "The original is at headquarters in Dublin. Now sit down and enjoy your drink."

Patrick shook his head then tore the photograph in half and threw the pieces on the table.

"You shouldn't have done that," Sweeney said. "But don't worry, we'll get another print for you."

"I'm going."

"Knee-capping is the usual punishment for insubordination. For something really serious it's execution. But we need you, Paddy me boy, in good condition and walking well."

Patrick marched to the door and wrenched it open.

". . . you have such a nice family," Sweeney continued. "They live a quiet and peaceful life out on Ennismore. We really would like to keep it that way."

"What do you mean?" Patrick asked, turning around.

"Your sister, Maeve. A grand girl. Good life ahead of her. Unfortunately it is sometimes necessary, in extreme cases, to inflict the punishment on one of the guilty man's family. Unfair, I grant you, but a necessity of war. There's a meeting we'd like you to attend next Wednesday. Eleven p.m., sharp. Be here!"

Numb with rage and frustration, Patrick couldn't wait to get back to the Castle. At one o'clock in the morning he was standing in the yard staring up at the windows of the women's quarters -- an area strictly out of bounds for all the male servants.

The third pebble he threw smashed a pane of glass and sounded like a gunshot. A moment later he heard voices and the sound of someone striking a match.

The window opened and a chamber-maid looked out, her head covered by a white sleeping cap.

"In the name of God, what's going on down there?" she called in a shrill whisper.

"I want to see Rosaleen."

"Well, you've got the wrong room. Who is it, anyway?" she added, leaning further out.

"Please get Rosaleen for me. I must see her immediately. It's very important."

"You're going to be given the sack for this, you know. Goin' around breaking windows and waking people up in the middle of the night. "

"Get Rosaleen!"

"Who the hell do you think you are!"

"I'm sorry, but I'm very upset. Please find her for me. I need to speak to her right away."

"She'll see you in the morning."

"No!" Patrick said, his voice getting louder. "I must see her right now!"

Several minutes passed. He was about to burst in when he heard the bolt being drawn back and the door swung slowly open.

"Oh! Patrick! God knows, I'm so sorry," Rosaleen said, staring out at him. "Sweeney said if I didn't get your . . ."

He slapped her so hard across the face that blood immediately spurted from the corner of her mouth. Staggering out of the door, she hit her head against the wall and fell to the ground.

Seeing in his mind the image of his sweet and gentle sister Maeve . . . Sweeney . . . the heavy caliber revolver . . .

forty-five bullet shattering the knee-cap . . . broken bone . . . blood and pain . . . Patrick lost control of himself and sitting astride Rosaleen started to throttle her.

Within seconds the hallway inside the door was filled with screaming women and girls, and Patrick felt himself roughly dragged upright, gasping in the vice-like grip of a man holding him from behind. The pressure increased like a band of steel around his chest and he felt his ribs beginning to crack.

"Hold him, McPherson, hold him while I hit him with this."

Patrick recognized Sharpe's voice in the darkness.

The blacksmith tightened his hold even more.

"Don't worry, I'll squeeze the bejaysus out of the little Papist bastard!"

When he came to, Patrick found he was lying on the stone floor of one of the cellars at the back of the Castle. He was numb with cold, and his clothes were wet from the water dripping off the walls. Holding his throbbing head, he felt his hair matted and stiff with blood. Unsteadily he got to his feet and tried to see out of the small barred window but it was too high up.

It was mid-morning by the time Sharpe brought him to the Agent's office.

". . . it is utterly extraordinary that I can't sack you," Robinson said when Patrick stood before him. "You should be jailed or horse-whipped, or both. But his Lordship says you're to have one more chance. It's ridiculous! And that little slut of a laundry maid refuses to place charges against you as well, and she won't even explain why. I suppose it must be some sort of sordid lover's quarrel," he snorted. "Get out of here, Castelan. The less I see of you the better."

That night, Patrick was unable to sleep. Every part of his body ached as he lay, fully clothed, wide-eyed in the darkness. Soon after mid-night, exhausted and in a semi-coma, he heard the noise of a bicycle free-wheeling along the dock.

Immediately he was wide awake,

"Patrick! Patrick!"

Recognizing Rosaleen's voice he got up, pushed open the hatch and climbed out on deck.

"I'm terribly sorry that I hit you," he began as he started up the gangway.

"I'm the one who should be sorry, the one who should be apologizing. Oh Patrick, I've got a deep sense of shame that I'll carry with me to my dying day. But Sweeney threatened to knee-cap me, and I was terrified. I knew that he meant it."

Patrick put his arms around her and kissed her cheek.

"I'm so very sorry," she whispered, "from the depths of my heart. If there's ever anything I can do to make it up to you."

"Hush now. Be quiet. There was nothing else you could have done. You had no choice."

THIRTY-THREE

P atrick arrived at Hanrahan's bar just before eleven o'clock the following Wednesday night. There were five men sitting around the table in the back room: Murtagh the headmaster, O'Shaughnessy, Kevin O'Malley, Sweeney, and a man Patrick did not know.

"This is Mr. McCarthy," Sweeney said, introducing him. "He's the liaison man for the operation, and has worked with Sir Roger Casement and the Irish Brigade in Berlin."

McCarthy seemed a very different type of IRA man, Patrick was thinking as he noted the well-cut suit and general air of refinement and sophistication. He was courteous, and spoke with a cultured, but not affected English accent.

". . . as the Central Committee Coordinator I outrank the rest of you at this meeting," Sweeney was saying, "except for Mr. McCarthy here who is in a different classification. Remember that everything said here is secret, and you are all bound by your oath of allegiance. Is that understood?" Sweeney added, looking directly at Patrick.

Patrick's expression didn't change: it was as if he hadn't heard what Sweeney had said.

Sweeney nodded to himself, as if making a note of something to remember, then turned to McCarthy.

"Let's get on then. The meeting is yours."

McCarthy nodded, thanked him and turned to the others.

"Just before the Easter Rebellion," he began, "the Germans sent us a shipment of arms aboard a large and very fast steam yacht, twenty thousand rifles with a million rounds of ammunition, mortars, machine guns, and bombs. They were to be landed during the night in Kerry, at the port of Fenit, loaded on a train and distributed throughout the west as far as Galway by dawn the following day. Who knows what would have happened if the British Army had woken up on Easter Sunday morning to face twenty thousand armed men, or what affect it might have had on the Western Front if the British had to withdraw a large number of troops and send them to Ireland. But, as you probably know, our people missed the rendezvous because the dates were changed at the last minute, and the guns and ammunition were lost."

He paused, looking at each one of them in turn.

"In spite of this fiasco, which was really our fault, the Germans are prepared to help us again. This time they will send a cargo-carrying submarine, the type they use to supply their U-Boats when they're at sea. The quantity they can carry for us is, of course, limited but if the operation is successful they're prepared to repeat it as often as necessary."

McCarthy paused again.

"In the past," he continued, "they've unloaded arms and ammunition into small boats some miles out then brought them ashore. They've also tried packing the supplies in containers, allowing them to float in with the tide. Neither of these methods has worked very well in the past and that is why we want to bring the U-Boat alongside a dock, unload it extremely fast and get back out to sea in the minimum amount of time. The problem, of course, is where to find a harbor that is big enough for a U-Boat, yet not guarded by the military or Coast Guard."

McCarthy unrolled a map of County Clare.

"They nearly all have a town or village around them, and are completely visible to the inhabitants as well as the RIC and the military. But," he paused and looked up, "there is one exception."

"The harbor at the Castle?" Patrick said in a quiet but clear voice.

"Yes, exactly," he replied, putting his index finger on the map.

"Will it be big enough for a U-Boat to enter and unload?" Patrick asked.

"Yes," McCarthy replied. "The German Navy, of course, have British Admiralty charts of this coast but they're concerned that the harbor at the Castle may have silted up because it is not used, and the soundings on the chart may no longer be correct. Has the harbor been dredged recently?"

"Not as far as I know. There's certainly no problem with the yacht going in and out but it doesn't draw more than one and half to two fathoms."

"The Germans want confirmation of the depths across the mouth of the harbor, within the harbor itself and alongside the dock where the submarine would unload. A minimum of three fathoms is needed, about eighteen feet. The information must be accurate, because if their U-Boat gets stranded and captured by the British they'd never trust us again. Can you," he asked, looking directly at Patrick, "get the depths for us?"

"How would I do it?"

"Use a fishing line and a lead weight. Tie knots every half a fathom, and count them as you pay out the line."

"Half a fathom?"

"Yes, about three feet. This drawing," he went on, taking a folded sheet out of his brief-case, "is a large scale map of the harbor. On it are the locations of where you should take the soundings."

"When will the U-Boat be coming?" Patrick asked.

"As soon as we can get the information to the German Navy they will start making definite plans," McCarthy replied. "They're anxious to carry out the operation and if it's successful they'll follow up with more. You see, for them it would be good value. To deliver a reasonable quantity of guns and ammunition to the IRA could result in keeping perhaps two or three British divisions tied down in Ireland which the Germans would otherwise have to face on the Western Front. How soon do you think you can get the information?"

"I don't know, but I'll start working on it as quickly as I can."

"Make it as soon as possible. The Germans are prepared to do this now, but if we delay too long they may change their minds and the whole operation could be called off."

THIRTY-FOUR

Patrick spent the next afternoon studying the map he'd been given, checking it for accuracy and dimensions.

The jetty where the yacht was moored stretched five hundred feet straight out from the shore, then turned at forty five degrees for another hundred and fifty feet to the lighthouse. The mouth of the harbor itself was about one hundred feet wide, and on the other side a breakwater extended out for about the same distance before joining again with the main dock.

Taking a fishing line, Patrick tied knots every half-fathom and attached a heavy lead weight at the end. Then he cast off in the dingy and rowed across the harbor to the other side.

To his surprise he found that against the wall of the main dock there was only one and a half fathoms, about nine feet. He continued on and at the extreme end, near the shore, it was even shallower. He held the oar vertically, thrust it down through the water and was able to touch the bottom.

Rowing back towards the jetty, he took soundings as he went and it was not until he was almost beside the yacht that he got a reading of more than three fathoms.

He tied up the dingy and climbed into the cockpit to

plot the depths on the map. When he had finished, it was clear that the only way for the U-Boat to unload would be to come alongside the yacht, then transfer the cargo across to the dock.

He looked at the map again. He still had to take soundings across the mouth of the harbor.

Next morning he was up on deck at 4 a.m., drinking tea and watching the stars fade in the first light of dawn.

By five o'clock he had fixed a rope across the mouth of the harbor hanging in a shallow curve, the marks he'd made every ten feet with paint becoming more visible as the sky grew lighter. By a quarter to six he was in the dingy taking his first sounding. Holding onto the rope at the first mark with his left hand, he began paying out the weighted line with his right, counting the knots tied every half a fathom as they slipped through his fingers until the line went slack as the weight hit the bottom.

He wrote the reading on the chart, then rowed to the second mark on the rope and put the fishing line over the side again. He continued in the same manner from west to east and had just completed writing down the last sounding when he felt someone was watching him. Abruptly he turned and looked up. Sitting on her horse, motionless beside the lighthouse, was Victoria, her elbow resting on the pummel of the saddle, her chin cupped in the palm of her hand.

"Patrick!" she called. "What in the world are you doing?"

Stunned, he gripped the rope, driving the nails of his fingers into the palm of his hand as he tried to think.

"Fishing," he replied, warily.

"Fishing?" she repeated. "What on earth are you trying to catch?"

"There're some very large fish that hover just here when the tide turns."

"But why do you have that rope stretched across, with all those marks?"

"So that I can hold my position at any point I want to."

Victoria was silent for a moment.

"Well, that's the funniest set of fishing tackle I've ever seen. And what's that large lead weight for?" she asked, pointing to the coil of line in the bottom of the boat. "And you've got no hook! What do you expect the fish to do? Hang on while you haul them in?" she added, laughing.

Patrick managed to laugh with her. "I've just lost the hook to a conger eel," he explained, looking directly up at her silhouetted against the brightening sky.

She was bareheaded, dressed in brown corduroy jodhpurs and a green sweater, the collar of her white shirt tucked neatly around her neck and her white cuffs showing above her gloved hands.

"It seems such a long time since I last saw you," Patrick said finally. "I didn't even know you'd come back. Do you know how to light the stove?"

"Of course," Victoria replied. "I'll start boiling some water for tea."

Nodding and smiling at him, she turned the horse's head and trotted back towards the yacht.

Patrick grabbed the fisherman's knife and slashed at the rope stretched across the mouth of the harbor. It fell into the water and floated just under the surface, weaving slowly backwards and forwards with the movement of the waves as it sank but the ends were still clearly visible especially where it was tied to the lighthouse.

Not knowing what to do, he replaced the knife in its sheath and started rowing back towards the dock.

As soon as Victoria had gone below he stopped and hid the clip board and map as best he could in the bottom of the dingy under the fishing line. Then he continued rowing again, trying to calm himself.

He clambered up onto the yacht and tied the mooring rope over the stern. Victoria was standing on the bottom step of the stairway, her head just above the hatch.

"It seems months since we've seen each other and made love," she said, "but it's only just two weeks."

Patrick leaned down and kissed her.

"Yes, it seemed a very long time," he said.

"Let's forget the tea and make love. Right now!" Victoria whispered. "I'll switch off the kettle."

Afterwards, they lay on their backs on the double bed in the Owner's Cabin, hands entwined, watching the netted pattern of sunlight and ripples reflecting through the porthole onto the white ceiling above.

"Victoria, I've got a little present for you," Patrick said.

"A present? For me? How lovely!"

"I'll go and get it."

He went to the crew's quarters and took a package from his locker.

"It's nothing much," he said handing it to her. "Just something to keep you safe in the future."

She opened it slowly, smiling and curious, and held up a silver medal of St. Christopher.

"There's an inscription on the back."

Turning it over she read aloud: "The twenty-fourth of September, nineteen fifteen. Oh darling, the day you rescued me from the sea."

She started to put her arms around him when he suddenly turned his head and stared out of the window at the stern of the yacht.

"Jesus Christ!" he whispered. "It's the Head Groom, it's Sharpe."

She sat up beside him and they both looked at the horseman who had stopped at the beginning of the jetty, uncertain what to do.

Without a word Victoria climbed over Patrick and grabbed her clothes. They both dressed in seconds then ran along the passage to the main saloon.

The clip-clop of horse's hooves came closer, then stopped just above the yacht. Victoria took a deep breath and standing straighter, she climbed the steps and put her head out of the hatch.

"Good morning, Mr. Sharpe. Looking for me?" she said.

"Yes, Lady Victoria," he replied, raising his cap. "When you didn't turn up for breakfast her Ladyship became worried. Several of us came out searching for you. I'm very pleased that nothing appears to be amiss."

"Oh, I didn't realize it had got so late. My horse became a little lame and I was giving her a rest. Patrick here very kindly offered me a cup of tea."

"Her Ladyship will be glad to know you're safe. Would you like me to ride on and tell her?

"Yes, Mr. Sharpe, please go ahead," she said. "I'll start walking with Daisy."

"Very good, me Lady," he said, tipping his cap, watching her come along the gangway. "I'll return directly with another horse for you."

Victoria untied the reins and called out in a loud, Ascendancy voice: "Thank you for the tea, Patrick, probably the best available in County Clare."

She started walking slowly, leading her horse by the reins until Sharpe went around the boat house and was out of sight. Then she stopped.

"Has he guessed?" Patrick asked, running to catch up with her.

"I don't think so. How long have we been?"

He took out his watch and opened it.

"Good God! It's almost half past nine."

"Oh no! Where on earth has the time gone? Oh to Hell with Sharpe, to Hell with everyone. I love you so much. Let's go back to the yacht."

Patrick shook his head and pointed behind her, towards the road to the Castle.

Victoria turned and they both watched a horseman come over the rise then trot briskly down the hill.

"Damn him to Hell! It's Sharpe again."

"Start walking towards him, but not too quickly."

They met when he rounded the boat house. He stopped beside them and jumped to the ground.

"I'm so sorry, Lady Victoria. I suddenly realized I should have given you my horse. I'm sure you'd want to get back to her Ladyship as soon as possible."

"How very thoughtful of you, Mr. Sharpe," Victoria said, taking the reins from him.

She put her boot in the stirrup and mounted in a swift,

easy movement. Crouching, she dug her heels into the horse's flanks and he sprang forward, breaking almost immediately into a canter. Patrick and Sharpe watched her ride up the hill until she crossed over the top and was hidden from them.

"There was a case a number of years ago in Tipperary," Sharpe said turning to Patrick, "that a daughter of the Ascendancy took a fancy to a handsome Papist lad. When they were caught fornicating together some of her father's Loyalist servants had to act to save the daughter from her temporary madness. They never found the boy again but it was said they castrated him with a broken whiskey bottle and it took him a long time to die."

THIRTY-FIVE

Patrick woke the following morning to the steady drumming of rain on the deck above. Cold and drowsy, he pulled the blankets more tightly around him and tried to go back to sleep but the image of Victoria kept passing through his mind and wouldn't go away.

He had never thought about her in the long term before, but now for the first time he pictured them married and living together. The gulf that separated them, he knew, was immense and probably unbridgeable if they remained in Ireland but if they started a new life in another country, Australia or America, somewhere far away, perhaps it would all be possible. When they were together, he ceased to be aware of the difference in their backgrounds, not even conscious of her Ascendancy accent. She was just the girl whom he felt, at their most intimate moments, must be the other half of himself, someone he loved dearly and could not live without.

A little later, as he rode up to the Castle through the fresh, damp morning air and cantered along the driveway, he began to feel light-hearted and carefree, and optimistic that somehow everything would work out.

He trotted through the gateway under the belfry then across the yard to the stables. Hungry for breakfast, he strode into the Castle then along the passage towards the kitchens.

Coming towards him was Rosaleen, carrying a large basket piled high with laundry. Seeing him, she quickly put it down and hurried over.

"Oh Patrick, thank goodness I've caught you," she said. "I'm so worried. They're all talking about you and some of ours have overheard the Prods say that Lady Stafford is taking Victoria away to Dublin this morning and they won't be back for a long time."

"Why?"

"I think, perhaps, that's what I should be asking you. They say she went out riding very early yesterday morning, alone, and when she didn't turn up for breakfast they thought perhaps she'd had a fall and was lying somewhere hurt. But it seems Sharpe found her with you, down at the yacht."

Patrick nodded, unable to speak for a moment.

"So it's true then," Rosaleen said, shaking her head in disbelief.

"I just gave her a cup of tea, that's all. I do know her. I pulled her from the sea."

"If it weren't for the fact you have a special position here the Prods would have had you out long ago."

"Well, what shall I do then? We only drank tea together. Are people saying there's more to it than that?"

"Patrick, me darlin' boy, a young man as beautiful as you and a girl as spirited as Victoria Stafford wouldn't be just drinking tea on their own for very long."

At that moment the door to the corridor swung open and Evans, the head clerk from the Agent's office, came shuffling towards them.

"Castelan! I'm glad I found you. Mr. Robinson wants to see you in his office. Nine o'clock sharp."

"Why?"

"You'll find out. Just be there. On the dot!"

At five minutes to nine Patrick was waiting outside the Agent's office, wondering why he had been sent for. He was still wondering at half past ten, and when he was finally ushered in at eleven o'clock he felt nervous and unsure of himself.

"His Lordship and the family," Mr. Robinson said, pronouncing each word carefully, "can talk to anyone they like and do whatever they like. However, contacts between servants and the Staffords must always, and I repeat always, be on a master-and-servant basis. It sometimes happens that when they are young some members of the landed gentry form friendships with Irish natives. But they should end as soon as they cease to be children and grow up. You have a special situation here at the Castle, and it is understandable that Lady Victoria should continue to feel grateful to you. She may, as a result, be more friendly than she realizes."

Robinson got up from his desk and stood looking out the window, his back to Patrick.

"Lady Victoria," he went on, "is leaving in a few minutes with her Ladyship for Dublin, where they will remain for the next few months. They wish to be near Lord Blaise who is to be transferred from England to the British military hospital at Leopardstown Park. When they come back at Christmas you will take great pains to have as little contact with Lady Victoria as possible." He turned around to face

Patrick. "I cannot stress enough how undesirable it would be, and very very dangerous, for you to ignore my instructions in this matter. Have I made myself absolutely clear?"

Patrick nodded.

"That will be all then. Remember you've been given this warning. It will be your only one."

THIRTY-SIX

Over the next few weeks Patrick tried to face up to the reality of himself and Victoria. When he was thinking rationally, he knew there could be no future for them together. Like it or not, the gulf that separated them was too great and they must use this break to try and forget each other. During the day he was kept busy but at night, when he was alone on the yacht, thoughts of her and the moments they had shared came back so vividly that he was powerless to resist them. Despite this, he felt he was gaining control of his feelings until the arrival, about a month after she'd left, of a letter.

He was called to the Agent's office and Mr. Robinson handed it to him. Turning it over, Patrick saw that the envelope had been opened and the flap glued down again with dark brown office glue.

"Mr. Robinson! This letter's been opened."

"I would remind you of the last time we met and what I told you then."

Patrick nodded slowly, and turned towards the door.

"It would be wiser, you know," Robinson said, stressing each word, "if you didn't reply. Understand this, Castelan, I am advising you not to send an answer."

Patrick went straight back to the yacht and put the letter,

unopened, on the chart table but as he looked at it he began to feel Victoria's presence in the cabin with him until she was almost there, sitting opposite him.

He weighed the envelope in his hand, put it down on the chart table again then picked it up once more. He opened it and took out a single sheet of notepaper embossed with the Stafford family crest.

Stafford House
Mountjoy
Dublin

15th September 1916

Dear Patrick,

I was sorry not to see you before leaving Ballinahinch last Thursday but we left in such a hurry.

We have had some marvelous news. My brother Blaise is coming back to Ireland to a convalescent home near Dublin. We are all so happy, and Mummy felt it would be better if we were near him.

We will be staying here for the next three months but hope to be home for Christmas.

Yours sincerely,
Victoria Stafford

Patrick saw that the envelope was postmarked nearly three weeks ago. Letters sent from Dublin were usually delivered to Ballinahinch the next day.

He read the letter again several times, trying to decide what she was really saying. The wording was stiff and formal, conveying just information, nothing more. Was she telling him not to forget her, that she would come back to him at Christmas? Three months away in Dublin was a long time, a very long time. Maybe she would meet someone else, a suitable young man of the Ascendancy. Perhaps it would be best for them both if she did.

THIRTY-SEVEN

All through October, Victoria and her mother visited Blaise in the military hospital at Leopardstown Park. With every visit he seemed to gain strength and was determinedly optimistic.

His head was wrapped in bandages but there were holes for his right eye, ear, nose, and mouth. His left arm had been amputated but they'd managed to save his left leg which was in plaster and held in traction from a frame over the bed.

"Darling, I have something to tell you," Lady Stafford said to Victoria as they drove up to the hospital one day in late October. "The doctor telephoned me this morning. He told me they'd removed the bandages from Blaise's head and that the skin graft on the left side of his face had taken very well, from a medical point of view that is, but he said it will be a great shock for us. So when we see him we must try and control ourselves."

"Oh Mummy, poor Blaise. I'll do my best."

"Yes, darling, I'm sure you will. It'll be very difficult but we must both behave as if he looks reasonably normal."

On either side of the driveway, convalescing soldiers dressed in hospital blue were strolling about or sitting on the lawn. Many were in wheelchairs or limping on crutches.

The car pulled up in front of the main entrance, and as the chauffeur held the door open the colonel in charge of the hospital came down the stairs to meet them.

"Good afternoon, Lady Stafford," he said. "I've arranged for the surgeon to see us in a short while to discuss Blaise's progress and to tell us what he suggests."

He and Lady Stafford walked together through the hallway of the house, Victoria following, into what had once been the library now converted into the colonel's office.

"Please sit down," he said pointing to the chairs on either side of his desk. "May I offer you something to drink?"

Lady Stafford and Victoria both shook their heads.

"Blaise has an indomitable spirit otherwise he wouldn't have pulled through. Such wounds would have killed most men, but he has an iron determination and the will to live that is almost as important as good surgery and hospitals."

"How fully will he recover?" Lady Stafford asked.

"Certainly not sufficiently to return to active service," the colonel replied. "Some limited duties perhaps. The surgeon can advise you better than I," he added standing up and introducing a doctor in a white coat who'd just come into the room, a man with an air of sadness and great fatigue about him.

"Your son has made a remarkable recovery," he said to Lady Stafford. "The blast from the shell struck him on his left side. We've been able to save his leg but the bones were so badly shattered that it has knitted shorter than it originally was, which means he'll always have to use a stick. However, he will be able to get around on his own, without any help, which of course is very good. His left arm had to be amputated in the field station just behind the lines. He took a lot of shrapnel on that side of his body, but luckily no vital organs were punctured and his heart wasn't damaged. Unfortunately the left side of his face was, and he lost his left eye. But on the positive side, his jaw has knit well and the skin graft across his cheek and side of his throat are fine."

Lady Stafford nodded slowly, her lips tightening.

"When you see him, it will be a shock and I ask that you hide this from him. He keeps asking for a mirror but I always delay this for at least one week so that the patient slowly begins to realize that he's not a pretty sight and starts learning to live with it."

Victoria began to feel sick and apprehensive. The thought of not being able to control herself, combined with the terrible hospital smell, made her feel dizzy.

"Bertie Mottram has usually been with us when you've been visiting Blaise, and I've asked him to be there when you come today. It will make the whole meeting a lot easier."

Walking down the corridor, Victoria thought of Bertie and her growing affection for him, a wounded war hero limping around with a stick, attractive and elegant even in hospital blue.

They entered Blaise's room and Bertie stood up.

"Good afternoon, Lady Stafford. How nice to see you, Victoria," he added. "Blaise is in fine form I'm glad to say."

Lady Stafford and Victoria walked across the room, each going to either side of Blaise's bed.

"Hello, mother," he said. "I probably won't win any more beauty contests but I'm still a going concern."

"Indeed you are, my dear boy," Lady Stafford agreed, leaning down and kissing him carefully on his right cheek. "I'm so glad you've got those wretched bandages off. You must feel a lot better and cooler without them."

"Yes I do, mother, thank you."

"Hello Blaise. You look fine," Victoria said, nervously kissing him on the forehead.

"Yes I do if you always sit on my right side," he replied laughing, his mouth pulled and distorted out of shape by the tightness of the skin graft. "What news of father?" he asked turning to Lady Stafford.

"He's very well," she answered, looking directly at him. "He wants to go back to France, of course, but I hope he stays on at the War Office."

Victoria dug her nails into the palm of her hand and fought to control the nausea she felt but her face was white and drained.

"Blazer, old chap," Bertie said, standing up with the help of his stick, "I'm going to take your sister out for a walk in the garden and flirt outrageously with her."

"What a good idea," Lady Stafford agreed. "Have a little fresh air. This must be one of the hottest Octobers on record. Blaise and I can have a nice chat together while you're gone."

Safely outside on the lawn Victoria said: "Thank you, Bertie, thank you for saving me. I couldn't have controlled myself much longer."

"I know. The first time you see that sort of thing it's a bit of a shock, particularly if it's one of your own family."

"But what's so terrible is that Blaise was such a handsome man."

"Victoria, don't worry. Believe me you'll soon get used to it and when you do you'll find you only see the brother you know and love. Please remember, Blaise could be dead, or wounded in a much more tragic way. We have men here who have lost both legs and arms and the sight of their eyes. By comparison, he's a bloomin' athlete. He'll be able to get around quite well with a stick and he may have lost his left arm but thank God he still has his right, the one he uses for drinking."

He laughed, and Victoria tried to laugh with him.

"Also he still has one eye, and in some ways a black eye-patch gives a fella a certain distinction."

Victoria stiffened suddenly, seeing an armless man sitting in a wheel chair, puffing a cigarette held to his lips by a nurse.

They walked on, passing men in blue sitting on benches or on the grass, smoking and talking. Some were silent, staring straight ahead, unaware of those around them.

"Believe me," Bertie said, "it's very easy for people in this place to go stark raving mad. Many do. It's absolutely essential here to take the best possible view of even the most terrible situation."

"And you?" Victoria asked.

"Oh, there's nothing wrong with me. My wounds are very minor. I took a little shrapnel in the right leg, that's all. I'll even be able to walk without a stick by Christmas and be back to active service. I've been incredibly lucky because I was only five or six yards away from Blaise when the shell burst. But that's war."

"When are you leaving?"

"I'm being discharged next week, and I'm going home to

England for about ten days to be with my family. Then I'd like to return here for a while to see how old Blazer is getting on."

"When you come back, please stay with us in Dublin. It would be marvelous for Blaise if you were close by, and Mummy and I would love it."

THIRTY-EIGHT

A Halloween Party was held in the hospital at the end of October and Lady Stafford, Victoria, and Bertie joined the witches and warlocks wandering around the lawns in the late afternoon sun. There were drinks for all who were allowed alcohol, and plenty of food. It went very well, everyone determined to have a good time.

Before it was over, the doctor confirmed that Blaise could leave the following week, stay at Stafford House in Dublin and just visit the hospital as an outpatient for the next month. He was likely to be discharged in early December and could return to Ballinahinch Castle in time for Christmas.

The day the family arrived home was clear and sparkling. The station platform was decorated with a bunting of miniature union jacks, and outside across the street hung a banner with the words, "Welcome home, hero of the Somme".

The town's Irish bagpipe band was assembled and some people of the town, though not many, were also there. Blocking the middle of the road and facing the station were the Protestant servants from the Castle, hostile and alien in their dark clothes and bowler hats. The blacksmith, the biggest of them all, had a bearskin tied around his chest on which rested a huge base drum. Beside him stood his son. He held to his lips, sideways to his mouth, the 'olde Orange flute' of Ulster, trilling up and down the scales, ready to accompany his father beating the drum when Blaise arrived. The Rolls Royce was parked directly in front of the station, a line of soldiers either side with fixed bayonets forming an honor guard. All became quiet as they waited, except for the trilling of the flute.

At last they heard the sound of the engine's whistle as the train reached the level crossing on the Limerick road, and a few moments later they saw it swing into view and coast down the last few hundred yards of track.

The station master himself opened the door of the Stafford family coach and the pipe band and the Orange drum and flute started the moment Lord and Lady Stafford appeared.

Blaise came next, levering himself slowly down the step. Despite his disfigurement and constant pain, he looked undefeated and confident, an arrogant glint clearly visible in his remaining eye.

Behind him in the carriage Patrick could see Victoria holding out his walking stick, her expression affectionate and concerned. She was dressed in elegant day clothes, her hair brushed back close to her head and her hat pinned clear of her face.

It was almost three months since Patrick had last seen her, and as he gazed at her his resolve melted away and he knew he still loved her dearly no matter what.

She stepped onto the platform, then turned back towards the train as a young British officer got out. Putting her arm through his, she laughed at something he said as they turned to follow Blaise.

He was an exceptionally handsome young man, strong and tall. His tunic fitted perfectly, he had medal ribbons above the left pocket, and his military cap was set at a rakish angle. From their expressions and the way they were smiling it was obvious they were captivated by each other.

For a moment Patrick couldn't think, and hardly saw Jeremy getting out of the carriage, blinking in the bright sunlight. When they were all seated in the car, the Rolls Royce moved off and Patrick backed into the crowd, hiding until it had passed.

Confused and angry, he helped to unload the Stafford's baggage.

"Look at all this bloody stuff," muttered one of the stable boys as he threw boxes of expensive Christmas presents up onto the cart. "Any one of these would have cost more than a year's wages. God! How I hate the British."

On the way back to the Castle, Patrick's mood wavered between anger and sadness, then jealousy began forming a hard, aching knot in his chest.

The family had dinner that evening in the small dining room. Patrick helped serve the meal. When he put a plate in front of Victoria she didn't look up, but continued talking without a break in her conversation with the young British officer. In his formal mess jacket he looked even more handsome, and had that sheen of arrogance and invincibility of the Ascendancy.

That night, Patrick sat in the main saloon of the yacht

drinking brandy from a bottle he'd taken from the bar when they'd cleaned up after dinner. In a welter of alcohol and self-pity he suddenly decided to leave the next day. He'd never see any of them again and they could go to Hell for all he cared.

Stumbling against the furniture he made his way to the Owner's Cabin, then remembering the times he and Victoria had spent there he struggled forward to his triangular cabin in the bow.

THIRTY-NINE

"Wake up, Patrick! For God's sake, wake up! It's very late and they're looking for you up at the Castle."

Groggy and confused, Patrick opened his eyes and saw the anxious face of one of the stable boys peering down at him.

"What's wrong?" he asked.

"The family are riding to Currafin House this morning and Mr. Sharpe needs your help. He's furious that you've overslept."

"Why does he want me?"

"To bring back the horses. The ride both ways is too much for Lord Stafford, so Mr. Carthew will meet them at Currafin with the Rolls."

Feeling unsteady, Patrick got up and after a shave and a wash in cold water he began to feel better. Dressing quickly, he ran along the dock to the stable, saddled his horse and rode up to the Castle at a fast canter.

Sharpe and some stable boys were waiting in the driveway but so far no one else had appeared. Lord Stafford's horse, an old cavalry charger named 'Waterloo', stood a full two hands higher than the rest but like Lord Stafford himself, although huge and impressive, was passed his prime.

Patrick trotted over to the group and stopped beside Sharpe.

"Did you sleep well, Castelan?" he asked.

"Sorry," Patrick replied. "We were very late last night clearing away after dinner."

Sharpe snorted and was about to say something when they heard the sound of the main door opening and the family, laughing and talking loudly, came outside. Lord Stafford, in a tweed jacket and cap, was first down the stairs with Jeremy close behind. Then came Lady Stafford, her riding skirt pinned up in elegant folds, and finally Victoria with the young British officer. Blaise followed them out and stood at the top of the stairway, leaning on his stick, calling out words of encouragement and assuring them he was much happier staying by the fire, reading the Dublin papers.

Through force of habit, Lord Stafford led the way and they formed an orderly procession going down the drive.

It was another cold day, with white frost covering the ground and sparkling in the bare branches of the trees. Patrick heard the young officer say that the air was so clear it was like looking through a gin bottle.

They went through the main gate of the Castle then along the road for about a mile before turning into the fields. Trotting and cantering for the next two hours they finally entered the Currafin Estate, and rode across beautiful park land that had been planted with trees fifty years before.

Sharpe stayed near the front of the group but at a respectful distance from Lord Stafford. The others were strung out behind, with Victoria last. Patrick brought up the rear and as they cantered steadily on, Victoria rode more and more slowly, dropping further and further back until she drew level with him.

"Did you get my letter?" she asked.

"Yes, I did."

"Well, why didn't you answer it?"

"You didn't say very much."

"I didn't dare to. I thought it might be opened."

"It was, by the Agent. I decided it was better not to reply. I thought while you were away I'd try to forget you. I know there's no future for us."

"I tried to do the same. But last night when I saw you serving at dinner, my heart stopped and I realized how difficult it was going to be. It's all wrong, you know. You looked so out of place. You're not a servant."

"I thought you didn't even notice I was there."

"I was very, very conscious that you were," she said smiling, reaching across and touching him briefly with her gloved hand.

"When can we meet?" he asked, glancing ahead at Sharpe and the others.

"I don't know. Part of me, the wise part, says we shouldn't go on seeing each other."

"I think you're in love with that British officer."

"Bertie? Oh no. I just like him very much. I did try to fall in love with him, I admit. Daddy and Mummy would be very happy, but . . ."

"Victoria!" they heard someone shout in the distance.

Feeling guilty they looked up. Lord Stafford had stopped and was waving impatiently to them.

"Oh dear, Daddy's calling me. I must go. Damn!" she

muttered, spurring her horse forward.

Although Patrick held back he could hear Lord Stafford saying to her: "We're going to gallop the last half mile, and present a magnificent sight to the Willoughbys, a charge by the Stafford family," he added, laughing.

"George, my dear, remember that Waterloo is not as young as he used to be."

"You really mean me, don't you, Clarissa? Well, I'll be all right and so will my horse. Are we ready? One, Two, Three. Charge!" he shouted, his arm thrust straight out as if he were holding a saber.

Waterloo sprang forward, nostrils wide. After a few strides he broke into a full gallop, with Lady Stafford and the others close behind.

Patrick was about to follow when Sharpe called out to him.

"Castelan! Where the hell do you think you're going?"

Wheeling his horse around he stopped and waited.

"I saw you hanging back, talking to Lady Victoria," he said trotting over to him. "I told you last September that the Loyalist servants would take the law into their own hands if they thought it was required. I believe at this moment we may have reached that point and action is perhaps now necessary."

FORTY

Rosaleen first saw Blaise from his right side when he arrived home for Christmas. The handsome face, the bright alert eye, the ready smile, the sweep of hair brushed over the right ear, it was all as she remembered.

She had started to smile to herself, pleased to see him again, when the British officer beside him said something. Blaise turned to laugh, revealing the red stump of his left ear under his army cap, the shiny red texture of the skin graft, the black eye patch, and finally the empty sleeve of his jacket. Rosaleen noted each in turn, then looked down at the ground in front of her and squeezed her eyes tightly shut.

When she looked up again he was already half way to the main door, his back twisting from side to side as he pivoted himself along on his good leg and the walking stick.

"That really is the most terrible waste," she whispered to the maid standing beside her. "He was such a gorgeous handsome man."

Two days later, as she came out of the servants' dining hall after breakfast, a cockney voice behind her said: "Are you Rosalind?"

Turning, she faced a British Tommy standing in front of her.

"Yes I am but Rosalind is an English name. It's Rosaleen in Ireland."

"Sorry. I thought that's what he said. It's my first time in the country. Haven't learnt the lingo yet."

He looked over her shoulder then glanced behind him.

"I'm Major Stafford's batman. He asked me to give you this. In private," he added, slipping an envelope into her hand.

She hesitated for a moment, then put it down the front of her dress. The soldier raised his eyebrows, winked, then tipped his cap to her.

Rosaleen hurried along to the laundry room, empty at that time of the day, and closed the door behind her. Leaning her back against it she took the letter out the top of her dress.

It was written on a British Army note pad, brief and to the point:

21st December 1916

> *Dear Rosalind,*
>
> *A lot has happened since we last met and I have missed you. I will be at the boat house tonight between 11 o'clock and midnight.*
>
> *Please meet me there.*
>
> B

Rosaleen smiled to herself and tore the note into little pieces, then put them back in the envelope.

Most of the day she thought about what to do. Should she meet Blaise, or just ignore him? If she didn't go he might be angry, and somehow she would suffer. Yet going all that way down to the boat house just to be with him didn't make much sense. She'd enjoy talking to him, of course, but she wondered why he still wanted to see her. Obviously he could no longer make love.

Just after eleven o'clock that night she wheeled her bicycle quietly across the yard, then cycled off down the driveway to the harbor. The air, chilled with frost, brought tears to her eyes but she pedaled fast and soon arrived at the boat house.

A vertical strip of light showed between the drawn curtains, and as she got closer she could smell the smoke from the log fire curling down from the chimney.

She tapped lightly on the door. A few moments later she heard the sound of a walking stick striking the floor and the shuffling gait of Blaise.

He opened the door with his good profile towards her.

"Rosalind, Rosalind," he said. "I'm so very glad you've come. Kiss me here on this cheek because the other side isn't so good."

She followed him as he limped back across the room to the fire, roaring and crackling up the chimney, and she could feel it's heat, comforting and sensuous on her bare legs.

"A snifter?"

"Yes, please," she said. "You developed a strong taste for brandy in me but since you left I haven't had any. I wonder if I'll ever be able to afford it myself."

"Perhaps when you get to America," Blaise said, pouring out two glasses and handing one to her.

Rosaleen laughed.

"Your health, your Lordship," she said, then suddenly she added: "To hell with this 'your Lordship' stuff. Your health, Blaise!"

"Quite right, Rosalind," he said sitting down. "Quite right."

He stretched out his left leg and rested it on the padded bench around the fireplace. Rosaleen sat beside him on the arm of his chair.

Blaise drank again, then putting his brandy glass on the table he placed his hand lightly on her knee. She looked down at him, smiling tentatively until she recognized the expression in his eye. It was simple and direct.

"You blue-eyed blonde-haired beauty," he said, a little embarrassed. "You deserve better than me. And this situation."

For a moment they were both silent and increasingly uncomfortable.

"You managed to pour out the brandy very well with one arm," Rosaleen said finally, her eyes bright and affectionate over the rim of her glass.

"One learns. One learns to adjust and do everything despite one eye, one arm, and about one and a half good legs."

"How did it happen?"

"Don't let's talk about it. War stories are extremely boring, except to those who've shared the same experience."

"Actually, I'd really be interested"

"Why?"

"Because I'm interested in you. A brave son of the Ascendancy, and a former lover."

"Former?"

Not knowing what to say, Rosaleen shrugged her shoulders then drank some more brandy. The fiery liquid ran down her throat and its warmth seeped through her body.

"It's a terrible thing that's happened to you," she said. "But you're still alive. Alive! And you've got a lot to live for."

"Have I? I won't be going back to the war, and I'm finished as a fighting soldier. But they may have a command for me here dealing with the IRA, although I hear they're almost finished and will soon fade away."

"That's what I hear too," Rosaleen replied quickly.

"Are you still determined to go to America?"

"Yes, yes I am. I want to get away from Ireland, to a place where everyone has the same chance."

"There're rich and poor in America, you know," Blaise said, shrugging his good shoulder. "You'll probably find that it's not all that different from Ireland if you're born poor. If you're born rich, then it's another story."

"If you were me, wouldn't you want to emigrate to America?"

"Yes, I suppose I would. I've never really thought about it. But I didn't make history. We're born into families, into circumstances we didn't make. You were born Irish and Catholic and I was born Protestant and Ascendancy. Neither of us is going to change that."

"Politics, Blaise me darlin', are a snare and a delusion."

He nodded and sipped his brandy. "For you and I to talk

politics is a waste of time. And worse, it may cause bad feeling between us and I certainly don't want that. You're much too important to me."

"Important to you?"

"Yes," Blaise said leaning forward. "Are you still saving to go to America?" he asked, patting her knee.

Rosaleen nodded, beginning to worry.

"I'd like to give you some money, if I may. A substantial sum of money. That is, if you'll help me."

Blaise looked at her intently, an expression of pleading in his eye, something Rosaleen had never seen before.

"You mean you want to do that business with the cane and have us make love like boys again?"

"No! That belongs in the past. It's terribly important to me now just to make love, to know if I can still make love. Will you help me?"

Rosaleen stared at him and his twisted, mutilated body and began to feel a strange and compelling sense of compassion. He was no longer an invincible member of the Ascendancy, strong and dominant. It was as if their roles were reversed.

"Please," he said, nervously wrinkling his forehead. "I'll pay you very well."

"Don't worry about that," Rosaleen replied, kneeling down beside him. "What do I have to do?" she asked.

"I'm terrible sorry," he said, glancing around in confusion, "but I'm afraid you'll have to do everything."

FORTY-ONE

Each year, the family had talked about canceling the New Year's Eve Ball because of the war but this year Lord Stafford was happy to hold it. He believed that 1917 would be the year of Victory.

As was usual on that gala night, all the bedrooms of the Castle were full. Lord Tremayne, Lady Stafford's brother, and his wife had been staying since Christmas but their daughter, Pippa, had not been with them and she didn't arrive until late that afternoon. Patrick was standing under the portico when the Hispano Suizza swept into view and pulled up at the foot of the stairs. He hurried down to meet her and opened the driver's door. She swiveled nimbly in the seat, one long leather boot appeared, followed by another, then ducking her fur hat under the low roof she stepped onto the driveway.

She hesitated for a moment, shaking out her furs, then held out the car keys between a gloved finger and thumb. Catching sight of Blaise standing at the top of the steps she called out: "Darling!" and thrusting the keys at Patrick without looking at him she ran up the stairway, graceful and agile as a young deer.

"How absolutely wonderful to see you again," Patrick could hear her say as she put her arms around Blaise's neck and carefully kissed him on his good cheek. "You look, well, terrific!" She drew back, blinked then repeated: "Really terrific!"

"Pippa! Pippa! Pippa!" he replied trying to hold onto her for a moment longer with his one arm. "You're even more lovely than I remember."

"I've been away in London," she said as he released her, "otherwise I'd have dashed over the moment I heard you were home."

"It's really absolutely marvelous to see you," he said trying to smile despite the skin graft.

"And it's marvelous to see you, darling," she said as Blaise pivoted on his walking stick and they went inside.

At nine o'clock, the band started playing a popular fox trot and the dance floor soon became crowded. Blaise remained seated, a fixed smile on his face, drinking whiskey. Patrick noticed that most of the time his eyes were fixed on Pippa as she flirted with the most handsome young men in the room. Bertie danced as often as he could with Victoria, who seemed very bright and stimulated, laughing and smiling as they spun around the floor.

At an intermission, Pippa finally came over to Blaise. He smiled up at her, his expression one of relief and gratitude, then ordered Patrick to bring two whiskey-sodas. When he returned with the drinks they were so deep in conversation that they didn't notice him.

". . . you're a hero, darling, but I'm not a heroine," Pippa was saying. "I'm really a very superficial person, and I'm awfully sorry. I know they say that love should conquer all but your wounds are just too much for me. Awful time to tell you . . ."

"My dear girl, I completely understand. That's exactly how I'd feel if I were in your shoes."

She started to say something but he interrupted her.

"Darling, don't. You mustn't worry about me. My life is with the Army now. I was never really interested in getting married, having children, all that sort of thing . . ."

Patrick backed away and put the untouched whiskeys down on a table.

A little later, as a lively waltz ended, he saw Victoria coming towards him, clasping the hand of an elderly gentleman.

"Patrick," she said, "Can I have a lemonade. What would you like, Sir Charles?"

"Not a thing, thank you my dear. That last dance was a bit too much for me. I think, if you don't mind, I'll sit down over there."

The moment he had gone, Victoria turned to Patrick.

"Can we meet?" she asked quietly.

Surprised, he paused for a moment.

"When?"

"Tonight?"

"Where?"

"My bedroom. About half past twelve," she whispered as she moved away.

Patrick watched her walking through the crowd, smiling and being charming to everyone, and wondered if he had the will power not to go. But just before half passed twelve he found himself walking across the hall, through the green baize door to the kitchens and up the back stairs to the second floor. Cautiously he looked out.

The corridor was empty but from the ballroom below he could hear the faint sound of music.

He stepped back behind the door and waited.

A few minutes later he saw Victoria appear at the top of the main staircase. She hesitated, looking around her before walking silently along the corridor and into her room.

She had just lit the candle on her dressing table when he tiptoed in.

"Patrick! Oh darling, I've missed you so much," Victoria whispered, rushing over to him. "I can't bear it any more! I've been so desperate for you, needing you, longing to be with you . . ."

They made love in her soft, warm bed, gently at first and then, as their excitement increased, with a reckless frenzy. Afterwards, clinging tightly together, Victoria held his head against her breasts and he could hear her heartbeat, steady and strong. They lay there completely still, warm and at peace, almost asleep, unconscious of time or anything else except the sweet contentment of being in each others arms.

Suddenly Patrick opened his eyes.

In the faint light of the candle he could see his footman's uniform thrown over a chair, and abruptly realizing where he was, sat up.

"What's wrong?" Victoria asked, half asleep.

"We must go. We must get back to the ballroom before they've missed us."

"Oh darling, let's stay a little longer. We may never have another moment as perfect as this."

Patrick gently kissed her, then went over to his jacket and took out the watch she'd given him.

"No, my love. We must hurry. It'll soon be half passed

one."

He sat down on the bed and held her hands.

"If you're really sure you want me then we'll leave Ireland as soon as I can get some money. We'd have a better chance in another country."

"Money? But I've money in Dublin. Lots of it."

Seeing his expression she said: "Oh darling, I know what you're thinking but it really doesn't matter if it's your money or mine. The important thing is for us to get away."

FORTY-TWO

The next evening Patrick strode into the servants dining hall for supper, full of optimism and hoping to find a way of seeing Victoria that night to discuss their plans. He sat down and started his meal, thinking of their future and dreaming of the life they would have together in a new land. There seemed to be only two places they might go, either Australia or America. He'd never known anyone who had gone to Australia so America was the place, somewhere where both he and Victoria could break completely from their own kind and start life together free of the prejudices and bitterness of the past.

". . . that's terrible news about Lady Dorothy," one of the grooms was saying to the man beside him. "She was a nice person. I remember her coming here for the hunting before the war. Always left a tip for those who looked after her horses."

Patrick was hardly listening and continued to eat, lost in his own thoughts until he heard Victoria's name mentioned.

"What's that you're talking about?" he asked looking up.

"Lady Stafford's sister. Haven't you heard? She was in a very bad car accident last night in London, coming home from a New Year's Eve ball."

"Oh?"

"Yes, and they left on the noon train for Dublin immediately after they received the telegram."

"Who left? What telegram?"

"Lady Stafford and Victoria, of course. His Lordship would have gone too if he'd been well enough."

For Patrick the days passed slowly. Victoria was constantly in his mind, and in one wild moment he thought of following her to London. Had she written to him? Did the Agent have a letter from her locked in his desk? Patrick's restlessness and frustration grew but in the second week of January he was summoned to a meeting in Hanrahan's Bar and forced to concentrate on something other than Victoria.

After a few remarks by Murtagh about the need for absolute secrecy, McCarthy sat down and started to speak.

"There are several days in early February that would be suitable, but the night of February the third would be the best, a combination of a high tide at three minutes passed two in the morning and a full moon."

"A full moon?" Patrick repeated. "Somebody might see us."

"To show lights of any type would be too dangerous. They've weighed it up, and decided that they need the full moon to navigate, and also to see what they're doing when they unload. The U-Boat will be running low in the water, with only its conning tower above the surface, until it is practically in the harbor, so the risk of being spotted is not great."

Patrick nodded.

"Also, the German Navy's thirty-day meteorological

forecast indicates cold, frosty weather about that time with calm to moderate seas."

He lifted up his briefcase and took out a large flashlight with a green and red lens, and a compass which he placed on the table.

"Do you know how to use a prismatic compass?" he asked Patrick, showing it to him.

"Yes, I do."

"The submarine will surface about one nautical mile southwest of the harbor. You should put the compass on something flat beside the lighthouse, and rotate it until the pointer shows a bearing of two hundred and twenty seven degrees, then hold the flashlight so that it's parallel with the pointer. The U-Boat will be approaching on the opposite bearing and should be looking straight at your light. Is that understood?"

Patrick nodded again.

"The all-clear signal is five green flashes at one second intervals, then a one minute pause, then the same pattern repeated over again. Start at two a.m. and keep on until you receive an answer from the U-Boat, and continue flashing green at five second intervals to guide them in. Any questions?"

"No, I understand."

"If there's any problem and the operation has to be canceled screw off the green filter and put on the red. The signal is ten red flashes, followed by one minute of darkness. Keep on doing that until you get an answer. Do you want me to go over all this again?"

"No," Patrick replied, shaking his head. "I can remember."

"I told them of the lack of depth on the west side of the harbor, and they said they could easily come alongside the yacht without causing any damage because they carry pneumatic rubber fenders."

"Are you sure?" Patrick asked. "Scratches on the side of the yacht would be hard to explain."

"When we discussed this in Berlin ten days ago," McCarthy said, "they assured me that German U-Boat crews of the supply submarines are very well trained and know their job. They transfer torpedoes and shells to other U-Boats out in the Atlantic, sometimes in very high seas. Maneuvering with precision within a small harbor will be no problem to them."

"How will they unload the crates with the yacht between them and the dock?" Murtagh asked.

"On a cargo U-Boat there's a crane that will be able to reach across. They'll unload the guns and ammunition in less than five minutes from the time they come alongside then be gone."

"Five minutes!" Murtagh exclaimed.

"Mr. Murtagh," Sweeney said in a tired voice, "let Mr. McCarthy finish speaking otherwise we'll be here all night."

"They'll come in for five minutes only, no more, and unload." McCarthy continued. "It will be our job to move the crates to the warehouse, but only after they've gone. There must be the minimum of activity when they're in the harbor."

"Don't worry about that," Murtagh said as they got up to go. "Our people will take care of the guns and ammunition as long as they get them ashore."

FORTY-THREE

By the end of January, Patrick was keyed up and tense all the time, and fearing he would make a mistake with the U-Boat signals he went over his instructions again and again. But Victoria remained constantly in his thoughts and his longing for her became an almost physical ache.

On the morning of February the third, in plenty of time before two o'clock, Patrick placed the compass on a flat granite slab beside the lighthouse and carefully aligned a bearing of two hundred and twenty seven degrees. The night, as predicted, was clear and cold, the moonlight so brilliant that he could read the dial easily.

At exactly two o'clock he started counting aloud: "One thousand and one, one thousand and two . . ." flashing the green signals at one second intervals. After he had completed a series of three, a green light out to sea winked in reply. Patrick stared into the darkness, his heart pounding so violently that he had to pause for a moment before he could go on.

He started again and continued flashing at five second intervals until, about half a mile out, he saw the U-Boat cross the band of moonlight shimmering on the bay, its conning tower clearly visible as it moved low in the water, running silently on its electric motors.

When it was about a hundred yards out Patrick could hear the sigh of compressed air and the U-Boat began to rise, water cascading from its decks as it surfaced. It moved forward again and a few moments later glided in the mouth of the harbor.

Once inside, the engines went into reverse, the water churned and foamed, and it came to a stop.

Patrick ran back along the dock towards the yacht then down the gangway to the cockpit where the others were waiting, their hands gripping the rail as they watched.

"My God!" said Murtagh, "that's the most wonderful sight I've ever seen."

The conning tower of the U-Boat had wide cargo doors which were already open. The unloading had already begun, and sailors wearing rubber shoes moved silently back and forth carrying wooden crates with rope handles out onto the deck as the U-Boat maneuvered closer.

Just before they touched, the rubber bags that had been strung out along the side were pumped full of air and noiselessly the yacht and the U-Boat came together.

McCarthy spoke with the captain in German while the others watched the crane swing the first load of boxes over their heads to the dock. Soon fifty or sixty were neatly stacked on top of each other. A sailor with a clip board and pencil had been ticking them off one by one and drew a line across the page when the last box was unloaded. He spoke rapidly in German then handed the list to McCarthy to sign.

The U-Boat prepared to leave. Its cargo doors were shut and the electric motors began to whir again. Slowly it pulled away from the yacht, the crew lifting the rubber air bags onto the deck as it moved away.

Patrick, Murtagh and McCarthy went up the gangway and walked quickly along the jetty to the lighthouse where Sweeney and Kevin O'Malley were watching the U-Boat reverse out the mouth of the harbor.

About a hundred yards from the shore it slowly turned. As the bow came around they could hear the hiss of air being expelled from the ballast tanks and, riding lower in the water until only the conning tower was visible, it went swiftly out to the open sea. Within a few minutes it was gone, and the bay became silent and empty again.

"So far so good," Sweeney said, pointing to a line of men who had already started carrying the crates to the warehouse on the other side of the harbor. "What I wouldn't give for a drink," he added, turning to Patrick as they walked back towards the yacht. "Do you have anything on that pleasure boat of yours?"

"There may be some brandy."

"Perfect!"

Sweeney settled himself in the saloon and took off his cap. Patrick lit the lamp, and the cabin filled with bright, soft light.

"Nice boat this," Sweeney said looking around. "Sure the Staffords must have everything. It'll be a real pleasure to take it away from them. Them and all the bloody Ascendancy."

Patrick opened the cupboard where the drinks were kept but there was nothing there. Remembering he'd left the bottle below, he said: "Wait a second, I'll have to get the brandy."

He went down the steps, walked along the passage to

the Owner's Cabin, then pushing open the door stepped inside.

Victoria, white with shock, was standing there, completely still. For a moment, Patrick could neither think nor speak nor move until he heard Sweeney shout from above: "Where the bloody hell is my drink?"

Getting control of himself Patrick looked intently at her and mouthed: "For God's sake, don't move or utter a word."

She nodded, watching him take the brandy bottle from the cupboard, then signaled that he should close the door behind him.

Patrick hurried back to the saloon and immediately poured two glasses of brandy, handing the larger one to Sweeney who knocked it straight back and asked for another.

"You look very peeky, me boy. Are you feeling all right?"

"Of course I am," Patrick replied, pouring him some more brandy.

"It's the strain and tension. You young fellows just can't take it."

Sweeney downed the second drink as quickly as the first, then stood up.

"We've got a lot to do before daylight," he said, stepping through the hatch to the cockpit. "Come on."

The men were now strung out around the harbor carrying the crates to the warehouse. In less than an hour they had all been stored, the door firmly locked and the key given to Patrick. At Sweeney's insistence he went with them as far as the estate wall, helping to carry some of the boxes they needed immediately. As soon as they were gone he started back along the path, running and walking, and arrived at the yacht out of breath, wondering what on earth he would say to Victoria.

He stood for a moment in the saloon, trying to pull himself together until, feeling calmer, he made his way to the Owner's Cabin. To his surprise, the door was now half open.

Carefully he pushed it wide and called her name. But the room was empty. She had gone.

FORTY-FOUR

Patrick spent the remainder of the night in the warehouse, sitting on the crates of guns and ammunition, worrying about Victoria. If only she'd waited and was still there when he'd got back he could have told her the whole story and somehow made her understand. But now he was becoming increasingly worried: had she rushed off to report what had happened?

As the morning sky brightened, he could make out the Gothic script stenciled on the wooden boxes all around him. On the one at his feet he read, "9mm Luger Parabellum".

Leaning down, he lifted the lid.

The guns were packed in rows. He opened one up and unwrapped the layer of oiled paper. The weapon he could see was similar to an automatic pistol but with a removable metal frame like a rifle stock. He found a case of 9mm ammunition and, taking several clips from it, practiced loading and unloading the gun until he felt reasonably confident. He then opened the next crate. It contained bayonets, short and stubby, not much longer than a knife.

The sun came up. The day passed slowly and by evening his hunger made him feel a little delirious. Although he knew it would be the first place the soldiers and the Constabulary would look, he decided to risk sleeping on the yacht. He took with him one of the guns, several clips of ammunition, and a bayonet.

He searched everywhere on board but there was nothing to eat, and when he woke up the next day he was ravenously, uncontrollably, hungry.

The morning was silent and peaceful. Everything seemed normal. Reckless from the lack of food he decided to take a chance and ride off to the Castle to get something to eat. He'd missed roll call yesterday but as no one had come looking for him perhaps it hadn't been noticed.

He joined the other servants for breakfast. Everyone treated him as usual: nothing seemed to be out of the ordinary. As he ate a second portion of breakfast, he learned from the other servants that because Lord Stafford was more seriously ill than anyone realized Lady Stafford and Victoria had rushed back from London to be with him. Also, it was reported that there now seemed to be something wrong with Victoria. She had stayed in her room for the last two days, and hardly eaten anything at all. It was ironical, someone pointed out, that she had come home because her father wasn't well and now she was ill herself.

As one day followed another, Patrick's fear of arrest began to fade away. He heard that Victoria was up and about again and, although pale, looked fine.

After a week had passed it seemed certain that she'd said nothing about the U-Boat. He was just beginning to relax and feel confident again when, one evening after supper, Rosaleen hurried towards him in the hall.

"Patrick!" she whispered, "Oh Patrick, something terrible has happened. Kevin O'Malley and two other IRA men were captured at a British Army road block last night. I don't know if they were betrayed, but they've been taken to Limerick army barracks. As Kevin is from Ballinahinch they've asked Blaise to go and help with the interrogation."

"Interrogation?"

"Yes, and when Blaise left this afternoon he took with him that big bastard of an Orangeman, McPherson, the blacksmith."

"Kevin and who else?"

"I don't know who the other two were, but Kevin was carrying a German gun, a very new model with a recent serial number, a gun they say that's only just appeared on the Western Front."

"Do you know anything more about it?"

"It had a funny name, something like 'para-belly'."

"Parabellum," he corrected her. "A nine millimeter Luger Parabellum."

"Yes! That's what it was, but how do you know that? Oh, Patrick, are you part of all this? If so for God's sake get out now while you have a chance. I don't want you on my conscience."

"Rosaleen" he said grasping her arm. "Where do you get your information?"

"Blaise, of course. He talks to me and I overhear things. Oh my God, for Christ's sake, Patrick, go! Go at once! If you're captured they'll probably hang you, and I'd never be able to forgive myself."

Two days later the news came through that Murtagh had also been arrested and taken to Limerick.

That night it was whispered in the servants hall that

Kevin O'Malley had died earlier in the day from what the Protestant servants called 'natural causes'. When his death was confirmed the following morning, the people of Ballinahinch hung black flags out of their windows and the whole town went into mourning.

The IRA moved quickly. The following night two British Tommies were kidnapped in Ballinahinch, lured into a trap, it was said, by some pretty girls.

FORTY-FIVE

The news about the kidnapping of the two British Tommies made Victoria feel, for the first time in her life, that she was living in a hostile and alien land.

That night, as she lay in bed she felt threatened, and a traitor to her own people. She tossed and turned, agonizing over what to do. Exhausted yet unable to sleep, she got up soon after dawn and walked across the room to the window.

She drew back the curtains and looked out. The rising sun, hidden behind masses of gray clouds, cast a stark white light across the tents of the British troops who had arrived the day before.

She glanced at the line of army lorries parked along the driveway, then over the lawn to the lake and the summer house beyond. Thinking of Patrick she remembered them making love there, of the intense pleasure followed by feelings of great tranquility and tenderness. It was hard to believe that he was an enemy.

The bugler sounded reveille, and almost immediately the camp stirred into life. She watched the soldiers coming out of their tents, and from behind the big marquee smoke from the cooking fires spiraled slowly upwards. A movement to her right made her turn her head and she could see the two open carriages filled with Catholic servants moving slowly along the road from the back of the Castle. She remembered her father's instructions to the Agent the night before: "Immediately curfew is lifted, get every damned Catholic off my land."

She realized that Patrick and his kind were at war with them, kidnapping their soldiers and murdering their people. The sick feeling and anxiety of the last few days abruptly returned. Allowing the curtains to fall closed, she went back across the room and lay on her bed again.

She knew she must now make the most difficult decision in her life: she couldn't put it off any longer. She was sure she would never meet another man she would care for as much as Patrick, but loyalty to her family and her traditions must come first. She had to tell them about the German submarine, and the names of the IRA men she had heard. The fact that she would have to admit that she and Patrick had been lovers would be terribly painful to her family, especially her mother, but she must do it. As soon as Blaise returned from Limerick she would tell him everything, then ask his advice how to break the news to her father.

She got up and washed her face with cold water. Glancing in the mirror she saw she was even paler, and more drawn, than the day before. Bracing herself, she went downstairs and found her mother reading in the Morning Room.

"Hello, Mummy," she said, kissing her forehead. "You're up early. How's Daddy today?"

"Not very well, I'm afraid. He's really the most terrible patient. It's almost impossible to keep him in bed, and the doctor says he must rest."

"I'm so sorry. Will Blaise be back today?"

"No, I'm afraid not but he said he'd return in time for lunch tomorrow."

"Not until tomorrow?"

Lady Stafford frowned, then peered closely at Victoria.

"You know, you're not looking at all well, darling. Are you feeling poorly again?"

"No, Mummy," she answered, smiling brightly.

"Is there something we should talk about, some female problem perhaps? I know I haven't been a very good mother in telling you about those sort of things because, frankly, it embarrasses me to talk about them. It's part of my generation. You young people are much more open."

"Don't worry, Mummy. It's not that. I'm fine," Victoria said, firm and positive. "I just haven't been sleeping properly."

"I think we all need a change. As soon as your father's well enough we'll go to Dublin for a while. That should cheer us up."

The next day lunch was served in Lord Stafford's bedroom. He was feeling much better and said he wanted to see them all. Freshly shaved, he greeted them propped up in bed on a lot of pillows and had that bright, imperious glint in his eyes that made Victoria think he had almost recovered.

"Good morning, Daddy," she said, kissing his cheek. "You're looking marvelous. I'm so glad."

"I'd be up and about if it wasn't for these damned doctors. But I am getting up in a day or two, no matter what they say. There's nothing wrong with me and I want to report to the War Office and get involved again."

"You may have to take it a little more slowly than that, dear," Lady Stafford said.

"Clarissa, I intend to take some part in this war. It will be the last one for our generation, perhaps for all time, and I'll be damned if I'll lie here in bed in Ballinahinch Castle until it's all over."

His eyes blazed with frustration and his face became very red.

"Dearest," Lady Clarissa said, sitting down beside him. "You'll be back there very soon then you'll miss the peace and comfort of Ballinahinch."

"Yes, yes my dear. Don't you think it's time we had something to drink?"

"What a good idea. I'd like a sherry. Victoria would you please pour? We don't want anyone disturbing us."

"I'll have the same," Lord Stafford said. "The doctor has forbidden me any drink at all but damn it, a little sherry can't do a person any harm."

Victoria smiled at him and was just about to reach for the decanter when Jeremy, a little breathless, came into the room.

"Father, I'm so sorry to barge in like this but Blaise has been delayed in Limerick and he's sent you this."

He handed him an envelope on which was stamped 'OHMS'.

Lord Stafford opened it and took out a type-written page. After reading it he looked up.

"Bad news, I'm afraid. They've found those two young Tommies. They've been executed by the IRA."

"Oh no!" Lady Stafford exclaimed. "They're just young

boys. Your age, Jeremy. How terrible for their mothers."

"Did Blaise say when he'll be back?" Victoria asked.

"No. Why?"

"I'd like to talk to him."

"What about?"

"About all this."

"Well, you can talk to me," Lord Stafford said.

"It doesn't matter, Daddy. It can wait. Why don't we all have some lunch?"

"Yes," Lady Stafford agreed. "Please ring the bell."

None of them ate very much, and for the most part they sat in silence. Immediately after they had drunk their coffee, Jeremy and Victoria excused themselves and left.

"Isn't it awful," Jeremy said as they went downstairs. "Let's do something to try and forget about it. Why don't we go for a ride or a walk?"

"I'm sorry but I don't feel up to it today," Victoria replied. "I think I'd prefer to be quiet. But I'd like to go riding tomorrow."

"All right then. What time?"

"Let's go early in the morning, about six o'clock? It's magical at that time of the day."

"Six o'clock it is. I'll go over to the stables and tell Sharpe."

Victoria went off to her room while Jeremy walked across the yard and found Sharpe in his office haranguing a stable boy who stood sulkily before him, nervously pulling at the threads from the ragged hole in his red sweater.

"We won't tolerate stealing," Sharpe was saying, "but for the sake of your father I'll give you one more chance if you return the money."

He broke off the moment he saw Jeremy enter.

"Good afternoon, m'lord. How can I be of service?" he asked, getting to his feet.

"Good afternoon, Sharpe. We'd like to go riding early tomorrow morning. My sister will take Daisy, and I think I'd like Toby. He's a fine galloper."

"He is that, sir."

"Will you please have the horses ready at six o'clock? We'll probably go down to the South Twenty."

That afternoon, the family had tea in the upstairs drawing room. Jeremy stood by the window, cup in hand, looking out at the gathering dusk. The movement of a cyclist coming through the arch under the belfry caught his eye. Something about him appeared familiar, and he recognized the stable boy he had seen earlier in Sharpe's office, the one in the old red sweater. He could see him pedaling fast along the driveway behind the Castle until he dropped down into the sunken road and vanished out of sight.

FORTY-SIX

"Red sky in the morning, shepherd's warning," Jeremy said as they stood on the stairs of the Castle waiting for the horses.

The sky to the east was crimson as the rising sun broke the line of the horizon and streaked the clouds in vivid hues of red. The lawn and bushes, and beyond them the bell tents of the army, sparkled with drops of dew. To the west, far out across the sea, clouds were already forming over Ennismore and beginning to drift towards the mainland.

"It's going to rain later."

"Yes," Victoria replied. "But the first few hours should be lovely."

Turning around they saw Sharpe coming towards them with the horses.

"I'm sorry I'm late . . ." he began.

"You're not late," Jeremy assured him. "We're early"

Victoria glanced at her brother, always anxious to put people at ease. But Sharpe doesn't deserve it she was thinking as she looked up at his hard face.

At that moment a bugler in the soldiers' camp sounded the reveille.

"There. Six o'clock exactly," Jeremy said. "You're right on time."

They mounted, and turned their horses down the driveway.

"Shall I come with you?" Sharpe inquired.

"Why?" Victoria asked.

"These are uncertain times."

She shook her head impatiently.

"Don't worry," Jeremy said. "We won't be going beyond the estate wall. We'll give the horses a really good gallop across the South Twenty and be back in about an hour."

They cantered off down the drive. Just before the main gate they turned into the twenty acres of park land where there was little danger of the horses stumbling because the ground was well drained.

"Race you to the south end!" Victoria cried.

"Right!" Jeremy shouted. "One, two, three. Go!"

Both the horses sprang forward in unison and within a short distance broke into a full gallop. Victoria felt the moist air rushing passed, fresh and cold on her cheeks, and crouching lower in the saddle she became as one with the horse, matching the rhythm of his stride, his breathing getting deeper, shoulder muscles working in unison with the thrust of his legs. She began to feel exhilarated as she urged the horse on, calmer and more relaxed than she had been for several days.

They galloped side by side, weaving through the trees, and reached the south end almost neck and neck.

Laughing and carefree, patting their horses heads, they walked them around in circles until they cooled off, then started back at a leisurely canter until Victoria abruptly pointed towards a grove of trees about a hundred yards ahead.

"What's that?" she said. "It looks like a riderless horse."

Jeremy blinked, squinting through his glasses.

"Yes it does," he replied.

"Whose can it be?"

They slowed down to a trot and made their way towards the horse grazing in a patch of lush grass, unaware of their approach.

Jeremy, a little to one side, slowed his horse to a walk and pointed with his riding crop.

"I think I see someone over there, a man lying on the ground."

"Where?" Victoria said, reining in her horse and going towards him.

"There. Partly hidden by the bushes."

Victoria leaned forward in the saddle and looked down.

"Judging by his clothes," she said, "he's not one of us. I wonder who he is?"

She slipped her feet out of the stirrups and slid to the ground. Cautious yet alert, she walked forward and stood over the man. He was lying face-down, his right hand covered by his body. Taking hold of his shoulder she started to roll him over when he jerked upright, thrusting a gun directly in her face.

"My God!" she exclaimed jumping back as two men holding revolvers came out of the bushes.

"If you behave yourselves," the thin-faced one with the twisted smile said, "nobody will get hurt."

Straightening up and becoming icy-calm she said: "The bloody IRA."

"That's right. Miss. Let me introduce myself. My name is Sweeney and I'm in charge of this part of West Clare."

"I don't give a damn who you are. Get off our land."

"Now, now, Miss. That's not very friendly. You see, we'd like you to come with us. We can make this nice and easy, or we can do it the hard way."

"What do you mean?"

"You're coming with us and it would be a lot easier if you came without causing any trouble."

At that moment the man behind Victoria threw a fishing net over her head, pinioned her arms to her side, then knocked her to the ground. She kicked and struggled but they drew the net tighter until she couldn't move.

Jeremy jumped down from his horse and ran over to her. "Let my sister go!" he shouted, pushing passed the men, trying to get to her.

"Now hold it right there," Sweeney said, pointing his gun at Jeremy.

Slowly he put his hands up.

"What shall we do with him?" the man beside Sweeney asked, shrugging his shoulders in a nervous gesture.

"He's no use to us, not part of the plan," Sweeney replied.

"But he could recognize us. You, me, and Brady."

"That's right. And we can't have that, can we?"

Sweeney turned his head slightly but still keeping his eyes on Jeremy he nodded towards the bushes.

"Take him over there and dispose of him."

"Dispose of him? Me! I couldn't do that, Commandant. Not in cold blood."

"Then you do it, Brady."

The other man shook his head.

"Why is it I have to do every damn thing myself,"

Sweeney said, affecting a weary voice as he tightened his finger on the trigger.

"For God's sake Commandant! Don't kill him! Let's take him with us."

Sweeney just laughed, closed one eye, aimed and fired.

Jeremy's head jerked backwards, he staggered for a couple of seconds then collapsed, dying without a murmur.

"No!" screamed Victoria hysterically, rolling over and over on the ground in a frenzied struggle to stand up. "No! No! No!"

"Will you keep quiet, girl!" Sweeney shouted, striking her across the side of her head with the barrel of his gun.

She quivered, then lay still.

"We must move quickly, lads. Somebody may have heard the shot up at the Castle, though I doubt it."

They took hold of the net, and lifting Victoria between them carried her to the estate wall.

Sweeney climbed up. The men hoisted Victoria above their heads and held her steady until Sweeney could grip the net and lever her onto the top of the wall. He paused for a moment then shoved her over. She landed on the other side with a heavy thud, next to a waiting car.

"Commandant!" the driver exclaimed, hurriedly getting out. "Maybe you've killed her, pushing her off the wall like that."

"Don't worry, O'Shaughnessy. She won't break. That bitch comes from strong Cromwellian stock."

FORTY-SEVEN

"You must leave today," Hanrahan said to Patrick after giving him breakfast, "and don't come back. It's not that I'm unsympathetic to the Movement, but I've a wife and children and a business to think of."

"Yes, I know," Patrick replied. "It was good of you to put me up last night. Tell me, have you seen O'Shaughnessy recently?"

"No. I haven't. Not for more than a week. Why?"

"I'd like to talk to him."

Patrick spent most of the day trying to find somewhere to stay but wherever he went there was no room, or they were afraid to help him. By late afternoon, tired and desperate, he thought of trying the Parish Priest. It was beginning to get dark when he started up the hill to the church and darker still when he knocked on the door.

"Yes?" the woman said as she peered at him in the gloom.

"I need a bed for the night and I thought perhaps the priest might help me."

"You're one of them," she said, nodding to herself. "On the run, is it?"

"No," Patrick said. "I can explain to the priest."

She began shaking her head, not listening to him.

"The Catholic Church does not take part in politics, particularly in these troublesome times."

"But still, I'd like to speak to him."

"It's impossible. He's not here anyway so I suggest you go into the church and say the Rosary," she said, a pious smirk curling the edges of her mouth as she closed the door.

He stood outside for a moment, uncertain what to do next. Thinking there might be a chance of getting back to Ennismore, he started walking down the hill towards the docks. He was just nearing the market square when he saw Rosaleen in the dusk on the other side of the street.

"Patrick, me darlin'," she called, crossing over to him. "What's wrong? You look awful. Have you nowhere to go?"

"I'm fine."

"No you're not. You're coming home with me. But for one night only, then you must move on."

The next morning he was awakened by Rosaleen's little sister standing in the doorway crying.

"Me sister's gone," she wailed.

"Gone!" Patrick repeated, sitting up in alarm. "Where's she gone?"

"A big car came in the middle of the night, a soldier driving it. He had a letter for her. She read it, then dressed and went with him. The children in the street say she's a whore. What's that? When I asked me Ma, she got angry and slapped me."

"I don't know. But don't worry, your sister's a very nice girl. Everyone likes her."

"Some people say everyone in the British Army likes her."

Patrick didn't know what to reply.

"Don't fret," he said taking her hand and leading her to the door. "I'll try to explain later but first I've got to get dressed."

Rosaleen's mother gave him a piece of bread and a cup of tea for breakfast. She asked him to please eat quickly then go. She stood watching at the window until he'd finished and was about to turn to him when she blessed herself and murmured under her breath: "Jesus, Mary, and Joseph, what's happened now?"

Patrick went over to her and looked out at the lane behind. Rosaleen had just leaned her bicycle on the railing and was running up the path towards them. The back door burst open and she rushed in.

"Patrick! You've got to go. At once!"

"What's happened?"

"I've seen the latest wanted list. Your name's on it."

"Are you sure?"

"Yes. A dispatch rider brought it an hour ago from the interrogation center in Limerick. Blaise left it on his desk."

"Where shall I go? I don't want to involve my family otherwise I'd try to get back to Ennismore."

"That's impossible. There's soldiers all around the docks."

"The Convent, maybe I could hide there."

"That may have worked in medieval times, but not in nineteen seventeen."

"O'Malley?"

"He has the money and the resources. He might help but I doubt it. But I know the foreman at O'Malley's coal yard. He's a friend of me Da's."

They hurried down the street towards the harbor, watchful for soldiers and ready to duck into a side street but there were few people about and none of them took any notice. When they came to the arch with the words 'O'Malley Coal Merchants' painted on it, Rosaleen turned to Patrick.

"Walk straight and tall, me darlin', like you didn't have a care in the world."

They passed under the arch into a cobblestoned yard where a horse-drawn cart was being loaded with sacks of coal, then across to the office building.

"You'd better wait outside," Rosaleen said, hooding her eyes and making a face at Patrick. "I'll be more persuasive on my own."

She was away a long time and Patrick was beginning to wonder what had happened when the door opened and she came down the steps towards him.

"He'll see you directly," she said with a wink. "I explained that Mr. O'Malley wanted him to give you a job and hide you, on account of you being a friend of Kevin's."

"For how long?"

"I told him two nights, but one step at a time. There's no point in thinking too far ahead."

The manager, breathless and agitated, appeared in the doorway then looked Patrick up and down.

"You can't stay here for long, you know. None of the lads or myself would give you away but it's too dangerous. We just don't want to be involved. But if Mr. O'Malley says to hide you for a couple of days then of course I will. Have you a gun?"

Patrick shook his head.

"What's in that?" he asked nodding towards the suitcase in Patrick's hand.

"Nothing but clothes."

"Have you got any weapons?" he asked again.

"He told you he hadn't," Rosaleen said, smiling agreeably.

"All right then. You can stay in the hay loft above the stables."

That night Rosaleen brought him food, also a razor, soap and a towel. She only stayed a few minutes, but said she'd be back soon.

A week passed without her coming to visit him again. Every morning the manager put pressure on Patrick to leave, but every afternoon he would relent and allow him to stay for just one more night. On the evening of the tenth day, Rosaleen arrived very tense and upset.

"What's wrong?" Patrick asked. "Has something happened?"

"Yes it has. Something terrible. Victoria Stafford's been kidnapped by the IRA."

"What!" Patrick whispered in disbelief. "Kidnapped? When?"

"Almost two weeks ago. The family kept it a secret, because they hoped to negotiate. But the bastards want ten of our men released from Limerick jail. They've given the British a forty-eight hour ultimatum."

"Ultimatum?"

"Yes. If they don't give in, Victoria will end up hanged like the two British Tommies. Jesus Christ! What'll we do, Patrick? We know that they mean it."

FORTY-EIGHT

That night Patrick left the coal yard and risked walking through the streets to Hanrahan's Bar. He had to have a drink, get some relief from the gnawing anxiety and helplessness he felt. Uncertain whether he'd be going back to the coal yard he took his suitcase with him, making sure that the gun and bayonet were carefully hidden and wrapped in his clothes.

"It's too late, almost curfew. Go away!" Hanrahan snapped when he opened the door.

Patrick pushed passed him and went inside.

"All right then. Just one drink. But if you're shot that's your fault. I'll get you a pint, but drink it here in the hall."

"Make it a whiskey. A double. And I don't intend to stand about like a beggar," Patrick called after him.

He tried to open the door to the back room but it was locked. Irritated, he rattled the knob two or three times and waited. Nobody came but as he turned away he heard the bolt being withdrawn. He looked around and saw the familiar face of O'Shaughnessy.

"Me old friend!" he said holding his hand out to Patrick. "How good it is to see you. Come in, come in."

"Are you alone?"

"Yes."

When Hanrahan returned with Patrick's whiskey, he was even more agitated.

"I'm sorry but I don't want you two staying here. I want you out of my pub, and out of my life before I get thrown into jail as well."

"You'll change your tune when Ireland's free," O'Shaughnessy retorted. "Then you'll be boasting about all the help you gave to the Movement."

Without a word he turned away, pulling the door closed behind him.

"To the memory of our dear friend Kevin O'Malley," O'Shaughnessy said, raising his glass. "And death to that bastard who killed him."

"Do you know who it was?"

"Yes. That big, bloody Orangeman, McPherson. The British Army are using him to do their dirty work for them. They've got pretty savage since they found the two Tommies."

"Who was responsible for hanging them?"

"Sweeney. He did the job himself. None of the other boys could stomach it."

"They were so young. Two conscripts, with no hatred for Ireland. I wouldn't want any part of an Irish Republican Army that does something like that."

"Discretion of the local commandant."

"You mean Sweeney?"

"Yes."

"Where's Victoria Stafford being held?"

O'Shaughnessy gazed into his glass.

"I've heard rumors you're sweet on her," he said, "that there's more between the two of you than just her gratitude."

"You haven't answered my question. Where is she?"

At that moment the door opened and Hanrahan looked in.

"For God's sake! Drink up the two of you. I want to lock up. It's already passed curfew."

Patrick got to his feet and walked over to Hanrahan.

"Out!" he said, opening his coat enough to expose the Luger pistol tucked in his belt.

Nodding, Hanrahan backed away without a word.

Patrick pushed the door closed behind him.

"Does Sweeney have her?"

O'Shaughnessy didn't answer. Patrick asked him again. This time he nodded.

"Don't you realize," Patrick said, sitting down at the table opposite O'Shaughnessy, "if the IRA start hanging women as well as young boys the cause of Irish freedom is finished. No one will support it. Every decent Irishman will turn away. The friends we have in America will be sickened, and there'll be no more money or support."

O'Shaughnessy knocked back the rest of his drink.

"Sweeney is not really the IRA," he said, his voice uneasy as he wiped his mouth with his sleeve.

"Then who the hell made him Commandant for West Clare?"

"I don't know how that happened. Orders from Dublin, but I think it was a mistake."

"O'Shaughnessy, the rebellion last year was led by good and honorable men like Pearse and Connelly and all the others, idealists and dreamers and poets, not twisted people, murderers like Sweeney."

"Look where it got us? The British executed all your

idealists and dreamers and poets. The rebellion collapsed. Michael Collins himself said next time we'll need to get real killers to win our freedom. I think he meant people like Sweeney."

"I'm damned sure he didn't mean killers of innocent people. O'Shaughnessy, let me quote something from the Proclamation of nineteen sixteen, Pearse's words which I remember very clearly."

Patrick leaned across the table.

"We place the cause of the Irish Republic under the protection of the Most High God, whose blessing we invoke upon our arms, and we pray that no one who serves that cause will dishonor it by cowardice, inhumanity or rapine."

"I too remember those words but they didn't get us anywhere."

"O'Shaughnessy, the Irish Republican Army you serve must be that of the executed heroes of nineteen sixteen, not Sweeney. Whether or not I was sweet on Victoria Stafford is beside the point. If she is found hanged like the British Tommies it will cause such a wave of revulsion on both sides of the Atlantic it will unite everyone against us and the British will put so many soldiers into Ireland that we'll be utterly crushed."

O'Shaughnessy shook his head in confusion.

"I obey orders. I don't make decisions. Maybe they'll release Murtagh and the others from Limerick jail and Sweeney won't have to hang her."

"They won't. The British won't give in. O'Shaughnessy, unless you tell me where Sweeney is holding her you'll be responsible before God, responsible for the death of an innocent girl."

"I need another drink."

"Where is Sweeney holding her?" Patrick asked again.

O'Shaughnessy stared at Patrick, his breath labored and audible. He was basically a simple man, a faithful follower, not a leader.

"In a farm," he said in a voice a little above a whisper. "About twenty miles away, up in the mountains beyond Gort."

"Do you know where the farm is?"

"Of course I do. I've been guarding her there for almost two weeks now, with Sean Brady and Seamus Kelly."

"Details, tell me the details," Patrick demanded, his voice becoming hard.

"Sweeney got to know where she and her brother were going riding one morning. Someone sold him the information and we faked an accident inside the grounds and trapped her. Then he shot that poor gentle soul Jeremy, point blank, with a forty-five. He didn't have to do that. By God, Patrick, you're right! He is a murdering bastard. He doesn't represent the IRA. And I think he's gone mad."

"Mad? Go on. What happened next?"

"We put her into the trunk of the car and got away without being seen. I was driving and we went like the wind up into the mountains to the farm."

"Who owns the farm?"

"It belongs to an old man married to a young girl. They've got no children. They say they're in sympathy with us, but I'm not sure."

"Haven't the army and RIC been out looking for her?"

"Of course they have. A British Army patrol came by the second day we were there but Sweeney knocked Victoria out. Brady grabbed the farmer's wife and we hid with her on the other side of the hill until the soldiers had gone. When we came back Sweeney said he'd made the old farmer stand in the middle of the room when the soldiers were there with both feet planted on the rug covering the trap-door."

"Trap-door? What trap-door? Describe the cottage to me."

"The cottage has three rooms and a cellar. There's a trap-door to it in the middle of the kitchen. Sweeney keeps her chained down there. It's dark and there's very little air. It's inhuman, but he says it's necessary so she's easier to control. In the beginning she put up a terrific fight when he tried to molest her."

"Molest her!"

"Yes. He's a dirty, evil man. He wanted her to . . ."

"To what?"

"Wanted her to . . . to accommodate him. But Christ, she has the spirit of a tigress, and as strong. She fought him to a standstill, and tore his face to ribbons with her nails. That's the reason he can't come into Ballinahinch himself. With the iodine on him he sure looks like hell."

"And then?"

"He knocked her senseless and chained her by the ankle to the wall. When she came to, he told her that she'd get no food or water until she submitted to him. She laughed in his face but he said in five or six days it would be a different story. He said he was going to break her spirit and that soon she'd be begging and pleading with him and do anything he asked."

"What did she do then?"

"She spat in his face. God knows, that woman has a powerful character, she wouldn't fear the Devil himself."

"How long is it since she's had food and water?"

O'Shaughnessy shook his head and smiled.

"Sure you couldn't let a woman like that die. Brigid, the farmer's wife, gives her food and water whenever Sweeney's asleep, or outside relieving himself. You know something?" he added after a moment's pause, "Brigid said a strange thing the other day."

"What did she say?"

"She said Victoria's going to have a baby. I asked her how in the name of God she knew that? And she said it was because Victoria gets sick when she wakes up in the morning. I really don't know what she meant. But look, Patrick, what we need is another drink. I'll go and get more whiskey."

FORTY-NINE

A few minutes later O'Shaughnessy came back into the room carrying a bottle of whiskey. It was new and unopened, and he had difficulty getting the wrapping off with his trembling hands.

"In the name of God what am I going to do?" he said, pouring them both a drink. "I'm supposed to obey the orders of my senior officer without question, aren't I?"

"Do you mean Sweeney?" Patrick asked.

"Yes."

"You don't have to obey the orders of a madman."

"But I've made a sacred oath."

"A sacred oath to obey the likes of Sweeney? That's obscene nonsense! Go and get a bible!"

"Why?" O'Shaughnessy asked, alarmed at the expression in Patrick's eyes. "Anyway, where would I find a bible?"

"Here, damn you," Patrick replied taking the crucifix from around his neck.

O'Shaughnessy drew back but Patrick grabbed his right hand and held it down over the cross. "I'm going to give you an oath you can honor and live by. You can swear, before God, swear that you will obey the principles laid down by Pearse, Connelly, Wolfe Tone, O'Donevan Rossa, Daniel O'Connell, Lord Edward FitzGerald, Charles Stewart

Parnell . . ."

O'Shaughnessy tried to pull away but couldn't move.

". . . and you will kill, if necessary, any man who defiles that sacred trust or betrays the dead generations in the fight for the freedom of Ireland."

O'Shaughnessy looked hard at Patrick then took a deep breath.

"I will! I swear to God, on the grave of my mother, that I will."

Patrick let go of his hand.

"How long have we got?" he asked, putting the crucifix back round his neck again.

O'Shaughnessy couldn't speak for a moment. He just stared at Patrick, then swallowed hard.

"How long?" Patrick asked again.

"Forty eight hours from midnight last night. That leaves a little over twenty four . . ."

"We need a car."

"I've got a car. It's registered to a farmer beyond Gort. Also I have a gun," he added, pulling open his coat, exposing a Webley forty-five in a leather holster under his armpit.

Patrick nodded. "I've a Luger and several clips of ammunition. And a bayonet. What do they have, Sweeney and the two others? I've forgotten their names."

"Brady and Kelly."

"Brady and Kelly," Patrick repeated. "What guns do they have?"

"Sweeney has a Webley, and a couple of hand grenades. He keeps them on the mantelpiece in the cottage. They're to be used as a last resort if the British Army find us. He says if they come he'll drop one into the cellar and close the trap door. Nothing down there could survive a blast like that."

"Brady?"

"He has a Webley too, like mine, and Kelly a Mauser automatic."

"You said the farm is about twenty miles away?"

"At least, and the last few miles are up a very steep, twisting boreen."

"Where are Brady and Kelly positioned? And where does Sweeney spend most of the day?"

"Mostly in the kitchen, near the trap door. He sleeps in the easy chair beside the fire, his revolver cocked on the table beside him. The other two, and myself, alternate watching the boreen about a hundred yards down from the cottage. We take shifts so there's always someone on guard."

"How long are they?"

"Four hours. We change at two a.m., then again at six, then at ten."

"So if we were to arrive at ten o'clock in the morning we would find both Brady and Kelly away from the cottage down the boreen, changing shifts?"

"That's right."

"Go on," Patrick said, "what about the farmer?"

"Well, he and his wife spend most of the day in the small bedroom at the back. Sweeney lets them out one at a time to feed the chickens and pigs, and cook the meals. The larger bedroom opposite the kitchen is where Brady, Kelly and myself sleep."

"Do they have dogs around the place?"

"One, half-starved, chained near the front door. He's on

a sort of hair-spring, barks at the slightest sound, and leaps at you when you approach."

"We'll need to deal with that dog. Get some rat poison, and a piece of meat."

O'Shaughnessy nodded.

"What time are they expecting you back?" Patrick asked.

"Tomorrow morning. I said I'd leave immediately after curfew with food, drink and news, if any, about our men in Limerick jail."

"Who would give you that information?"

"If there was a message Hanrahan would have it."

"Who else knows the location of the farm?"

"No one."

"Not even the Central Committee?"

"No. That was the way Sweeney wanted it, for security reasons."

Patrick paused for a moment and took a sip of his whiskey.

"If you're stopped on the road by a British Army patrol how do you explain yourself?" he asked.

"I have papers saying I'm a farmer and registered at Ballinahinch Constabulary Barracks."

"Are you?"

"Of course not, but I play the fool and they never check."

"I explain I'm driving a big car because I'm a prosperous farmer who supplies meat to the British Army. I also have these," he said, laughing as he took a set of false teeth out of his pocket. "They're bloody uncomfortable but I wear them when I'm driving. Prosperous farmers aren't usually toothless."

Patrick nodded then took another drink from his glass.

"What are the chances of driving there in the dark?"

"Not good. The patrols are very active at night, and any movement on the road or sound of a motor is easy to pick up. The best time is exactly when curfew's lifted. The soldiers going off duty are anxious for breakfast and sleep. Those coming on are often still half awake, and hung over from the previous night's beer."

Patrick poured more whiskey into both glasses and they drank in silence, each lost in their own thoughts.

"Could you kill Brady and Kelly if it were necessary?" Patrick asked.

O'Shaughnessy shook his head. "Not Kelly anyway. We were at school together, and his family are close to mine. I'd be lying to you if I said I could kill him."

"Could you knock him senseless?"

"Yes, I could do that, but I couldn't kill him."

"And Brady?"

"He's a nasty piece of work, a bit like Sweeney. But these men trust me," O'Shaughnessy went on, his face wrinkled with concern. "Really, I couldn't kill either of them."

"Well, what about Sweeney?"

"Yes, if it were necessary I think I could, but maybe we can rescue the girl without killing anybody?"

Patrick nodded.

O'Shaughnessy sighed with relief and started to pour another drink.

Patrick covered both glasses with his hands.

"No. We've had enough tonight. We must be sharp and alert tomorrow."

FIFTY

Patrick and O'Shaughnessy slept fitfully, their heads resting on their hands spread out on the table. By five thirty they were wide awake and ready to go.

Keyed up and alert they moved swift and silent through the deserted streets then passed the church into a quiet residential area where doctors, bank managers and other leading citizens of the town lived.

O'Shaughnessy had left the car at the house of a sympathizer whose son had been killed in the fighting of Easter Week. They opened the gates, and walked quietly up the driveway to an eight cylinder open tourer with a canvas top and a large trunk fixed at the back.

"She's powerful and fast," O'Shaughnessy whispered, "could outrun most British Army vehicles."

He got behind the steering wheel, released the hand brake and Patrick started to push the car down the drive. It gained momentum then bounced out onto the road as Patrick jumped on the running board and climbed in.

"Say a prayer the engine turns over," O'Shaughnessy said pressing the clutch pedal to the floor, "or we'll have to stop and crank it by hand."

He eased it into gear then slowly lifted his foot. The car juddered violently two or three times, then the engine began running smoothly. Although dawn was breaking, O'Shaughnessy switched the headlights on.

"Why are you doing that?" Patrick asked.

"Because if we're spotted, they'll think it's a British Army vehicle that's been out all night and on its way home. By the time they realize we're not, we'll be gone."

They drove out of Ballinahinch, traveling fast, passed the turreted gateway to the Castle then continued northwards towards the distant mountains. The sun was already showing above the horizon, and birds were singing in the trees as the new day began.

O'Shaughnessy was joking and talking loudly, the speed and power of the car exciting him. He put his foot down harder on the accelerator and Patrick watched the speedometer needle creep slowly up until they were doing fifty miles an hour, leaving behind them a plume of exhaust smoke and flying gravel.

They approached a curve in the road where it turned into a shallow valley with a running stream. They rounded the corner and had started to descend towards the bridge when they saw ahead of them a British Army road block.

"Jesus Christ! We're lost!" O'Shaughnessy muttered pressing his foot on the brake.

"Be quiet! Smile. Look agreeable," Patrick said, giving the impression of calm he did not feel.

They pulled up a few yards short of the bridge, in front of a Vickers machine gun. Two soldiers squatted behind it drinking tea. A sergeant, leaning against a Crossley lorry, also had a cup in his hand.

"Better search them, Corporal," he said wearily. "Maybe they're a couple of bloody IRA."

"It's after six o'clock, Sarge! I don't give a bugger if it's the commandant-in-chief himself. I'm for bacon and eggs, and a spot of kip."

"Corporal! Don't talk like that, or I'll have you on a charge," he replied without conviction as the machine gunners pulled the belt of ammunition from the breach and started dismantling the gun.

The sergeant watched them for a moment then sighed and finally came over to the car.

"Your papers," he said. "Although if you are the IRA I'm sure you'll have a very fine set indeed. Let's see them anyway."

O'Shaughnessy showed him his identification card with its stamp from the Royal Irish Constabulary in Ballinahinch.

"And you?"

Patrick gave him his pass to the coal yard.

"What are you carrying?"

"Food and groceries," O'Shaughnessy replied, pointing to the parcels on the rear seat.

"And what's in the big trunk on the back?

"Oh, just bombs, rifles, ammunition, grenades, that sort of thing," he answered, smiling inanely.

The sergeant yawned.

"Save your bloody humor for another time. Where are you going?"

"To my farm."

"And you?" he asked, looking at Patrick.

O'Shaughnessy leaned forward. "He's coming to work for me at the farm."

"Can't the bugger speak for himself? Are things slow in the coal yard?"

"Yes," Patrick said. "There's very little work anywhere these days."

"Shall we be on our way, sergeant?" O'Shaughnessy asked, nodding his head, trying to extract a positive answer.

"We'd better check you out first. You'll have to follow us to Rathdown, to our headquarters."

He walked over to the lorry, climbed up beside the driver, and they moved off. O'Shaughnessy engaged the gears and they followed close behind.

"Where the hell is Rathdown?" Patrick asked.

"About ten miles up the road."

They drove in silence for about half an hour, too tense and worried to speak, until they came to a large village. The buildings on either side of the Royal Irish Constabulary barracks had been commandeered by the army, and for additional space they had pitched tents in the town square. A row of Crossley lorries were lined up one behind the other and khaki-uniformed soldiers seemed everywhere.

Patrick and O'Shaughnessy were brought into the office of the duty officer.

"Where were you going so early in the morning?" he asked. "You broke the curfew?"

"Oh no, your honor," O'Shaughnessy said. "We didn't start moving a moment before six o'clock. We'd loaded the car the night before in order to have an early start and we left as soon as curfew was lifted."

"All right. But where are you heading?"

"To my farm, your honor, in the mountains beyond Gort," O'Shaughnessy replied, rummaging in his coat pocket and taking out some papers which he thrust at him. "I own good land, the finest for grazing, and raise cattle which I sell to the British Army."

The officer seemed disinterested, and glanced frequently at the large map covering the wall behind him. He stood up while O'Shaughnessy was talking and traced his finger over a certain area, then picked up the telephone.

"I want a second sweep through Sector Blue Four. Yes, every farmhouse, barn, woodland, everything thoroughly checked. Also, telephone the Royal Flying Corps at Limerick and ask if they can help us again with an aeroplane."

He put down the receiver and turned to O'Shaughnessy once more.

"We'll check your identity," he said. "If it's all right you can go. Deirdre," he called to his secretary, "get the RIC in Ballinahinch, give them these men's names, and confirm that they're on their list of approved residents."

A few moments later they heard her crank the telephone and say: "Please connect me with Ballinahinch Exchange."

While she waited she looked from Patrick to O'Shaughnessy then back to Patrick again.

"Ballinahinch Exchange? Would you put me through to the RIC barracks. Yes, I'll hold on."

After a pause, she pressed the receiver tighter to her ear and said in a loud voice: "I can't hear you! Speak up! This is the British Army, Rathdown. We have two men here and we would like to confirm . . . what, not until eight? Hold on."

The officer looked inquiringly at her.

"It seems, sir," she said, "that the files are locked up, and the secretary who has the key doesn't come to work until eight o'clock."

The officer shrugged his shoulders, then glanced at his watch. "Well, it's only a quarter to seven. Better put them under guard, and bring them back in about an hour."

FIFTY-ONE

The cell was bare except for two bunk beds.

"What on earth are we going to do?" O'Shaughnessy began but Patrick glared at him, signaling with his eyes that someone might be listening. Nodding, O'Shaughnessy started talking about cattle and the great prices the British Army were paying for beef on the hoof.

The minutes ticked slowly by.

At five minutes to eight, they heard the key turn in the lock and the door was opened by a soldier.

"Come along you two. Get a move on!" he said, giving them a shove with his rifle butt.

Through the open door of the office, Patrick could see the secretary typing a letter. Sensing that he was watching her, she looked up, her eyes narrowing slightly as she glanced at him.

"Sit over there!" the soldier ordered, pointing to the bench in the passage.

Just before the hour, the clock on the wall began to strike eight.

"I'll try the RIC now, sir," Patrick heard the secretary say, bright and efficient, to the officer.

Patrick stood up and moved to the open doorway, watching her intently as she briskly cranked the telephone and asked again for Ballinahinch Exchange. When they answered she stared directly into Patrick's eyes and said: "Please connect me with the Royal Irish Constabulary."

His gaze was as steady and unblinking as hers.

She looked away for a moment, across to the officer, then turning back to Patrick gently put her index finger on the telephone cradle, disconnecting the line.

"Yes," she said calmly, sitting up straighter. "This is the Duty Officer's secretary at the British Army post at Rathdown. We have two men here who were stopped at a road block this morning. They claim to be residents of Ballinahinch and we need confirmation of their identities."

She read out the names and addresses then said: "Yes, I'll hold."

Silence -- except the tapping of the secretary's pencil on the top of the desk.

"Yes, I'm still here," she said.

Although her head didn't move, her eyes did and focused on Patrick.

"So both check out all right then? Thank you very much, goodbye."

She put the receiver back in its cradle, then breathed in before speaking to the officer.

"Very well," Patrick heard him say. "Tell the sergeant to fill out a report and let them go."

Fifteen minutes were needed for the sergeant to finish and by a quarter to nine they were finally on their way.

"How long will it take to get there now?" Patrick asked as the car accelerated up the street.

"Maybe an hour. Should I try to drive a little faster?"

"No, the last thing we want is an accident."

"God must be with us," O'Shaughnessy said as they cleared the town. "Only Divine Intervention could have made the officer's secretary a member of the Women's Brigade."

Patrick nodded, curt and abrupt.

"You told me that they change shifts at ten o'clock. Exactly at ten o'clock?"

"Yes."

The road began to wind and climb into the hills. O'Shaughnessy changed gear frequently trying to keep up their speed but the road grew steeper and they were forced to run in low gear for longer periods. After a few miles the engine began to overheat. The thermometer, set in a circular gauge on top of the radiator, showed a reading in the red part of the dial, but still O'Shaughnessy did not slow down.

"How far now?" Patrick asked as wisps of steam began to appear around the radiator cap.

"Several miles to where we turn into the boreen, and from there it's at least two miles up the mountain."

"Well, we can't go on. We must let the engine cool a bit. If we don't, it'll overheat and seize."

Around the next corner they came to a short level stretch. O'Shaughnessy put the car into neutral and they coasted slowly to a stop.

"Leave the motor going. That way the fan will keep running," Patrick said, getting out to stretch his legs.

A moment later he frowned, his eyes on the front of the car, listening. O'Shaughnessy listened too, then leaning forward tried to hear through the windshield.

"It sounds funny," he said as the throb of the engine became louder.

Jerking his head back, he looked over Patrick's shoulder and pointed.

"Jesus Christ!" he shouted. "It's not the car! It's an aeroplane!"

Patrick turned and stared upwards.

Flying directly at them, a few hundred feet off the ground, he could see the silhouette of a plane growing rapidly before his eyes -- wings, struts, landing wheels, sunlight reflecting on the spinning propeller.

Instinctively they ducked as it passed over in an ear-shattering roar just above their heads and made a climbing turn to the west, the goggled face of the observer in the rear cockpit clearly visible as he swiveled in his seat to keep them in view.

Moments later it returned, flying just above the fields, the pilot craning his neck to see over the machine guns in front of him.

"What shall we do!" O'Shaughnessy shouted. "We're finished. Let's make a run for it."

"Shut up!" Patrick yelled at him. "Leave it to me."

The plane approached again, this time from the east and, as it drew near, Patrick waved at it then held his arms out wide in despair and mimed that the car had broken down. It passed behind them and wheeled around in a wide circle, then came straight at them waggling its wings in acknowledgement.

"What do you think they'll do?" asked O'Shaughnessy.

Patrick shook his head.

"I don't think we looked suspicious and they don't seem to be in a hurry to get back to their aerodrome," he said gazing after the plane. "They're flying towards the sea."

The car engine had now become cool. They started off once more but with Patrick driving this time. Fifteen minutes later, O'Shaughnessy nudged him and pointed ahead.

"There," he said. "The road to the left."

Patrick slowed and changed to a lower gear before turning into the narrow, rocky lane.

"Let's go over it again," Patrick said bringing the car to a stop. "I'll get into the trunk and you drive up to the guard. Whether it's Brady or Kelly you'll stop, get out, and ask how everything is. Then you'll say you have a Luger Parabellum with you, and offer to show it to him. Walk with him around to the back of the car, and when you're sure he's close enough for me to easily reach him, open the lid. Before he knows what's happening I'll have knocked him senseless. Is that completely clear?"

"Yes."

"If for any reason I'm unable to do this, you must immediately grab his arms until I can get out of the trunk. No matter what happens, he mustn't have time to get to his gun and fire a shot. If he does, then Sweeney will hear it and kill her. Do you understand, O'Shaughnessy? Sweeney will kill her."

FIFTY-TWO

The car moved slowly up the rutted lane.

Patrick lay on his back in the trunk, his gun beside him. He pulled the stubby bayonet from its sheath and held it across his chest. It was pitch dark, and smaller than he'd realized. His shoulders touched either side and there wasn't room enough for him to stretch out his legs. Feeling he must have some air and light, he tried to push open the lid but it wouldn't budge. He pushed again, much harder but it was securely locked from the outside.

Panting and sweating he began to panic and was about to start shouting when he heard the sound of O'Shaughnessy shifting down into a lower gear, and the car slowed to a stop.

"The top of the morning to you, Brady," he heard him say. "You'll be glad to know I've brought a drop of whiskey with me as well as everything else, so we'll be able to have a few jars tonight."

"Grand," Brady replied. "Just what the doctor ordered."

O'Shaughnessy started to tell him about the Luger Parabellum but he stopped in mid-sentence.

"God! you gave me a fright. Is that you, Kelly?"

"Who else do you think it is?" The other voice said.

"You're both here," O'Shaughnessy almost shouted.

"Look," Brady exclaimed, "if you're going to yell like that they'll hear you in the next parish. Why are you shouting?"

"I'm not! I'm just surprised. It's good to see you both."

"Yeh. Well we were a bit late changing guard and anyway Kelly here had to answer an urgent call of nature. But enough. Did I hear somebody speak of whiskey? There wasn't anything for us last night, neither whiskey nor Guinness, nor potcheen, nothing fit for a man to drink."

"If you two heroes need a drop right now, then you shall have one," O'Shaughnessy said.

Patrick heard him fumbling in the supplies at the back of the car, followed by the pop of a cork.

"Cheers," one of them said, "first today."

O'Shaughnessy responded, then asked: "How's our visitor?"

"No idea. Himself never lets us get near her, not even for a peek down the trap door. God knows, she must be almost dead by now without any food or water. Maybe himself will have only a body to hang tonight."

"Does he really mean to go through with it?" O'Shaughnessy asked.

"Of course he does. He's crazed, gone mad. He spent all last evening making the sign he's going to put around her neck, embellishing it with all sorts of designs, squiggles and curly queues. It starts off saying, 'John Bull, you never thought we'd go through with it, did you?' Then a lot of stuff about total war."

"But is it right to hang a woman?" Patrick heard one of them ask.

"Didn't I tell you what he said? Total war. Men, women, and children. Why are you suddenly getting so squeamish,

Kelly? You didn't seem to have much trouble hanging the Tommies."

"I didn't do it. I just held them for Sweeney to put the noose on. Anyway, that was different. They were enemy soldiers in uniform, and in any case it wasn't me who hung them."

"But you were there. You took part."

"Christ, I know I was! But a woman, sure it's not right to hang a woman, unless she's committed murder or something."

"Here, have another drink. Don't think of it as hanging an individual. We're at war with the British, and Sweeney says we're hanging an Ascendancy bitch who represents those blood-suckers. God only knows the suffering they've caused our people for hundreds of years."

"Heh!" O'Shaughnessy exclaimed. "That's enough whiskey. You know the rules. No drinking before nightfall. If himself gets the whiff of it on our breath, he'll put us on official reprimand."

Patrick heard one of them hammer the cork into the bottle with his clenched fist, then felt the movement of the car as it was put on the back seat.

"Where's that Luger Parabellum you said you had for me, O'Shaughnessy?"

"Not now. There's only one of them and there are two of you. I don't want to be the one to cause bad feelings."

The other two laughed.

"That's very sensitive and considerate of you. In any case, himself will probably take it. But let's have a quick look, for it's a darlin' weapon."

"Forget it. We're late already."

"I don't give a damn if we are. I want to see it."

The top of the trunk was jerked open and light streamed into Patrick's eyes, blinding him.

Panicking, he grabbed at the silhouette above him and drove the bayonet straight through the man's throat. Blood foamed out over the handle, trickling down Patrick's wrist. Sickened, he sat up and struggled to get out.

The other man, stunned, started slowly reaching for his gun. Patrick sprang forward and hit him across the head with the side of the bayonet knocking him senseless.

"Sweet Jesus!" O'Shaughnessy yelled. "You've killed Kelly!"

"I didn't mean to. There was no other way."

"But you have! You said you'd only knock him out!"

Patrick turned away, revolted and shocked by what he'd done. He started to sit down on the running board of the car when he saw Brady dragging himself along the ground towards his gun.

A revolver shot . . . the trap door pulled open . . . an explosion -- Patrick dived forward and without a moment's hesitation thrust the bayonet deep into Brady's back. He stiffened in sudden spasm, then lay still.

O'Shaughnessy started screaming uncontrollably. Patrick grabbed him and clamped his hand tightly over his mouth.

"Quiet!" he whispered. "For Christ's sake, be quiet!"

"You didn't give them a chance, either of them," O'Shaughnessy stuttered when Patrick let go of him. "You didn't say you were going to kill them. They were my friends. We were at school together."

"I never meant it to happen this way."

Trembling, O'Shaughnessy lit a cigarette and inhaled deeply. "I can't go through with it."

Patrick pretended he hadn't heard.

"You will drive up to the cottage, park in front of the door, and unload the supplies. When everything is brought inside you will come out. If other IRA men have arrived leave the car there but if Sweeney is alone, drive it around to the barn."

Speaking slowly, stressing every word, Patrick continued.

"Assuming there is only Sweeney, go back to the door and throw the piece of poisoned meat to the dog, making sure it falls where he can reach it. Then go into the cottage again and get Sweeney to have a drink of whiskey from the bottle that's poisoned. He drinks so greedily he'll gulp it down before he tastes the strychnine."

FIFTY-THREE

Shaughnessy finally calmed down and got into the car. He threw his cigarette away, hesitated for a moment, then started the engine and drove off up the hill.

Patrick hid the two bodies behind a stone wall. Thinking of Victoria chained in the cellar, he realized he felt nothing for them. No regret: no shock: no feelings at all.

He came back into the lane and kicked some loose dirt and pebbles over the trail of blood, trying to hide it but it made little difference.

He glanced around him, then at the sky, listening and scanning the horizon. It was completely still and quiet, no sound except for the bleat of sheep in the distance. Keeping his head down, he moved round the hill until he was opposite the cottage. Cautiously, he peered out from behind a boulder.

In front of him, about fifty yards away, O'Shaughnessy was unloading boxes from the car while Sweeney stood in the doorway, smoking. Each time O'Shaughnessy passed, the dog lunged at him, growling and pawing the ground, straining at his leash.

When Patrick saw them both go inside, he settled himself and prepared to wait. About ten minutes later O'Shaughnessy came out, followed by Sweeney who watched him get in the car and drive around to the barn. He stood there for a few moments gazing down the lane, then at his watch, then at the lane again. Frowning, he turned abruptly and went inside.

The moment he was out of sight, O'Shaughnessy came back across the yard unwrapping the piece of meat. As he approached the front of the cottage he threw it towards the kennel. The dog sprang forward and caught it in his teeth before it hit the ground. Tearing at it he swallowed it in lumps. Suddenly he seemed to struggle, howled, and slumped forward.

Sweeney came to the door again, holding his revolver. He looked all around then caught sight of the dog stretched out, inert and still. Cautiously he went up to it and turned the lifeless body over with his foot.

"Let's have a drink, Commandant," O'Shaughnessy said going over to him. "It'll steady the nerves."

Sweeney shook his head and motioned him inside with his gun. O'Shaughnessy went ahead. Sweeney backed into the cottage, glanced this way and that, then slammed the door behind him.

Patrick retreated a few paces then crouching down he started running until he came to the other side of the hill. Cautiously he broke cover. Sprinting across the open ground passed the barn, he hid behind it. When he got his breath, he peered out to study the cottage.

The only window at the back was in the small bedroom where the farmer and his wife were. Patrick could see the curtains were tightly drawn.

Taking a deep breath he ran silently across the yard. Edging slowly beside the cottage wall and around the chimney, he worked his way to the front. Crawling along the ground he kept beneath the window sill until he reached the doorway. Keeping his back to the wall, he stood up then pressed his ear against the door and listened.

No sound from inside: it was as if everyone were dead.

Holding his breath, he lifted the latch and eased the door open with the barrel of his gun.

"So you're our mystery visitor," Sweeney said, grinning.

He was standing in the middle of the room, the rug on the floor kicked aside, holding a hand-grenade directly above the open trap door. In the corner stood O'Shaughnessy, hands high above his head.

Sweeney nodded towards the gun in Patrick's hand. "That's a fine looking weapon you're carrying. It looks to me like a nine millimeter Luger parabellum. Very effective, particularly for fighting in close quarters."

Patrick raised the gun so it pointed at Sweeney's stomach.

"I would think," he continued, "that you could fire several rounds in a second, but in this situation what counts are split seconds, in fact just one split second. If you hit me, even if the first shot kills me, I'm bound to drop this grenade and it will fall straight through the trap door. As you can see, the pin is out."

"Sweeney, let's talk."

"I'll do the talking for the moment, Patrick me lad. Now, look at it this way. From a standing start, from where you are now, it would take you three seconds to get down into that cellar. It's so bloody dark and filthy there it'd be a long time before you'd find the grenade. And time is something you don't have."

"All right, Sweeney, let's make a deal."

"What sort of a deal?"

"Your freedom for her life. There's a car outside. Just go."

Sweeney threw back his head, laughing.

"That's almost like asking me to do something and promising to remember me in your will."

The smile faded.

"Now you listen to me, and I'll tell you my proposition."

He paused for a moment, turning his head slightly, and Patrick could see the red scratch marks from Victoria's nails embedded in his cheek.

"First of all, I'm older than you, and I'm not afraid to die. In some ways I'd welcome it. But you're young, you haven't had your life yet. Also, I think you have a strong feeling for that young lady down there," he said, pointing with the hand-grenade through the trap door. "She's a beautiful young girl, although she looks bloody awful right now, so let me make this very simple. Either you put that gun on the floor very gently, or on the count of three, no perhaps five I'll be generous. On the count of five, down goes this grenade, and up comes pieces of your little friend."

He laughed but didn't take his eyes off Patrick for an instant as he started to count.

"One. Two. Three."

Patrick didn't move.

"You're pushing your luck, Patrick me lad. Four!"

Patrick nodded then laid the gun carefully on the floor.

"Now that's better. Good boy."

Something in his peripheral vision made Patrick's eyes flicker for an instant over Sweeney's shoulder. The farmer's wife, Brigid, had appeared from the small bedroom and stood frozen in the doorway.

"Tell me, Sweeney," Patrick said, speaking quickly, "what has happened to the IRA? When I was young we were taught that the fighters for Ireland's freedom were heroes and brave men. Today they seem to be people like you with nicknames like 'Knee-capper'. Or perhaps they'll give you a new one, 'Hangman'. Young conscript soldiers, or women, you don't care. It's all for the Movement. All for the love of Ireland."

"Patrick, me boy, you talk too much. And it's all drivel."

Brigid tiptoed further into the room and was now about two paces from the open trap door.

"In order for the IRA to succeed," Patrick went on, "you must have the support of the masses. The majority in any country are fundamentally decent, and wouldn't support the likes of you. You're mentally sick, you're a murderer. . ."

Brigid sprang forward and kicked the trap door closed with her right foot. Sweeney dropped the grenade, spun around and fired.

The bullet passed over Brigid's head as she dropped to the floor, snatched up the grenade and hurled it through the open window.

Patrick ducked down and grabbed his gun. Sweeney fired twice in quick succession, missing both times. Then the grenade exploded in front of the cottage and pieces of glass and window frame flew across the room. Darting forward, Patrick struck Sweeney violently across the side of his head. He staggered backwards a pace then fell to the floor and lay still. When he was sure Sweeney was unconscious Patrick pulled up the trap door.

He peered into the darkness below then drew back for a

couple of seconds. The airless stench was overpowering but he started to lower himself until his foot found the top rung of the ladder and he clambered down.

Standing at the bottom in a pool of light from the opening above, he could just make out the shape of a person in the corner. As his eyes adjusted he was able to see it was Victoria pressing herself tightly against the wall. Feeling his way forward he moved across the floor and reached out to her.

She didn't move, or make any sound at all, and for a terrible moment he thought she was dead. Then he felt her shudder, and choking and catching her breath, she began to cry.

He heard a movement behind him, then Brigid's voice. "It's all right, it's me, Brigid. I have the key."

Groping in the darkness, she found Victoria's ankle and undid the padlock that held the chain. Between them they carried her to the ladder and with O'Shaughnessy's help got her through the trap-door into the room above.

When Patrick emerged he saw Victoria lying full length on the floor, sobbing almost noiselessly, Brigid cradling her head. Her face was bruised, her clothes torn and filthy, and her hair so matted and knotted it stuck out from her head like a grotesque golliwog. Her ankle, lacerated by the chain, was covered with caked blood.

"My love," Patrick whispered as he knelt down beside her, "what has he done to you."

Before Victoria could answer, Brigid jumped to her feet.

"Christ!" she screamed. "He's got the other grenade!"

FIFTY-FOUR

Patrick hurled himself at Sweeney. He fell backwards, dropping the grenade before he could pull the pin. By the time he sat up, Patrick was standing over him.

Slowly he raised his gun and Sweeney, crab-like, retreated into the corner.

"Why don't you go ahead and shoot? You don't have the guts, do you?"

Patrick looked at him, then at Victoria, then calmly turned back and fired two bullets, one into each kneecap.

Sweeney screamed, grabbed his knees, rolling over and over on the ground, hysterical with pain. Blood soaked through his trousers and began seeping between his fingers.

Patrick kneeled down again beside Victoria, taking her in his arms. The crying had stopped and she slowly started looking around the room.

"I'm sorry about all that weeping," she said. "It's over now."

She got to her feet with Patrick's help but her legs buckled under her.

"Leave her with me," Brigid said, "I'll look after her. The first thing she needs is a bath. I'll heat some water."

Patrick carried Victoria into the back room and placed her gently on the bed.

"Can you manage?" he asked Brigid.

She nodded, waving him away.

Patrick returned to the living room and looked at Sweeney. He had pressed himself tightly against the wall, and was rocking back and forth, trying to get away from the pain.

"What are you going to do with him?" the farmer asked. "A British Army patrol, or some of his IRA friends, could be very troublesome for Brigid and me."

"Don't worry. We'll see you're all right. First, they're two bodies in the lane that need to be buried."

"Put down a bog hole would be better. They'd never be found."

"Do you know where?"

The farmer nodded.

"O'Shaughnessy," Patrick said. "Stay here. We'll be back in a little while. Watch Sweeney. If he makes any trouble, shoot him."

About an hour later, they returned. Sweeney was still sitting in the corner, groaning.

"Any problems?"

O'Shaughnessy shook his head.

"We'd better start making plans to leave," Patrick said, looking around. "Whose briefcase is that?" he asked.

"Sweeney's."

Patrick picked it up and laid it on the kitchen table.

"What are you doing with my briefcase?" Sweeney asked, his voice contorted with pain. "Those are my clothes and personal possessions. Don't touch them."

"You travel light," Patrick said, snapping open the locks.

He lifted the lid then stepped back, shaking his head in amazement. "It's full of banknotes."

He picked up a bundle and read aloud from the paper wrapper. "One hundred pounds, Royal Hibernian Bank."

"What did you say?" O'Shaughnessy said, coming over. "Jaysus! There must be tens of thousands here. Have you ever seen so much money in your life?"

Patrick heard the bedroom door open and turning, saw Victoria and Brigid coming into the room. Victoria, though gaunt and thin, seemed calm and in control of herself. She was clean and wore a red skirt and blouse, and a black shawl of Brigid's.

"I'm fine now," she said.

"Are you sure?" Patrick asked, looking closely at her.

She nodded, started to say something then held up her hand, signaling them to listen.

Faint but distinct, they heard the sound of an engine, laboring in low gear. O'Shaughnessy moved quickly to the door. Standing to one side he leaned his head just far enough to see out.

"Oh my God! It's a British Army lorry, coming up the boreen," he whispered over his shoulder. "They're stopping. Lots of soldiers. They're going to surround the cottage!"

Victoria stooped to peer through the window.

"We've got a few minutes yet," she said then added in a quieter voice as she walked across to the kitchen table, "there's something I must do before they come."

She picked up Sweeney's revolver, checking there were bullets in the magazine as she walked towards him. She held the gun rigidly in her extended arm then hooked the trigger hammer back with her thumb, raising the barrel until it was pointing straight into Sweeney's face.

"No!" he screamed. "No! No! No! Haven't you done enough to me? I'll never walk again. Please have pity on me."

"Pity? For you?" Victoria shook her head. "Look at me. Look into my eyes. Look into the barrel of this gun and see again the face of my brother Jeremy."

Sweeney cringed away, trying to make himself smaller, pressing more tightly against the wall.

"Damn you!" Victoria shouted. "Look at me! This is the same gun you killed my brother with."

He turned to her, eyes wide.

"It wasn't me who killed him. It was one of the other men . . . it was . . . it was Brady who did it. For the love of God, I swear it wasn't me who killed him."

Patrick could see her knuckle grow white as she pulled the trigger. In the confines of the cottage the gunshot that followed was deafening. Sweeney's head jerked back, then fell forward, leaving a crimson burst of color on the whitewashed wall.

Victoria stared at Sweeney's body slumped on the floor, murmuring in a quiet and detached voice: "With a big blue mark on his forehead, and the back blown out of his head."

"What are you saying?"

"It's Kipling," she said, throwing the revolver down at Sweeney's feet. "I always thought the words were graphic. And they are."

O'Shaughnessy moved away from the door.

"Quick, they're coming. Out through the kitchen or we're dead."

Patrick went to Victoria and put his arms around her

then held her tight. They stood for a moment in silence, looking at each other, unaware of what was going on around them.

"You must go, my love. Now!" she said kissing him firmly on the lips. "You'll have the best chance in Dublin. I'll be there waiting for you. Stafford House, Mountjoy."

Patrick nodded. "A week," he said. "Perhaps less."

He picked up the gun, grabbed the brief-case and followed O'Shaughnessy through the kitchen door.

The shrill sound of a whistle, soldiers shouting, rifle shots. Crouching, Patrick sprinted across the yard and jumped over the low stone wall. O'Shaughnessy, fifty yards ahead, was running down the hill in a straight line, as fast as he could. Patrick heard the crack of a rifle, then three more shots in quick succession. O'Shaughnessy pitched forward, rolling over and over, then lay still.

Moments later Patrick reached him. Kneeling, he gently turned him onto his back. His chest was already soaked with blood, his eyes lifeless and unseeing.

A bullet thudded into the earth at Patrick's feet. Shaking himself, he darted forward, crouching and weaving and dodging through the gorse bushes until he reached the bottom of the hill. Ahead of him was bare bog land -- no cover at all.

He looked behind him. The sun had set. In the twilight shadows he would be a difficult target: in fifteen minutes it would be dark.

Hiding behind some rocks, he fired several shots over the heads of the soldiers coming towards him. They immediately dropped to the ground, the whistle blew and they began to regroup.

Putting another clip of ammunition into the gun, Patrick breathed deeply, then waited.

FIFTY-FIVE

Patrick expected a reply from Victoria to his letter within a day or two, but a week had already passed and his life had became a monotonous routine centered around the arrival of the post, with long walks between morning and evening deliveries.

Soon he knew most of Dublin south of the River Liffey quite well. He'd visited all the areas where there'd been fighting, and had walked several times through the center of the city looking at the gutted buildings and burnt out shell of General Post Office.

During the second week of waiting, he decided he would go to Mountjoy, and walk passed the Stafford's house. He had been determined, when he first arrived in Dublin, to stay away but now, as he rode in the tram through the gathering darkness, he felt he would be safe.

Stafford House was a large Georgian mansion which dominated the street, and through the railings he could see the windows of well-lighted rooms, warm and comfortable in contrast to the raw March evening outside. He walked along on the opposite side of the street, passed the house and looked down the cobbled lane leading to the stables. He crossed over, and walked back directly in front of the house, peering through the railings, hoping to see Victoria or at least some sign of life, but saw none.

He continued on around the block, then came to the house from the other direction. It had got darker, and the windows appeared to glow more brightly in the dusk but still he couldn't see anyone inside.

He had passed the house four or five times when a policeman came out of a side street and stared closely at him. Realizing he was about to be stopped and questioned, he turned up a lane and ran.

That night, Patrick telephoned Stafford House.

"Is Lady Victoria there?" he asked in what he hoped was an English accent.

"May I ask who's speaking?" replied the butler.

"Barrington, David Barrington"

"Would you please hold the line? I'll see if Lady Victoria is available."

He waited, tense, his heart pounding, and after what seemed like several minutes he began to think they'd been disconnected. Then he heard Victoria's voice.

"Hello?"

"It's me, Patrick."

She didn't answer but he heard her breath.

"It's Patrick," he said again.

"Yes, how are you David?"

Her voice was clear, and a little too loud.

"Did you get my letter?"

"No, David, I didn't. But I'm awfully glad to hear from you. Are you staying long in Dublin?"

"Is someone listening to you?"

"Yes."

"Just answer yes or no. I wrote to you ten days ago. You didn't get my letter, is that right?"

"Yes."

"The post is very reliable. Someone must have intercepted it."

"I don't think so."

"I asked you to write to me."

"Let's arrange to meet. I know Blaise would love to see you after all this time."

"Tomorrow?"

"I'm not sure."

"Do you know St. Stephen's Green?"

"Yes."

"Do you know the statue of the poet, just opposite the Royal College of Surgeons."

"Yes, I do."

"I'll be there tomorrow at twelve o'clock, then every day at twelve o'clock until you come."

"That will be fine. It's so nice to hear from you again. Goodbye David. I'll tell Blaise you telephoned."

The next morning was cold but clear, with sunlight glistening on the white frost covering the grass. The only bright colors in the park were the mallard ducks on the pond, moving back and forth between groups of children and pensioners, throwing them pieces of bread.

At about eleven thirty, Patrick passed the statue of the poet, paused to read the inscription then walked on. A man in a heavy overcoat sat on the bench opposite reading the Irish Times, and behind him a gardener was busy picking up pieces of paper with a pointed metal stick. Patrick continued until he'd reached the southwest corner of the park and went out through the gate to the street. Turning to the right he walked along the iron railings parallel to the path inside that he'd just come down. As he drew level with the bust of the poet he could see that the man sitting opposite wasn't really reading his newspaper but was studying each person as they passed.

Patrick continued on to the main gate opposite Grafton Street. Two policemen were there, checking people who entered the park. In panic, he ran across the street, just missing an on-coming tram, then forced himself to stop at the corner and look around him.

On the opposite side of the street, among the parked cars, was a large black Daimler. In the back sat two British officers, both watching the main gate of the park. One had a black eye patch, and his army cap was pulled down, hiding the left side of his face.

EPILOGUE

In November 1919 the Black and Tans arrived in Ireland with orders to pacify the country by whatever means necessary. Within a few months they had succeeded in uniting the Irish in a way their own leaders never thought possible.

Patrick rose through the ranks of the IRA, and by the time the treaty forming the Irish Free State was agreed in late 1921 he was the veteran of many successful operations. When the general amnesty was declared, he returned to Ballinahinch.

* * *

After several months on Ennismore he came back to the mainland the following June to attend, with the O'Malley family, the 'open house' at Ballinahinch Castle.

As they went through the main gate of the Castle O'Malley turned to his wife.

"Within a few years all this will be mine, all mine. Not bad, me darlin', for a humble shopkeeper like myself."

They drove along the driveway in silence until Kathleen

pointed ahead.

"Look!" she cried, her voice shrill with excitement. "Now that's a sight I thought I'd never see."

They had reached the brow of the hill. Ballinahinch Castle stood before them, and from the topmost turret flew the Irish tricolor.

On the west lawn several hundred people from the town, self-conscious in their best clothes, were mingling with the few members of the Ascendancy who had decided to attend. Seeing the O'Malleys arrive, the Parish Priest hurried over.

"Is Lord Stafford here?" O'Malley asked, looking around at the crowd, smiling at everyone. "I'd really like to meet him under these particular circumstances."

"No." the priest replied. "It's said he's ill in London, and that Lady Clarissa is with him. The Family is represented by Blaise, and Victoria with her husband."

Patrick tensed.

"Who did she marry?" he asked. "Someone of the Ascendancy?"

"No. Some English titled gentleman."

A roll of kettle drums interrupted him and Patrick saw Blaise mounting the stairs to the dais, adroitly pivoting himself with his stick, lifting his good leg up a step at a time.

He was followed a moment later by Victoria.

Patrick watched her climb the stairs, elegant and graceful, and impossible thoughts of turning the clock back raced through his mind until he remembered the bitterness of her betrayal, and the acute pain and longing for her afterwards. He continued with his eyes fixed on her, trying to feel anger and hate, but there was none.

She sat down beside a British officer, about thirty years old. Blaise and the other speakers, whether Irish or of the Ascendancy, made very similar speeches stressing that all hatred must be put aside in the newly created Irish Free State, and from now on the Ascendancy and native Irish would enjoy a period of unprecedented co-operation and prosperity.

Patrick stood beside Kathleen O'Malley, their shoulders brushing lightly together, but he hardly heard the words that were being said as he gazed intently at Victoria, more beautiful than he remembered. She was looking straight ahead, serene and untroubled, a faint smile giving her face a pleasing expression until, moving slightly, she caught sight of him.

For a long moment they stared at each other then slowly closing her eyes, Victoria turned away.

* * *

A year later, Patrick and Kathleen were married by the parish priest. The wedding was the most lavish in the history of the town. They spent their honeymoon in Monte Carlo, the location chosen by O'Malley as appropriate for his daughter. It was followed by a long visit to the shrine of St. Bernadette at Lourdes.

* * *

Although many of the Ascendancy stayed on in Ireland, Lord Stafford never returned to Ballinahinch: he could not accept the new Irish Free State.

Blaise, feeling cheated of his birthright, hung on but by 1928 most of the good farming land had been sold off to maintain his life-style until only the Castle itself and several hundred acres of bog land remained.

He continued keeping Rosaleen as his mistress, but she had to live in London because die-hard members of the old IRA had threatened to kill her if she set foot in Ireland again.

By 1930 Blaise was chronically sick, a combination of war wounds and excessive drinking. By the winter he was declared bankrupt, and the Castle and what remained of the estate put up for sale. Two days before the auction took place he drank a bottle of whiskey, put the barrel of his service revolver into his mouth, and pulled the trigger.

* * *

O'Malley bought the Castle and the remaining land cheaply. The only people bidding against him were the Christian Brothers, who wished to turn it into an orphanage, and the Sacred Heart nuns who wanted it for a new convent.

Patrick now spent most of his time in Dublin taking care of O'Malley's business interests there. It was an arrangement that suited both him and Kathleen the best.

Six months later, one Sunday after O'Malley and his

wife had slept off their mid-day dinner, Patrick and Kathleen went with them in the new Packard limousine to look at Ballinahinch Castle.

They turned in from the road and drove through the opening where the gates had once been. The turreted lodges on either side were partly demolished, bricks, rafters, and slates all neatly stacked, ready to be hauled away. But the wrought iron arch over the gateway, with the Stafford family coat of arms in the center, was still in place.

As the Packard drove under it O'Malley said: "I'm preserving this archway to erect over the entrance of that new pig farm and slaughter house I've bought down in Tipperary."

"What's happened?" Patrick asked, bewildered.

"You'll see," O'Malley said, his eyes growing small and hard as he gazed directly ahead of him.

They drove along the driveway, now overgrown and neglected, then crossed the rise and started descending into the valley.

Patrick sat back, his eyes wide.

Where once the Castle had stood now was empty sky. Everything was gone except the tops of the foundations which formed intricate rectangle and square patterns through the grass and weeds. The lawns and ornamental gardens had run wild, and an atmosphere of desolation and violence lingered all around them.

Patrick stared at O'Malley, grinning from ear to ear, a cigarette wedged firmly in his mouth below an arch of nicotine on his upper lip.

"Michael?" Mrs. O'Malley said as the car stopped in front of the stone stairway that used to lead up to the main door of the Castle.

"What is it, me dear?"

"You forgot the summer house," she said, pointing across the rank grass.

Patrick turned to look.

It was still there, partly covered with ivy, the white paint weathered to a dull gray.

"Good God! So I did," O'Malley replied. "You can rest assured it'll be gone tomorrow. All gone," he added, shaking with laughter. "The Staffords came with Cromwell in sixteen forty nine, but it was the gombeen man Michael O'Malley who saw them out in nineteen hundred and thirty!"

* * *

By 1932, Patrick felt more and more convinced that his life had no meaning. He drank heavily, began to get fat, and his hair started to thin. He could buy anything he wanted yet seemed to have nothing. The only consolation was his mistress, a dancer in the chorus line at the Theater Royal.

* * *

At the Curragh races of 1938, Patrick was making his way from the Members Enclosure to the grandstand when an exceptionally beautiful, blonde-haired woman passed him. There was something about her face, and the quick expression in her eyes, that seemed familiar.

"Patrick me darlin', don't you recognize me?" she asked.

The voice had the lilt of West Clare in it and as he turned around he shook his head in disbelief.

"Is it really Rosaleen?"

"Rosalind," she corrected him in a clipped, upper class accent. "Rosaleen died many years ago."

"Rosaleen, Rosalind, you look absolutely marvelous."

"I should do, considering the amount of money I spend on myself. It's my life's work."

"Isn't it dangerous for you to be in Ireland?"

She shook her head.

"That's a long time ago, and anyway I'm now married to a very wealthy man, Sir Stanley Bradshaw. Formerly," she added, with a twinkle in her eye, "Stanislaus Bradouski, a Polish Jew and a rag peddler. He's just bought himself a title. It's ridiculous, isn't it, but my name's Lady Rosalind Bradshaw."

She threw back her head, laughing, and Patrick laughed with her.

"Do you have time for a drink?" he asked.

"Of course. My husband's fully occupied for the moment, trying to ingratiate himself with some trainers because he feels we need a stud farm to go with the newly purchased title."

They went into the bar. The most prominent drink on display was champagne.

"What would you like?"

"Some of that, of course. A bottle of Veuve Clicquot."

Patrick ordered.

"It's really great seeing you," she said in the accent Patrick remembered. "It takes me back fifteen years. But damn it! It's no good."

"Why not?"

"Because now, with you, I'm becoming relaxed and myself again. Something I haven't been since Blaise died. Let's drink to him," she said raising her glass, touching Patrick's. "I think he was the only man who ever really loved me, and extraordinary as it may sound, the only man I ever loved."

Rosaleen blinked and glanced away, then gripping her glass forced a smile.

"I heard you married Kathleen O'Malley, and that you're very rich."

"True."

"Are you happy?"

"What is happiness?"

She started to answer but broke off as a bugle sounded outside announcing the next race. People around them were quickly finishing their drinks and the bar began to empty.

"I must go," she said, slipping gracefully off the stool. "Stanley will be looking for me to bring him luck before he places his next bet."

Patrick stood up and held out his hand.

Rosaleen took it in hers and kissed him.

"It was a tonic seeing you, me darlin'. I might suggest we meet again but we can't put back the clock."

She paused, and Patrick could see the sparkle had gone from her eyes.

"The past is the past," she finally said, then added, "let it rest in peace."

Patrick watched her threading her way towards the grand-stand, quick and slim and graceful, until she was hidden in the crowd.

* * *

The following Monday morning Patrick sat down in his office and began to deal with the business correspondence his secretary had put on his desk. He flipped through it but couldn't concentrate. Meeting Rosaleen and seeing her once more had brought back memories that he'd been controlling for many years. Now they were vividly alive again.

He was weary of O'Malley and the business of making even more money than he could possibly use, and tired of life with nothing to live for.

As he leafed through the letters, thinking he'd look at them later, a large registered envelope with a London post mark caught his eye. Underneath the address was written: 'To be opened by addressee only'. Seeing it was from a law firm whose name he didn't recognize, he reached for the paper knife to open it.

Inside was a letter, folded around a small envelope on which was written, in Victoria's hand, 'Patrick Castelan, Esq.'

He picked it up and stared at it, at the familiar writing he hadn't seen for so many years. For a moment he was too shaken to move, then getting control of himself he began to read the solicitor's letter.

14th August 1938

Dear Mr. Castelan,

About four months ago, when the illness of Lady Victoria Glendenning became obviously terminal, she visited our offices and gave me certain instructions, including the request that the enclosed envelope be delivered to you after her death.

In addition, there was a directive to provide a Trust fund for a beneficiary to be named by you. The payment of interest on the capital should commence on the 7th of September 1938, and be paid quarterly thereafter. Financial arrangements have already been made and all payments will come from Lady Glendenning's estate.

To comply with the foregoing, I would be most grateful for your instructions in due course...

Patrick became cold. All warmth and life drained out of him as he looked down at the envelope lying on the desk in front of him. He hesitated, then reached for the paper knife again.

23rd March 1938

Dearest Patrick,

Our daughter was born in London on the 7th of September 1917. Her name is Patricia Anne (I hope you approve -- Patricia for Patrick, and Anne, my second name, which the family never used although I preferred it to Victoria).

She is in the Dominican convent in Richmond, Surrey, registered as Patricia Anne FitzWilliam, which was my mother's maiden name.

Patricia will be twenty-one on the 7th of September this year and I intended setting up a trust fund for her that would give her an adequate monthly income from her birthday onwards. As I'll not be able to make these arrangements myself, I'm asking you to do so.

Blaise knew more about us than we realized. The Secret Service were listening to our conversation when you telephoned Stafford House and they prevented me from meeting you. The next day, Blaise showed me an intelligence report saying that you'd been killed while resisting arrest, and it was not until June 1922 when I saw you at Ballinahinch Castle that I realized he had lied.

By then, so much had happened that I thought it was too late for us to start our lives again. I know now that I was wrong as I am sure that Patrick, Victoria, and Patricia would have been very happy together, and it seems unfair that it was not to be.

With fondest love,
Victoria

ACKNOWLEDGMENTS

Much thanks to my daughter Sarah and my son-in-law Ramin for their Herculean efforts in designing and publishing this book.

John Flanagan was a young man when he left his native Ireland in search of adventure. To begin with he joined Her Majesty's Colonial Service where he experienced first hand the twilight years of colonialism. His first novel *Tambu* was inspired by his time in British West Africa. Like an 'international gypsy' John has lived in and explored many different countries around the world, a number of which he vividly brings to life in his novels. With his wife Jill, he now lives in London, his writing inspired by a lifetime of travel.

www.ingramcontent.com/pod-product-compliance
Lightning Source LLC
Chambersburg PA
CBHW031202020726
47499CB00002B/452